Every Time He Leaves

Anna Karington

To Jonathan, who left without saying goodbye.

.

Chapter One

I adjust a flower arrangement on an accessory table and make sure the appetizers look aesthetically pleasing. My mother is responsible for hosting the Women's Club's annual charity event, and I agreed to help out, as I usually do. This wasn't a great idea, since I have plenty of work to catch up on, but considering I bailed on Mom's past two events, I had to step up to the plate.

A few yards away, two waiters cross paths before a cluster of guests. The room is packed, which surprises me, since last year was a bust. From my work as an event coordinator, I've learned this is the nature of charities and fundraisers—depending upon the year, some are more fashionable than others. One year, breast cancer support is all the rage at the expense of heart disease or Parkinson's. The next year, Alzheimer's gets all the attention and the color pink makes people want to vomit.

As much as I'm a fan of helping people, the sorts that show up to these charities seem more interested in write-offs and appearances than generosity. How appropriate that my mother is involved in the sort of ostentatious events that cost as much to host as they manage to raise for whatever organization or group they're benefiting. I can't judge, though, considering I work for a major organization that exists exclusively to profit off major nonprofits.

"Sis." I whirl around. Janet holds a plate covered with fragments of glass.

"What in the—"

"I had an accident," she says. It reminds me of when we were little and she approached me covered in red marker, terrified Mom would discover what a mess she'd made in her room.

"What is it?"

"Maybe a really expensive statue…"

"Oh, God."

Mom asked for permission from the Atlanta Historic Society to use the Kinderly House, the mansion of a wealthy family known for prestige in the arts community. The place is decorated with beautiful and surely expensive furnishings.

Janet holds the plate out. The moment I take it from her, I will have silently agreed to take responsibility for what she has done. However, that's my life with her, so I figure I might as well take it now.

"That's what insurance is for, right?" she asks.

I glare at her. She always makes light of the messes she makes. Maybe as an older sister, I have a harder time seeing the amusement when I'm always the one who winds up in trouble. Did Janet get yelled at for the red marker incident? No. I was evidently negligent by not keeping an eye on my little sis to make sure she stayed out of trouble. And Mom made her rage clear with a red-faced fit and a few thrown stuffed animals.

I gaze at the mess, my mind reeling through possible solutions. "I'm just going to find somewhere to stick it until I can get my head on straight, okay?"

"I have to get some more flour to the crêpe chef outside anyway," Janet says as she heads off. It doesn't surprise me that she found a responsibility that would put her as far away from this as possible.

I curb my frustration by reminding myself that she has always here to help Mom with these gatherings, which is helpful since I'm considered the official event planning expert and somehow end up responsible for making sure everything goes off without a hitch. My current job stems directly from Mom's involvement in these sorts of events, since I have been doing this since my late teens. Mom always has some party or another to throw or attend. She sits on the boards of several charities and committees, and each requires various events that I have been involved with (in some form or another) for many years.

I navigate through the crowd with the glass-covered plate, occasionally pulling it out of reach of patrons who are either so unthinking or so blind that they reach for it, expecting to snatch a glass of champagne, I suppose.

A tug at my shoulder.

I turn to Kelsey, my older sister. The black dress she wears has a severe dip between her breasts, exposing an ample (yet surprisingly not inappropriate) amount of cleavage. She has always dressed like she's trying to capture the interest of a new man, even when she was married. Despite my familiarity with her outfits, I can't keep my gaze off the crack between her breasts. Sometimes when I look at them, I can't help but blame them for Janet's and my modest chests, like some part of me believes, despite the scientific impossibility of it, that Kelsey selfishly hoarded the good boob genes.

"Lana, I want you to meet my friends!" she exclaims. Kelsey has been in town less than a month. After her divorce was finalized, she moved into a condo in Buckhead. She's always been good at making new friends, so I'm not surprised she's created a girl gang.

"This is Carol Radner..." She indicates a blonde in a black jump-suit. "...and this is Melanie Farrar." Her gesture shifts from Carol to a girl who, despite her freckles, must have dyed her hair a darker shade because it is far too vibrant to be real. "This is my sister, Lana," Kelsey says.

"Pleased to meet you," Melanie says, extending her hand. We shake, and then I shake hands with Carol.

"Glad you all could make it," I say, eyeing the demolished glass in the plate I'm still carrying—my not-so-subtle way of alerting Kelsey to the issue I'm trying to handle right now. Hopefully that will excuse me from this meet and greet.

Unfortunately, no one seems fazed by the presence of the mess. "Kelsey tells us you're in event coordinating," Melanie says.

"Working to be. I'm still in training, technically."

"Lana's being modest," Kelsey says. "She's been doing this stuff forever. And she's with Farcon & Williams."

Carol's eyes widen as if she's impressed. It makes me regret where I work, since I don't work there to get this sort of attention. "You must be incredibly busy, then," Melanie says. Farcon & Williams handles mega-million-dollar nonprofit accounts. If a charity needs to host a money-making fundraiser, our company is assigned the responsibility of putting together everything from the venue and entertainment to the advertising. Our company works off of commission for each gig, so it's in our best interest to make sure each client's fundraiser makes as much money as possible.

"I just started a little over a year ago," I say. "I used to freelance until Farcon & Williams approached me."

"She's being modest," Kelsey insists. "She's in charge of a fundraiser at the end of the month. Isn't that right?"

I don't want to discuss this, especially since my career is riding on this opportunity. Up until this event, I have been at the mercy of my superior, organizing with her. This is the first fundraiser I'll be managing on my own, and the past few weeks have been incredibly hectic and unnerving, to say the least. A recent billing fiasco with our last major client has left us scrambling for an internal audit, one that has hardly given me time to focus on the fundraiser that will determine my future with this company.

"What's the event?" Carol asks.

"We're working with the Damon Gray Foundation. They raise money for educational programs for children with special needs."

"That's wonderful," Carol says.

I try to sneak away again, offering a polite, "I'm sorry. I really need to—"

"Need to spend more time with me now that I'm back in town," Kelsey says. "You know, I've been here the past three weeks, and I think I've seen you a whole two times."

That's because some of us have to work. I'm not going to say that, but it must be easier for Kelsey when her biggest daily worry is who she will find to play tennis with or go shopping with at Phipps Plaza.

"Just give me a call and we'll set something up," I say, hoping to refresh her memory about all the times she hasn't called me to set up plans. I'm fairly sure the only reason she brought it up in front of her friends was to distract from her own negligence. I stare at the plate again and say, "I should really..."

Kelsey waves to a girl nearby. "Hey, Marisol!"

"Oh, who's that?" Carol asks, eyeing someone behind me, and judging by her impressed look, it's an attractive man.

"I don't know," Melanie says, "But I think I should find out."

Their distraction gives me the perfect opportunity to escape. I whirl around and head for the door.

I'm about to pass this mystery guy. I don't want to check him out because if he's as attractive as they let on, I don't want to make the same vacant, doe-eyed look that Melanie and Carol did. As I pass him, I keep my gaze straight ahead, but a part of me is just too curious. I have to look, don't I?

As I catch a glimpse of his suit and tie out of my periphery, I admit there's no reason I shouldn't enjoy the aesthetic beauty that Carol and Melanie appreciated. I take a quick peek— then do a double take before stopping in my tracks. A force behind me pushes me forward. Though I manage to stay on my feet, the plate flies out of my hand, crashes against the floor, and explodes—ceramic shards from the plate mixing with the glass statue my sister destroyed. Even though I just royally fucked up, my attention can't remain on the glass. I turn back to the man who just walked back into my life: Jarek Dean.

My thoughts race through a series of questions: *What is he doing here? Where has he been all these years? What do I do? How am I going to clean up this mess?* I turn from him and start picking up the glass. I want to believe he's a figment of my imagination. There's no way I could be seeing this phantom from my past.

He kneels beside me and assists, picking up shards with those thick fingers I remember weaving through the wires and pipes under the trunk of his scratched and mud-patched truck. Why is he here? Why is he helping me? What's going on? Is this a dream? A nightmare?

"I'll get a broom," I say to him. I'm curt because I don't know how I should react. I'm in shock. It's been years since I thought there was even a chance of seeing him, so what am I supposed to do now that he's found his way back into my life?

I don't wait for him to respond. I hop to my feet and head to the kitchen, which is isolated enough that I'll have an opportunity to search for a broom and have a nervous breakdown.

As I push through the swing door, I see it's as empty as I hoped. I bury my face in a nook between the fridge and a pantry.

It's difficult for me to pinpoint the emotion I'm feeling most. I have a few ideas about how I *should* feel. Angry. Hurt. Devastated. I vacillated between these emotions when he destroyed me nine years ago.

My heart beats so fast I wonder if I'm about to pass out. *Get it together, Lana. Just get it together.* How am I supposed to get it together when the man who left me isn't just standing out there, but probably waiting for me to return with a broom? Where the hell is a broom around here anyway?

My worry about that stupid glass statue has evaporated. My only concern is Jarek Dean. He didn't just leave me. He left my family at a time when we needed him most, after Daddy passed away. After all my father did for him, after all the care and tending—after he treated Jarek like he would treat a son. For Jarek to dismiss us like that was too much for me. It filled me with rage, beyond anything I thought possible. It was more than the abandonment of my family, though. The night before he left, I was filled with grief over Daddy's death, and he was there for me. He held me in his arms. He stroked me gently and soothed me with tender kisses. We had a beautiful, magical, sensuous experience—my first experience—and the next morning, he was gone.

I haven't seen him since, and I never thought I'd see him again, so having him walk back into my life like this has left me in shock. Frazzled as I am, I know one thing for sure: he won't destroy me again. I won't cower from this or him, because I'm not that little, helpless girl he so easily wounded.

I search through the nearby cabinets and closets. When I find a broom and dustpan, I march back into the main auditorium, like a soldier heading into a battle. *You can do this. You can do this.*

I return to the mess and Jarek. He's collecting the fragments with the suddenly incredibly helpful Kelsey, Melanie, and Carol, who are on their knees helping him gather the shattered glass and ceramic shards.

"I've got a broom," I announce as I approach, calling off the ill-intentioned maids. The girls hop up, as if they would have preferred to be anywhere but on their knees. In fairness, I'm sure they would do anything on their knees if it involved Jarek.

He stands, his shoulders and chest bulging in a slick, navy-blue blazer. Beneath a curl in his golden locks, his eyes are locked in a cringe, as if he's struggling to see something in the distance, as if he's seeing something disturbing. That piercing gaze used to catch me off guard and make my voice rise a few octaves, but I doubt he can have that effect on me now. But even just kneeling here, I find he stirs so many of those early emotions, the ones I'd feel when I caught him working shirtless on his truck in the driveway.

I sweep up the mess, pissed at my body for warring against my feelings like this.

"Lana," Kelsey says behind me, "It's Jarek. Don't you remember him?"

How could I forget him?

"I hardly recognized him at first," she continues. "Can you believe it? He's here for business. Isn't this an amazing coincidence?"

"That's lovely," I say, sounding as underwhelmed as I can manage. I'm trying to let him think I don't give a shit, but I worry it will let him know how many shits I really give.

After I collect the pieces into a pile, I kneel and sweep them into the dustpan. I stand back up, keeping my eyes everywhere but on Jarek. I head off with the mess to dispose of it in the kitchen.

I empty the dustbin in the trash and hurry out the back door. The chilly spring air wraps around me. The temperature will surely protect me from the party guests, discouraging them from venturing outside. It'll permit me a moment with my thoughts, allowing them to wander where they've wanted to since I set eyes on him again.

They drift back to the day we returned home from the movies, discovering a broken front door and missing artwork and décor. Daddy had a disappointed look in his eyes while Mom raced around frantically, taking inventory. A police officer came to the house, and Daddy and Mom gave him a tour as he took photos and left with Mom's list of missing items. Several days passed before the police phoned to let Daddy and Mom know they'd caught the culprit, who had naïvely sold several of our pieces to a local pawn shop.

Despite Mom's insistence on a hanging, Daddy refused to press charges. The burglar was a vagrant, a homeless kid who'd pawned our belongings to buy food. Daddy wasn't a vengeful man, and his generosity was one of his weaknesses, so much so that for many years, our family struggled because of what little money he left behind—something Mom manages to bring up every chance she gets.

Shortly after the discovery of this burglar, Daddy introduced him to us. I was thirteen at the time, and I didn't understand why he was insistent upon us meeting him until, after great turmoil with Mom, we allowed him—this criminal—into our home. He bought Jarek new clothes and got him a job with Jermaine Quagley, the local mechanic, who trained him so that Jarek could work off his debt for some of the things he'd broken during the burglary.

Daddy fixed up the garage for this deviant, who after a very short time became a son to my father and a friend to me. I can't say he was such a friend to my sisters. He was closer to Kelsey's age, but she seemed as enthusiastic about him as Mom was. I, on the other hand, found we always had a very good time whenever we watched TV together, which was how it began. After dinner, we'd sit in the living room and watch Jeopardy and then whatever movie we could catch on cable. He was so kind, sincere, and funny that it was easy for me to let my guard down. After even more time I found myself feeling something deeper for him, something I finally acted on after Daddy's death. I nestled against him for comfort, and in my weakness, he took me—with a passion and intensity that was all I could have ever dreamed of. I believe it may have been the severity of my depression that made it stand out above all the other experiences I've ever had, but that would be the last night I ever encountered Jarek Dean. He left the following morning, without so much as a goodbye, breaking my heart in two, snapping it like a twig, and leaving me dying inside. I don't know that it was because I wanted our relationship to be more serious, though I did. More than anything, I needed a friend, and my family needed someone strong to keep us together. We had nothing. We were on our own, struggling to survive, and Daddy had left us in greater debt than Mom had realized.

In a very short time, I lost the two men who meant most to me, and I was devastated. Until I saw him just moments ago, I didn't even know what had become of him. I imagined he'd run off and found sanctuary working as a mechanic, but he's wearing an awfully nice—and what I assume is a tailored—suit for a mechanic.

What will I do? How can I approach him when all I want is to slap him across the face? However, I can't spend the rest of my evening hiding. I don't want him to know how he's affected me all these years later. I return to the auditorium, grab a glass of white wine from the nearest waiter, and regroup with Kelsey and her friends. If he's going to see me at this event, it won't be as someone busting her butt off to keep the function moving, but as someone who's so preoccupied with her magnificent life that she's hardly thinking of him. While looking everywhere but at this man from my past, I'm acutely aware of where he is at all times. I position myself between Carol and Melanie so I can keep an eye on him while he chats with Janet. He makes a comment that she laughs at before downing a large gulp of wine. I feel betrayed. She should be my ally. She's my sister, after all. However, I can't blame her. I never spoke to her about what happened—never told her how much he broke my heart.

I sort through myriad fantasies: storming across the room and slapping him across the face, pulling him aside and berating him in a nearby hallway, retrieving one of the Kinderly family's decorative statuettes and breaking it over the back of his head. There are so many ways to punish him...all of which he deserves. But I feel any sort of punishment is admitting I've been hung up all these years, and he doesn't deserve to know that. He doesn't deserve that satisfaction. Although, if I nabbed one of the kebob sticks from the appetizer table and stabbed it through his neck, that satisfaction would be short-lived.

I'm not inclined to dwell on these sorts of sadistic thoughts, but they must stem from years of repressed aggression towards Jarek. How else could I feel toward the man who wounded my family and my heart? Through my peripherals, I see one of Janet's friends dragging her away from Jarek. I catch him glancing in my direction before heading toward our little group. I haven't been listening to the conversation since Carol brought up a travesty of her disagreement with her contractor about the tiling in her bathroom, a plight I doubt I'd sympathize with even if I wasn't so distracted.

As he grows nearer, I wonder what he's doing at the Women's Club's charity function. My body stirs with emotions similar to the ones I experienced at sixteen, when I started to see him as someone I was interested in being more than friends with. My face feels clammy and warm. My heartbeat quickens. He shouldn't affect me like this. If anything, he should evoke rage. However, I can't deny this feeling within me—one that wishes he would wrap his arms around me, cradle me, and tell me he loves me. I curse my body, my emotions, as I did when I caught my first glimpse of him tonight.

I thought I'd come a long way from feeling these sensations around him. My mind and body should know better than to permit them. Where are my survival instincts? Shouldn't they kick in and help me feel total disdain for him—the sort that doesn't have any lustful impulses attached to it?

But in the same way I know I'll never be able to shake him from my thoughts, some part of me will always feel connected to him. When we were together, he activated a part of me—something I've attempted to recall in past experiences with my boyfriends, using my imagination just to get close enough to the fantasy of those feelings so I could reach my destination. I'm not proud of those imaginings, but they're not about what I *wish* would arouse me, they're about what *actually* arouses me—what I crave. Whether I like it or not, I crave Jarek, and I always have.

I wonder if this sensation lingers because of how close we became those nights when I'd stay up watching TV with him, lying in his lap. Or was it those days when he'd tease me before I ran off to school? Perhaps it was that impulse that made me give in so easily to him when I was most alone. Whatever the reason, as he slips around Kelsey and approaches me head-on, I'm face-to-face with the man I thought I'd never see again—the man who I never should have had to encounter again.

I work to conjure a greeting. As much as a part of me wants to lash out at him, to find some way of hurting his body as much as he hurt my heart, I must be civil. Not just because I don't want to cause a scene, but also because I don't want him to have the satisfaction of thinking of me as another desperate fling, like those girls who frequented his dormitory his first and only year in college.

"Hey, Strawberry." My nickname is like a knife through my heart because it refers to a different time, a better time, when Jarek and I would take a ride in his pickup truck, listening to old cassette tapes of Willie

Nelson and Prince, singing as loudly as we could on our way to enjoy milkshakes at the local ice cream shop.

I recall one of many times waiting in line, the sun stinging against my flesh. Jarek wore a sleeveless tee, his shoulders and cheeks burnt red. He laughed at me as I bobbed about to a song he didn't recognize that came from a small, duct-taped radio on the chrome counter before the window where the attendant would take our order. As we reached the counter, Jarek ordered for both of us: strawberry for me, cookies and cream for him. I continued my little dance, which the attendant and Jarek laughed at, but I just kept doing it anyway, because it was making him smile.

Those were much happier times—times I don't want to reflect on because he doesn't deserve the nostalgia.

"Hey, Jarek," I reply. I'm not curt, nor am I overly friendly. I'm matter-of-fact. It's the best front I can muster right now. I look into his eyes, sapphire-blue, stunningly more beautiful than any eyes I've seen since I first met him. I ball my hand, squeezing to encourage myself to be strong. I can't show my weakness, how I desperately want to run off, and even though I knew he was approaching me, I didn't imagine it would take so much effort to be strong. As I look into those eyes, I want to cry—not for my present self, but for the girl who was tormented by his abandonment, by not receiving so much as a telephone call from him. You're a murderer, Jarek Dean. You murdered my heart and there's nothing anyone can do to change that.

Since him, I've never found the sort of passion we shared that night. I've never felt that explosive chemistry, that intensity that left me reeling, as if I'd been overtaken by some powerful surge of electricity. His passion, his caress ruined me for those who came after him, and that, along with so many other reasons, has left me despising him.

"How did the cleanup go?" he asks.

"It's all taken care of," Kelsey replies by proxy, as if I need someone to respond on my behalf. However, I'm relieved she's given me a moment to consider how I'm going to respond to all this. "She was just so surprised to see you," she says.

"I was," I admit, looking directly into his eyes. I'm conquering some great fear, not because I'm fearless, but because I won't be defeated. It reminds me of when I was scared to go in the woods at night as a kid, so I mustered the courage by encouraging Janet to sneak out with me. She didn't last long, but I persisted. I wouldn't be defeated.

"What brings you here?" I ask. That sounds too eloquent for casual conversation, like I'm in an old movie, like some of my favorites that Jarek and I used to watch together. However, I feel keeping my words to a minimum is the best I can do.

"I'm in town on business, and a friend of mine invited me tonight to see if I might be willing to donate some money to the foundation." *Donate money?* I assess his suit once again. Surely he can understand why I'm puzzled about him A) having money and B) donating it to anyone.

"He's a CEO," Kelsey says. "What did you say you do? Something to do with engineering? Oh, I feel so stupid. It's totally escaped me." She says it the way she used to talk to boys, with her blonde, I'm-too-stupid-to-think attitude. I'm sure that since it has to do with money, she hasn't forgotten what he does for a living.

Jarek chuckles, as the boys always do when Kelsey is oh-so-coy. "Engineering," he says coolly.

My Jarek is a CEO? That's absurd. Not that he wasn't intelligent. He just never struck me as terribly ambitious, and I don't mean that in a bad way. He just didn't want an extravagant life. He wanted a simple one. His big dream was to own a double wide and have cable. When he left, he must've transformed into someone entirely different from the Jarek I knew.

"How have you been, Lana?" he asks, as if he doesn't want the attention on his newly acquired riches.

"I've been really good," I say, and while I don't feel as if I've been particularly bad, I'm overcompensating because I don't want him thinking I've been living anything other than an amazing life without him. He doesn't need to know what he's done to me.

I'll play cool and sweet as pie so that you think you meant so little to me that it hurts you. The problematic nature of my approach is that it may be exactly what he wants. Would he prefer I was unaffected by my past? How could I be unaffected by it?

"It's good seeing you again," I say to him. I turn to Kelsey. "I'm going to check on Mom." I look back at Jarek. "You know how she is." I offer a friendly smile, and as I turn, I can tell by the pout on his face that he's disappointed by my departure. Perhaps he thought he had an opportunity to make amends. If that's the case, he's out of luck, because I can't offer him that.

I search for Mom, but I run into Janet alongside her husband, Kirk. "Good to see you again, Lana," he says.

"You, too," I reply. He wears a flannel shirt, tucked into slacks. He looks adorable next to my sister. They've always been an adorable couple. However, I could never shake a sort of resentment I've felt toward him. It's not that he's awful to her. On the contrary, he's always been Janet's most doting partner. And he's never been anything but an angel to me. I believe my resentment stems from when they began dating. Since then, I've felt distant from my sister. Janet and I used to get along so well...far better than Kelsey and I. When Kirk came along, sweeping her off her feet faster than Romeo with Juliette, everything other than Kirk fell out of her vision. It was as if she could only love one person at a time, and it had to be him. Despite her living fifteen minutes away, I hardly ever see her. And while she used to cite work as her excuse, she recently became unemployed when her school laid off several employees, and she still hasn't offered to spend any time with me. Kelsey's the same way. Now jobless and husband-less and back in town, she hasn't managed to conjure up a moment of time. Although it's forgivable with Kelsey because we were never that close. We didn't understand each other, it always seemed. With Janet, it's as if she needs to keep away from me to conceal some great secret. Janet has always been incredibly secretive, and it only worsened after Daddy passed. She didn't unleash a red-faced, wide-mouthed performance like Kelsey did. She, like me, fell silent. It may have been better if either of us had taken to Kelsey's approach, as her efforts left her with dozens who were eager to aid her through the dark times, whereas Janet and I shut out the world. She used to see a therapist, but I figure she had as much trouble opening up with her as she does opening up with anyone.

"How's life been treating you?" Kirk asks.

Right now, not so great. "Just fine," I say

"Kirk has to go to Dallas for work this weekend," Janet says. "He's doing some big software installation. Evidently, the guys who handled it before really messed up."

"Yeah," he adds. "Can't say I'm doing that much better. What's happening with you?"

"We have a major internal audit week after next because of a problem with our last client, and I'm in charge of a fundraiser that happens to be the weekend after the audit."

"Oh, God."

"So what are you going to do while you're in Dallas?" I ask, trying to turn the subject away from me.

"Aside from work, I'll probably just hang out with some of the guys. Poor baby. Don't want to leave her here all by her lonesome, but..."

"Aw," Janet says in her most cutesy voice. "Baby'll be just fine." I've heard their back and forth referring to each other as 'baby' before, but it's not something I like to hear. No one's a baby here. Also, I find when he uses 'baby' to describe my kid sister condescending. If any of my exes had attempted to call me baby, I would have thrown a tantrum that would have probably earned me such a title. I don't need a man talking down to me, and neither does Janet. She doesn't have this sort of feminist view of the issue, though. I think she sees it as some sort of privilege to earn the title. And Kirk's use is innocent enough, but it's not going to keep me from secretly wishing he'd find a new nickname that didn't make him sound like a pedophile.

"We should have a girls night while he's gone," Janet suggests, and I'm pleased by the look in her eyes because she appears to genuinely want to do something with me. Although, knowing Janet, she'll just want to down a bottle of wine, and my presence has never been required for that.

"That'd be great, Janet. Just let me know when." I know I don't have the time, but I'm willing to make it for Janet. She smiles. It's been a long time since I've seen her look excited about the possibility of doing something with me.

As the event comes to an end and people start to leave, I settle beside a table, sipping a glass of white zinfandel. I've never been one to turn to alcohol for comfort, but the more I talked to Janet while she tossed them down, the more convinced I became that, considering the events that had transpired, I needed something to take the edge off. As Jarek approaches me again, I'm pleased I've made the decision. This little glass of wine has given me a bit of courage and maybe I'll get through a discussion with him. Although I'm also terrified it might have loosened me up so much that I'll blurt out some confession about that night or about how I feel now.

Why shouldn't I fuss at him about it? I have every right to be furious. However, it feels like in doing that, he'd be winning. I refuse to cave to a tantrum. That's not me. That's something Kelsey would do after some date slighted her. I remember when her ex-husband disagreed with her at a dinner party. I thought she was going to throw him out the window. She went into a tirade, berating him as if he were a toddler who'd done something against his mother's wishes. That's not what I'm looking for. I don't want him to see me mad. He doesn't deserve that. I'll keep my cool. I'll be so cool he'll even question if I remember what happened all those years ago. But wait—I can't be that aloof. Then he might realize I'm faking it. I have to be clever about this. I have to acknowledge what happened, but act as if so many years have gone by that naturally I don't have any major feelings about it anymore.

"Hey again, Lana," he says. The guilty look on his face reminds me of the first day he introduced himself, when he knew he had been wrong to rob us.

"So you've been doing well?" I say, attempting to direct the conversation.

He smirks a smirk I remember seeing frequently, a sort of false-humble expression that he'd get whenever he told a joke in just the right way—jokes that caught me so off-guard I couldn't help but drown in laughter. "I hear the same about you," he says.

"I'm not exactly a millionaire." *Exactly? Ha. I just barely make five figures.*

"I hardly do the word service."

"Really?" I ask, looking over his suit. "Did you wear a lot of designer suits before?"

He rolls his eyes. "It comes with the package." Speaking of package, I can't help but sneak a glance. I'm hoping it will look smaller than I recall, but the bulge suggests the contrary. Surely it hasn't gotten bigger...or smaller in my recollection. Neither of those things seems particularly likely. I'm not sure I'd even be willing to take that thing now—after having years of practice with other men. I must have been a very bold girl...or just incredibly naïve.

Why am I even thinking about his penis?

"So what's this business you're in town for?" I ask, more to redirect my own line of thinking than to actually discuss his business affairs.

"I came down to check out an engineering start-up. I'm interested in acquiring it." *But never interested in acquiring me.*

"Where are you usually?" I ask, worried my emphasis might stress the years that went by without me knowing where he was.

His expression turns sad, as if he caught the dig. "San Diego."

"Do you like it in California?"

"Can't really complain about the weather, that's for sure."

"Well, that's—"

"Hello, you," Kelsey sings as she slides between us. She throws her arms around him. I can't help but resent them both for the display. This wasn't something she would have done back when he lived with us. I recall occasions when she'd tell him to clean up because he smelled like sweat, but I never understood her issue with his scent. He smelled wonderful to me. It's no surprise that a new suit, new hairdo, and considerably larger bank account go a long way with Kelsey.

"Are you outta here?" he asks with a smile, one I wish he'd worn when he first saw me.

"Yeah. I have to get home. It's late." Late? What she means is she's getting the hell out of here so I can do the real work.

"It was good seeing you," Jarek says. "And sorry to hear about—"

"Don't worry. I'm fine. It really was over *long* before the divorce was finalized."

"I'm still sorry to hear about that." Kelsey giggles that awkward giggle she does whenever she doesn't know how to respond to a comment. I guess that was the way to survive the various idiots she surrounded herself with in high school, but I can't figure how it benefits her as an adult. But who am I to question Kelsey's skills? She's been wooing men far longer than I have...and with far better results.

"How long will you be in town?" she asks.

"Until my business here is resolved."

"We need to go out. Catch up."

"That sounds great."

"How about this week sometime? What's your number?" Before she finishes her sentence, she has her phone in hand. She keys away, preparing to take his digits. I don't make any movement to take out my phone. I hope it's clear I'm not interested. A glance from Jarek assures me he's noticed.

I wish I could gauge that look. Is he bothered by my disinterest? Or is he just wondering why the girl who was head over heels for him isn't desperately scrambling for her phone?

He gives her his number and then looks to me and folds his arms, giving me a look that I always interpreted to mean, "I know what you're doing."

"There's this great new restaurant over in Buckhead," Kelsey says as she puts her phone in her Gucci purse and slides the strap up her shoulder. "Do you like sushi?"

"Love it," he says, but it's clear by the look he gives that he doesn't, and I figure that hasn't changed because he never liked sushi. I want to call him out on it, but I'm not going to give him the satisfaction of knowing I've kept that memory all these years.

"We must go," Kelsey says.

"That'd be great."

"I guess I'll see you soon then." She tosses him a seductive glance. I wish I couldn't read her so well, but when she bats her eyes in the most transparent way imaginable, how could anyone not know what she's up to? Leave it to Kelsey to fall for a guy after he fell into a big wad of cash, but I suppose millions is more than just a wad of cash.

"Make sure to say bye to Mom," I say, giving Kelsey a glare she knows she deserves—the sort I used to give her when she would conveniently need to go to the bathroom after dinner, leaving Janet and me to tend to the dishes. Considering how busy this event has been, I'm already worried it'll just be me and Janet cleaning up. I would have thought Kelsey could make time during at least one of the few events she comes to, but I'm obviously mistaken—as I always am when it comes to Kelsey. "You might just want to see if she has something you can do before you go," I add.

"I would, but I really need to get home. I have an early brunch I have to get to tomorrow." How silly of me. I guess those of us who don't have brunches scheduled are in charge of the dirty work. In Kelsey's narrow-minded vision of the world, my job isn't as important as her brunch. She turns to Jarek, as if to avoid the glare I continue to stare her down with. "So good to see you again. Now, don't disappoint me. I expect a call, because I'm going to be real sad if you head off without so much as hanging out with me." Maybe they can have cocktails and talk about how much money they have.

I admit I'm jealous. I'd love to have half as much money as either of them, but considering I'm not totally unfortunate, I don't really have anything to complain about.

After she leaves, an awkward silence stretches between Jarek and me. What are we supposed to talk about? What could we possibly talk about?

"Your mother told me you're a big wig at an event management company," Jarek says, breaking the silence.

"Mom's exaggerating, as usual. I'm with the company, but I'm pretty much still in training. I'm organizing a major fundraiser for one of our biggest clients, so that will determine my future there."

"That sounds promising."

"Far from a CEO. I guess all our little math sessions paid off after all."

His grin widens. "Clearly."

"You're welcome for scaring you off so you could become super-successful." Dammit. I can tell by how quickly his grin falls that this wasn't the right thing to say.

"Are you seeing anyone?" he asks, I guess trying to change the subject. I want to lie so I don't seem like a spinster who's been all alone and bitter without him, but I have no desire for word to get around so I'd have to answer to Mom, who will surely interrogate me: "Why haven't I heard about this mystery man? Who is he? What does he do?"

"I'm pretty focused on the job right now," I explain. "I'd better go mingle. It's been nice talking again." By nice, I mean super-stressful and let's not do it again.

I abandon him yet again and work with Janet to return the mansion to its usual state.

In the middle of the commotion, I speak with Nancy Frader, the woman who helped us organize the event. After relaying Janet's run-in with the glass statue, which I claim was my own run-in, she gives me a twisted expression and a few curt words before leading me into an office, where she digs out paperwork for me to fill out. Though she's upset, I can tell she's feigning a sort of cordial attitude. My mother is too active in town politics and social gossip circles for a woman like this to piss off one of her daughters. However, if Nancy knew how little Mom would care about her going off on me, I'm sure she'd eagerly share all her thoughts about property destruction in this ostentatious mansion.

Once I finish the paperwork, I head back to the kitchen, where I assist some staff members with packing supplies and loading them into the catering van. When we finish, I take Mom's dishes, many of her own which she brought to the event because she didn't think those offered by the service were fancy enough. I wash them in the kitchen sink. As I'm working through trays, Jarek steps in. Is he lost?

"Anything I can help you with?" he asks.

"All good here."

"Really?" he asks. "Your mom said you could use some help." Of course she did. She'd say anything so she could continue chatting with her hoity-toity buddies. While it bothers me she's avoiding the cleanup for *her* event, it's worse that she sent him back to see if I needed help. I never spoke to her about what happened, though I would have thought my own mother would have some idea that things weren't good between us. Perhaps it's a lot to ask, especially of a mother who never seemed to understand me, but I would have thought it reasonable to assume she would have known I felt something. I guess that's silly because had she realized that, surely she would have approached me back then and consoled me about my loss. However, she assumed it was just part of my grieving over Daddy.

"She was mistaken," I say.

"Nonsense," Janet says. She steps through the swing door, walking around him and setting a stack of plates on the counter beside me. "If she doesn't need the help, then I sure do." My tension relaxes as I'm filled with hope that he'll be following Janet around, not me. They head out together and I continue my work with the dishes. As I reach the end of my task, I work nearly as hard scrubbing grime off my arm as I did to get it off the pans.

Mom saunters through the doorway, her eyes red, as they usually are when she's had a few glasses of wine or a couple of strawberry daiquiris. She wears a designer dress— I'm not sure of the brand, but the top is brown and cuts off diagonally at the waist, giving way to the black lower half of the dress. A set of pearls draws some attention to a spot of inflamed flesh on her chest, just above her augmented breasts. Mom's skin has always been incredibly sensitive, so there's no telling where the inflamed spot came from. Perhaps it's a bit of perfume from one of the guests, or perhaps it's merely a dry patch, which Mom develops more and more frequently these days.

She beams, which is nice considering that after events like these she usually has a foul expression on her face. It appears this one was a success. Although the fresh batch of Botox she received last week, which makes her forehead appear swollen, could be responsible for the stiff, seemingly-pleased expression she wears. Perhaps it's frozen that way. However, she's not whining about anxiety attacks, so I believe I'm not misunderstanding her mood.

"This has been wonderful, hasn't it?" she asks as she sets a tray of wine glasses on the counter beside me. "Although Charlene didn't make it, and you know how I need her to help with the anxiety. She's good at keeping everyone entertained so I don't have to be put on the spot, but even though tonight was just on me, I guess I did fine." The gleam in her eyes assures me she's feeling fairly proud of how well she did.

She's about to head back out when she turns back to me and says, "Jarek is sure looking handsome, isn't he?"

Ah! This is why she's beaming. "And *successful*," I say, stressing what she's actually noticing. Mom may be a fan of his today, but I remember how she used to treat him. In the beginning, I believed her contempt was understandable. He robbed us, after all. What mother would be excited about her daughters being around a criminal? She was just protective, or so I thought. But while she used that as her logic, it became clear once we saw how good-natured he was, when he went out of his way to volunteer with me every time I helped out with some food drive or fundraiser in impoverished areas, that her issue was exclusively with his lack of money. While Mom is well known around town for her work with charities and how willing she is to assist with causes that benefit the sick and poor, most of these events began with my father, who spent what little time he had on this earth trying to give away the money he'd managed to acquire through his knack with real estate investments.

While Mom threw lavish parties, Daddy read to children at hospitals and went around door-to-door delivering presents to families at Christmastime. Mom wouldn't have done those sorts of things. Mingling with the poor has never been her forte. I recall a party where she said,

"You don't want to be around them. They're so unpleasant and miserable, and the longer you're around them, the less you want to give them anything—let alone money. Donate from a distance because it's the only way you'll ever be able to keep doing it." God forbid she set eyes on the actual horrors of those less fortunate than herself. I think she sees that as being like Lot's wife during Sodom and Gomorrah, as if she'd turn back and transform into salt. If the legend ended with her turning into diamonds, I doubt she would have had much of an issue, because I've developed a strong suspicion that Mom really believes you can take it with you.

"I know, I know," Mom says regarding Jarek's success, as if that's a perfectly valid reason to appreciate him now. "Did you ever notice a spark between him and Kelsey before? I saw her approach him and how she just lit up. Don't you think they would make a cute couple?"

"What?" I ask so severely that Mom gives me an incredulous look. "I mean, I didn't notice anything. Do you think he's interested?"

"Have you seen Kelsey? Of course he's interested." Mom has never hid her praise of Kelsey's beauty, though I'm not sure she's at fault for that. Kelsey is objectively beautiful—legs long as broomsticks, plenty of breast, and silky blonde hair that waves to her waist. She's a goddess. It seems Mom's ovaries decided there was only room for one gorgeous daughter, because while Janet and I aren't lacking, we've always paled in comparison to Kelsey and have been treated appropriately so.

Being around Kelsey has assured me that the world is a much better place when you're considered gorgeous. You're nice because you can afford to be nice. No one gets frustrated with you. Few challenge you, because surely whatever divine authority gave you beauty also provided brains—or if it didn't, surely there's no reason you should be forced to endure the pain of intellect. Brains and ingenuity were never Kelsey's specialty, but they never had to be. She just needed that smile and the gleam in her eyes that, for some unknowable reason, has always been present.

"It's been long enough that she's surely ready to move on anyway," Mom says, referring to Kelsey's divorce. But I'm hung up on her obsession with Jarek being great for my older sis. Why not me? Because I'm not interested. I've been hurt so much that I *can't* be interested again, but Mom doesn't know that. How can a mother not understand her daughter as much as mine doesn't understand me?

"He's not going to be in town long," I say, "so if she wants to make anything happen, she'd better get on it."

"I'm sure she will," Mom says, a sly smirk on her face as she snatches some of the silverware I've stacked on a towel beside the sink and sets it in a plastic container on the table behind me—actual silver, because when the service offered aluminum, I recall her saying, "What will the girls say? I'll be a social pariah!"

Jarek enters the kitchen and approaches Mom. "Anything else you need help with, Ms. Raeven?"

"No, Jarek, but thank you so much."

"No problem."

"Have you seen Janet?" I ask Mom.

"She left with Kirk about thirty minutes ago," Jarek replies.

"What? She said she'd drive me home."

"You can get a car," Mom says.

"That's like forty dollars from here." Mom looks unfazed by my hesitation at spending that much on a ride back. If I'd been smart, I would have driven myself rather than accept the ride from Kelsey.

"I can drive you," Jarek offers. My arms tense. Why would he suggest that? Why doesn't he know how awkward this should be for him? Did my cool act leave him thinking we're buddies?

"I can take public transit," I say.

"It's on my way back to the hotel."

"Don't be ridiculous, Lana," Mom says. As I catch her expression, it's clear she isn't considering anything other than the get-out-of-jail card that is Jarek, because I'm sure she knows how pissed I am that I've been ditched and have to fend for myself.

I'm trapped between a rock and a hard place. If I go back with him, I'll have to make conversation with the guy I despise for what he did to me. If I insist I won't, he'll know just how mad I am at him.

I force a smile. "Perfect."

Chapter Two

On the drive to my place, I glance around uneasily. My body is stiff as I keep still so he won't catch me fidgeting or see me doing anything that indicates how uneasy I am. I want to be in control—or at least appear that way—even as I'm working desperately to keep from reliving the most painful moments of my life over and over again.

"Your family seems to be doing really well," Jarek says.

"We're fine," I say. "I think Kelsey's happier now that she's divorced than I ever saw her when she was married. And Janet's actually talking to me, so that's a treat." Why did I say that? That's something I would have confided to him back in the day, but not now. He doesn't have a right to know the details of my life, so why do I feel compelled to share with him? It's hard not to, because there's something disarming about him, something about his manner right now that makes it hard not to be swept away by him all over again.

"Why doesn't she talk to you?" he asks.

"It's nothing. We've just been distant these past few years. Ever since she got married."

"Is she okay?"

"I'm sure," I lie. I hope she is, but I can never tell. Every time I see her, it's like she's crying out for help. There's something in her demeanor that makes me feel like I need to come in and rescue her, but I can never tell from what...I'm not sure if even she really knows. It may just be the mere discontent with where she is in her life.

Jarek pulls up alongside my apartment building, hidden in darkness. "Do you live in Mug-Central?" he asks.

"It's the streetlight across the street," I say, indignant at the suggestion that I live in a bad neighborhood. "The city hasn't come out to fix it."

He smirks, as if he's pleased to have gotten to me with his tease. I grab my purse and push the door open. "It was nice to see you again," he says.

"Nice to see you again, too," I say as I scoot out. I start to shut the door behind me, but stop.

This isn't good enough.

I don't want to shut this door and send him away. Something deep inside me wants him, and I chastise the urges, but they beckon me, give me an idea. If I can, why shouldn't I get to enjoy another moment?

It's a terrible idea—to bring him back in and feel those same twisted emotions that I felt when he went away before, but maybe it will be therapeutic. Maybe by inviting him in again, I'll have control this time, because I'll know what he's going to do—how he's going to leave me again.

Don't do it!

As bad an idea as I know it is, I can't stop myself from reopening the door, ducking to look at him, and saying, "You wanna come up for a drink?"

His eyes light up. *Is he glad I've offered him another chance? Does he see it as an opportunity to redeem himself?* He shouldn't. That's not what this is. It's not his chance to get back in. It's my chance to be in control—to take charge of the experience I had no control over. Because that's what I deserve—a moment to turn him away, a moment to show him how much I don't need him.

It won't be that easy. A part of me will feel those same sensations I felt so long ago and be overpowered by them, but he won't catch my act. He doesn't know me as well as he did back then, and he won't know I'm faking when I convince him I'm so over him that I can have a fleeting night of passion and dismiss him without giving him so much as a second thought. That's how powerful I am, and there's nothing he can do to take that power from me.

As he steps across the threshold, into my apartment, I wonder how I let it get to this.

In all the years after he left, I never thought we'd end up here. Countless times, I imagined standing up to him, hating him up close, but being with him now, I feel hope well within me. It frightens me because I know nothing can really come of this.

You always seem to win, Jarek. You always did.

I loathe myself for this desire to feel those same exciting emotions he once evoked in me. *Don't do this*, I plead with myself, because as much as I've assured myself it's vengeance, I know better. I wish I could delude myself into thinking that's all it's about, but I can't.

I flip two switches on the wall beside the door, turning on the orange bulb before the entry and the white kitchen fluorescent lights. I make my way to the kitchen, which connects to the living room. I take note of the Captain Crunch box I left out this morning, and I know there's a bowl of cereal and a spoon in the sink that I need to clean. My heels click on the white tile of the kitchen floor as I approach an island in the center of the kitchen. The black onyx top glistens beneath the white light. I can tell by my movements that I'm at least subconsciously working to draw attention to my swaying hips. I turn my head to Jarek ever so slightly, a clear seduction that I hate myself for. How can I be doing this? Why would I even entertain this after all he's done?

But I deserve it. I deserve another night...and yet, I worry it'll just leave me wanting more, as it did so long ago.

I'm different now. I won't be that girl again. I'm in control. I'm the one who's going to leave him wishing he'd given me his everything when he had the chance.

"I thought you'd..." he begins, and I can tell by the look in his eyes he wants to take me back to that night, and I don't want to go. "...be upset about—"

I turn back to him and rest my lower back against the kitchen island. "The past is the past."

Though I know I can't just toss it off like I wasn't upset. Jarek will know it's an act, so I'm more careful in my approach as I lean back against the island, pushing my hip forward to stress my form. I'm not Kelsey, but if even half the chemistry of our past still lingers, my tricks will be as effective as they once were.

"I can't say I was ecstatic," I say with a forced chuckle. "It wasn't the most noble of exits, and I was pretty mad at you for a while after. But what else should I have expected? I was a kid. We were both kids. Stupid kids."

"Yeah," he says, a trite acknowledgment of his behavior. *You hurt me so much. How can't you see that? How can't you read my thoughts and see the pain I still feel because of what you did? The Jarek I knew could have read that...would have seen how much I'm falling apart inside right now. He would have saved me from the pain.* Maybe that version of him only existed in my imagination.

"That was a long time ago, though," I say. "I'm not sure I can even remember the details." I think I'm doing a good job, but I worry I'm trying too hard. He steps across the living area carpet, onto the tile. The click of his shoes isn't as loud as my heels—a slow, steady tap, emphasizing how fast my heart is racing right now.

As he grows nearer, I have to look up to see him. Our positions leave me feeling submissive. I want to fall into his arms and let him do with my body as he pleases, because I know exactly how satisfying it can be, but I have to fight this primal urge.

At least for now.

"Regardless," he says, "it was a shitty thing to do."

"I've done plenty of shitty things since then, so I can't claim to be an innocent."

I haven't done anything nearly as cruel to another person as what he did to me. But tonight...I just want to lose myself in this. I can face the regret tomorrow. I can handle that insurmountable pain another time—not now.

He approaches me and caresses his thumb against my cheek. It's the way I remember him touching me before our last experience. It almost does me in, but he doesn't get to be in charge. I leap at him, pressing my lips against his, cupping my hand around his neck, pulling him close.

He pushes me away.

Will he stop this? Will he reject me? Maybe it would be better if he did. That might offer me the closure I desperately seek. *Give that to me, Jarek. Deny me right here.*

"Do you really want to do this?" he asks, reminding me of a similar sentiment he expressed last time. I attempt to vanquish it from my thoughts.

My conscience begs me to reconsider what I'm doing. That's the weak child within me. She doesn't have a right to speak right now. She doesn't have a right to vocalize her opinion when her childishness has only caused me heartache. She's not in control of this moment. And neither is he.

"Jarek, Jarek, Jarek," I say. "I'm not the girl you once knew." I kiss him again, the way I would a guy I'd picked up for the night. However, I can't deny the warmth of his lips and breath, the sensation that spreads through me as our flesh meets. He wraps his arms around me. I trust I won't have any problem getting him to fall into my trap—to watch me take it, enjoy it, and walk away. Regardless of how much it will hurt tomorrow, it'll help knowing I had a moment where he didn't leave me like I meant nothing to him. Not this time. Never again, Jarek.

His lips abandon mine and trail down my neck. I throw my head back as he kisses down to my chest. He rubs his hands up and down my sides, his fingers caressing, stroking and kneading, sending sensations up and down my body—sensations that bring me to life, make me feel a whole other level of arousal and intrigue. He feels so good. Why does someone this wrong for me, someone who's caused me such pain, have to send these delicious feelings rippling through me? Shouldn't it hurt? Shouldn't it be so unbearable that I couldn't even consider a moment like this?

He grabs the bottom of my dress and lifts it over my head, exposing me. I won't be the only one standing in such a vulnerable state, though. I always hate that in movies, when the girl is butt-naked and the guy has all his clothes on—especially if it's a fancy suit like the one he's wearing. I unbutton his blazer and toss it over a stool beside the kitchen island. We work together, me unbuttoning his shirt while he kicks off his shoes and drops his pants so we're both in our underwear.

He removes his shirt and pulls off a white tee beneath it, revealing a beautifully sculpted six-pack. He's more ripped than I remember. He's clearly been working on his body, maybe at the gym, maybe because he was born to have this incredible physique. Whatever the reason, it's gorgeous, and I allow my gaze to delight in every crevice.

I press my lips against his chest and move down into the dip between his pecs. I rest my hand on his side as I trail down his torso, taking in the scent of the delicious cologne he wears and a bit that I know is him, a fragrance that smells as good as it did back then. While I enjoy the topography of his body, I imagine how I will ravage him. I kiss to his obliques, where I follow one of his v-lines, seemingly pointing to the expanding bulge in his black boxer briefs. I yank them down and behold his fully erect penis.

There it is. I remember when I was so eager to pleasure it. Now I just feel as if it took advantage of me. What right did he have to take that from me when he never had any intention of giving me more?

I settle on my knees, and rather than pleasuring his dick, which I am sure he wants, I run my tongue around his balls, tasting him. His penis twitches, assuring me of his satisfaction. I grab his ass cheeks and claw my nails into his flesh just a little too hard, so that he groans. *You're mine, Jarek.*

Who is this wicked woman within me? I can't claim ignorance, because I know her too well. She's the bitter, resentful creature Jarek created—a monster that has dwelt within me since that tragic day. And now Victor Frankenstein has returned to face the beast he gave life to.

I stand and step to him so that our torsos are flush. As I gaze into his eyes, I find I'm challenged. I don't see the terrible man I wish I saw. I see the boy I fell for, the same boy who I wanted so badly but who didn't want me back.

I shift my gaze. I can't do what I must if I'm looking in those beautiful blue eyes. Not if I'm filled with sympathy and hate, such confusing emotions to handle at one time. To distract myself from the thoughts that duel within me, I kiss him again. It replaces the pain with the profound lust I have for him. He spins me around and I follow his lead until my back is pressed against the wall beside the front door. His movements are gentle, but forceful enough to show me he wants to be in charge. I want him to ravage my body, but that's not how tonight is going down. *You're not calling the shots.*

I slide out from between him and the wall and shove him forward so that his chest presses up against it. I wrap my hands around his torso and feel the grooves in his six-pack, those powerful muscles that shift with each breath. How many sit-ups does it take to get a stomach like this? I envy his body. I'm sure it takes him a fraction of the time it takes me to maintain my own form. Of course, there's also the element of genes. I recall how he walked around with a six pack when we were younger. He didn't have to work for it then, like some guys. My ex, Todd, had to go to the gym just to keep his stomach flat, but starvation was the only way he would have achieved the kind of definition that seems to be a gift the gods bestowed upon Jarek.

His head falls back as he delights in the pleasure I'm permitting him. He doesn't deserve it. I question if I should even give him the benefit of this moment, but I've come too far. I must stick with the plan: show him I can give him this and not feel anything afterward—or at least, appear not to.

I grip onto the shaft of his cock and stroke it up and down, massaging my thumb across the head, feeling pre-come lacing my flesh. A part of me wants to stick it in my mouth and taste him, but that won't be happening tonight. He grunts a familiar grunt, one that has returned to me again and again when unbidden thoughts of that night have forced their way into my brain, despite my attempts to focus on anything else. Sometimes I attempt to watch a movie. Sometimes I read a book. Sometimes I go through endless series of Wikipedia articles. None of these occupations can shake his guttural sounds made in passionate moments from my thoughts. Those thoughts haunt me, and I know they always will.

I release his dick and slide my hand down his thigh, feeling his flesh, taut against his firm muscles. I stroke my hand around his hip and caress his ass. It feels just as I remember. So smooth, so supple. I love it!

I press my lips against a depression in his shoulder blades and kiss softly across his back. As I feel the crown of his head on my forehead, I can't help but enjoy the moment. This is how close I wanted to be to Jarek for so long. This is a moment that felt so good in that time when I allowed myself to get lost in him, and I decide, though I want to get my revenge, I can let that wait until after this experience. Right now, all I want is for him to take me—to make me his—to do as he chooses.

I grip his shoulder, spin him around, and kiss him again. He swoops down and scoops me off my feet. The power, the intensity of the move, the exhibition of his masculine power, allows me to lose myself as he kisses me. He has me, and I feel safe again. What could be safer than lying in his arms?

He pries his lips from mine, and I guide him into the bedroom, where he places me on the bed, moving his face down my body. His nose and lips assault my flesh, shifting about, leaving me wanting so much more, wanting him inside me. I want him all over me. As much as I want him to own me, there's a line I won't allow him to cross, because he had a chance to have me however he wanted. He had the chance to do as he wished, and he didn't take advantage of it. He let it slip away. His loss...and mine, too.

His lashes brush my belly as he blinks, the sensation coupling with his kisses and sending waves of energy rushing up and down my body, stirring goosebumps across my chest and arms. The sensation is powerful, and another surge rushes up my spine and feels as if it's spilling waves of delight, like a river dumping these delightful sensations at the back of my head.

My cheeks tickle. My fingers prick. I want him inside me. I want to feel his thrusts, and in a moment, all those delicious sensations I experienced so long ago are reawakened. It hurts feeling it now, knowing I've been with enough guys to know how rare it is to feel these intoxicating highs. I never felt this way with Brad, Jesse, or Todd. This sort of stimulation was anomalous compared to my experience with Jarek, but it felt like what I was always reaching for, and now it's here again. It must be whatever potent pheromone he emits. How else can someone feel this kind of chemistry with another person?

He cups his hand under my back, pulls my body closer to his face, and kisses up and down my belly. His movements are so rapid, so primal, it feels as if he's missed my body as much as I've missed his. It's the sort of attention I've longed to receive from him—the sort of appreciation I wanted to feel—the sort of sensation that stirred such life in me, and brought me to climax that first time.

He leans back and gazes at me. What's he doing? As much as I could read Jarek in the past, I'm not sure what this look means. Is he thinking about how he left me? Is he thinking about leaving me right now? Regardless, just having his gaze on me makes me feel so important, as if I'm the only thing in the world that matters to him. Tomorrow, I'll realize that isn't the case.

He slides his hand up my thigh and gently removes my panties, pulling them down my legs and discarding them on the floor. He trails his fingers back up my leg until he reaches my clitoris. I toss my head back so I'm looking at the concrete ceiling. It looks different, as if something's changed, though every crack and divot appear the same as they always have. Everything in my place seems new, beautiful, magical, but I know it's only because Jarek's affection has transformed my perspective of everything around us.

Soft flesh and warm, wet saliva delight my senses. Flicking, teasing sensations sporadically stimulate, and what nerves aren't aroused are left waiting in suspense, as if they hope they will be fortunate enough to experience those same sensations. Rushes of energy, like volts of electricity, spiral up my body. They feel so good. Knowing this will be the last time I get to experience them makes me want to soak them up, to engrave them into my memory forever, to collect them and ensure that I never forget how amazing this feels.

He kisses up my body again until he reaches my face. Then he pulls back and gazes at me. I want those eyes on me, but at the same time, they make me feel so vulnerable that I almost need him to look away. But then I wouldn't be under his spell, so I refuse to do that. *Dammit, Jarek! You have me all over again. Take me. Punish me for this desire that pools through my body. Tear me like no man has ever torn me because I deserve the cruelty for wanting something that is so bad for me.* I'm an addict, and he's my drug. I shouldn't want him, but I can't help my desire to feel all this over and over again. Worse than anything, I know that when it ends there won't be any way for me to get it back.

I pull away from his gaze and scramble to the nightstand, retrieving condoms and lube.

"Look who's all ready," he says. I'm sure he thinks I'm a slut for having condoms and lube ready to go. It's really the opposite. I bought the unused pack several weeks after my break up with Tom, when I was about to go on a date, but the guy was a prick so they went unused. So if anything, they mark what a prude I've been. However, he doesn't have to know that. I toss him a glance, raising a suggestive eyebrow to keep an air of mystery around his suspicion.

I start to tear the condom wrapper open, but he snatches it from me. "I got this, thank you very much," he says as he opens the wrapper and slips the condom over the head of his dick, rolling the edges down his shaft with a proficiency that assures me he's done this with plenty of other women. He opens the bottle of lube and lathers his shielded dick. I don't know how much he'll need though, considering how wet I am.

I lie across the bed, awaiting his entry. He slides forward, his knees gliding across the duvet, pushing my legs apart as he maneuvers inside me. I instinctively roll my head back and grip his arm. Though there isn't a lot of pain *yet,* I know what's coming, and if it hurts even fractionally as much as it did that first time, I need to brace myself. But I know he won't invade me aggressively. Even in that first experience, he was so gentle. He stroked his finger across my face and kissed me tenderly, as if reminding me that, despite the pain, he cared for me.

He strokes his hand up my side and presses his lips between my breasts, kissing his way back up to my cheek, until he's making his way around my jaw and up to my ear. As his breath hits my earlobe, my body quakes. Body heat radiates off his face and hits my cheek. I feel pressure building inside me. I try to relax, to allow the invasion, but the occasional muscle spasm resists, and I know it's only making it more difficult on me. Once again, I'm my own worst enemy.

He pushes forward boldly, until I feel as if I can't take it much longer. I assure myself I can. I've taken it before, with far less experience. I grip his arm, hoping it will distract me from the sting, but as I start to adjust, I feel the pressure in me relax as he pulls back.

He leans down and kisses me. It starts as a soft, sensual kiss, but as it firms, it feels more passionate. I kiss back, taking in the warmth of his mouth, licking his wet tongue, feeling a rush of heat, like a fever, overtaking me. He wraps his arm around my neck and pulls me close, kissing as if he's missed holding me as much as I've missed being held by him. He slides back in, powerfully, forcefully. The intensity of the move is too much for me. I pull my lips away from his and groan. He freezes, a worried expression on his face, and I can tell he's terrified his last insertion was too intense.

"I'm sorry," he says quickly, "I didn't—" I put my finger over his lips.

"I'm not a little girl anymore," I say.

I'm not that girl who couldn't handle it—that girl who was so nervous and uncertain. And even though I can feel certain parts of me reluctant to embrace the severe obstruction, they'll have to bear it however they can, because I insist. I smile a twisted smile, one that I can tell by his relaxed expression gives him relief. He slides back in, and it's just as intense as the last time. I grind my teeth and grunt. He thrusts and thrusts, each time sending my thoughts back, as if opening a portal to the past. I wander through blissful sensations I haven't recalled in such a long time. These corridors of ancient memories fill me with sensations I've long forgotten, ones I almost believed for such a long time couldn't exist for someone my age.

I drift back to that night.

"I'm so scared," I told him.

He looked at me with that loving gaze, those sapphire blue eyes glistening in the lamplight. He nestled his face against mine and whispered, "I don't want to do anything you're not comfortable with."

His shirtless, slightly burned flesh was warm against me as I lay beneath him, exposed. His jeans, the only barrier between us, scratched at my legs as he caved to the movements that his body encouraged him to make, as if preparing him for those he would make when he reached his final destination.

My fan didn't work, so the room was filled with a thick July air that forced beads of sweat across my face, and the heat from Jarek and the experience of being so close to him only made it worse. I struggled to breathe, though I wondered if that was because I was still recovering from the funeral I'd witnessed the day before.

A stray lock of my dark brown hair lay across my eye. Noticing the obstruction, Jarek passed his thumb across my forehead, freeing my vision so that nothing could taint my view of him and his soft, loving gaze. In that moment, I couldn't have felt more safe.

I tightened my hold around him. "But I want it, Jarek. I need you. Please, Jarek."

Jarek kissed me again, for what felt like the thousandth time, but it still wasn't enough. I didn't think I could ever get over that kiss—that it could ever mean anything other than something magical to me.

He stroked his hand across my belly and promptly leaned down and kissed it, burying his face against me. My flesh felt as if it was on fire. I tossed my head back and savored the attention, the affection.

This moment feels just as delicious, as carefree. As my body rises nearly to the peak of excitement, I hear the distant memory of the words he whispered, with lips caressing my ear as he spoke just before my climax: "You mean everything to me, Lana."

My muscles spasm furiously, my head bobbing back and forth as I feel these powerful sensations explode through me. The intensity of my climax scatters my memory, chasing it back into the corners of my mind.

As Jarek continues his movements, his face twisting in a way that assures me he's close, I feel terrible for my mind's betrayal. How could I consider using such a moment to reach a powerful climax? I curse myself, but it doesn't keep me from enjoying the final bit of pressure and the settling of Jarek's body that assures me he's finished.

Chapter Three

He lies beside me, resting peacefully. The deep breaths he takes assure me no matter how much I stir, he won't be disturbed, which is a relief because I'm not sure how easy it will be for me to rest after what has transpired. Though my relief after the pinnacle of our excitement temporarily scattered my thoughts, I find them drifting back to that last day, before our encounter.

I sat on a rock at Lake Dreyfus, just a few miles from the house. It's where I would often sneak off to, sometimes to work on homework, other times just to think. That day, I needed to get away from the hustle and bustle that had followed the news of Daddy's death. An aneurism seemed to me the most mischievous of thieves, the sort that, without warning, could come into someone's life and destroy everything they had held so dear.

The smell from the lake, accentuated by the hot day, was rank. Two mallards swam side-by-side. I wondered how one would feel if the other was suddenly plucked from the world by an owl or a hawk. Such a disturbing thought for a seventeen-year-old girl to have, but since hearing the news about Daddy five days earlier, the world had turned dark, as if a shadow had suddenly been cast over a place that had once enjoyed too many days of sunshine.

"You okay?" came a voice from behind me.

At first, I resented the voice, because I enjoyed my solitude, and most importantly, I didn't want to be caught in my grief. However, as I turned and saw Jarek behind me, his face as worn and tired as my own surely was, I couldn't help but appreciate that if anyone understood how much I loved Daddy, it would be one of the greatest recipients of his love.

He sat beside me on the rock, as he'd done on many occasions when we'd slipped away to this place to enjoy the afternoon together, him sharing stories about the girls at college and me telling him about my own drama with my friends in school. The last time I saw him, I was particularly hateful as he described a girl he was interested in. I'd shouted at him about being as sleazy as every other guy, but I knew better, because it was really jealousy. Since he'd left for school, his absence had stirred something within me, alerted me to something I felt for Jarek that was much stronger than friendship. We hadn't made up since that incident, but in light of recent events, I couldn't find a decent reason to be upset with Jarek. If anything, he was my only companion, the only one who could, with a single look, know exactly how I felt, exactly how much pain I was in.

Without a word, he wrapped his arms around me and held me close. Even with the heat joining his to make me feel as if I was suffocating, I didn't care. I would have rather suffocated in his arms than anywhere else.

My body trembled. I hadn't noticed until his arms were around me. The tears fell, and soon I felt him trembling as much as myself. We shared our grief in a place that had once been so magical to us both.

I shake myself from the memory. What's the point of dwelling on the past except to torture myself? I gaze at Jarek, a once sympathetic and understanding creature who had at some moment turned cold and become my nemesis.

I wake as if from a dream. Last night was surreal. When I was little, I had a dream about our dog Barry returning. He bounced about, running in circles and chasing after finches. We picked up right back where we left off, me throwing sticks across the yard and Janet teasing him with slices of ham before offering them for a reciprocal lick to the face, something that seems increasingly disgusting the older I get. Barry had been dead for two years, and when I woke to discover it was only a dream, I was devastated. Nearly as devastated as when I had similar dreams about Daddy.

Surely last night with Jarek wasn't real...just another cruel dream, one that makes it seem as if my own mind is warring against me, wanting me to endure emotional turmoil.

It couldn't have happened. I haven't seen Jarek in so long, and nothing's occurred to suggest he would come back into my life. However, as my thoughts clear and sensations linger in my body, I know it was real. My neck stiffens.

Don't look, I tell myself, because I'm terrified if I roll over and look at the other side of the bed, he'll be gone. That's what I should expect from a night like that. That's what he's left me knowing must be the outcome.

As I turn, I discover I'm right.

I didn't want to be. Why couldn't I have woken when he got up? What time did he leave? Why did he leave?

No! I shouldn't be asking that question anymore! But there's a little girl in here who isn't strong enough to handle this, and her emotions come racing back to me in the most powerful and painful of ways. Tears stir in my eyes. I rub my face against the duvet furiously. I shouldn't feel this way! I knew this was coming! It's not the same, but it is. I feel that awful emptiness that I felt after Daddy was gone.

Why did I fall for this trick? Not Jarek's trick, but my own deception. Why did I convince myself I could bear this one-night stand with someone who evoked such powerful sensations within me? How could I be so stupid as to believe I wouldn't feel those same emotions—or that I could handle them? *I'm such an idiot.*

The door creaks open. I shift my gaze to the intruder—not just in my room, but my life. My face turns bright red, because he's caught me in the most vulnerable, most embarrassing of moments. I wipe my face against a pillow beside me, working to appear as if I'm wiping the sleep out of my eyes.

Jarek approaches, his boxers low, giving me a view of those impressive curves outlining his obliques. My gaze lifts to that taut navel surrounded by the muscles in his swollen abdomen.

"'Morning," he says, kneeling on the edge of the bed. He leans close and offers a kiss. I don't fight it. I don't know why, because I'm furious with him, but it wouldn't make sense for me to show it, not now that I've worked so hard to put on a front to convince him I can get over him, that he means nothing to me anymore.

As he pulls away, I say, "'Morning." I don't want to say much more. Too much talking seems like something a desperate girl would do to keep him around.

"Sorry. I had to slip out to make a call. I have to head out soon. Got a meeting I need to get to."

"Oooh. Sounds fun," I say, trying to keep my cool, but I can't help but feel that going so far out of my way to appear cool is just making me sloppy.

"I was going to ask if you wanted to have dinner tonight." *Dinner? Really?* What does he think this is? A part of me wants to say yes. She's that same naïve girl who needs me to protect her because she's a moron who believes this means something.

"That won't work," I say. "I have plans."

"Maybe tomorrow, then?" *He's going out of his way to make plans with me?* It only makes me want to say yes more, but what's the point? He'll just leave me like he did before, and this is my chance—the one I wanted last night. I can show him I don't care any more than he did back then.

But the little girl in me reminds me that he might want something more. *Don't be stupid, Lana. He's seen you for a night. He doesn't even know who you are. Who you've become. This isn't the Jarek you knew back then. This is a stranger.*

"I might have something then," I reply. His expression turns serious, as if he's detected my meaning. "Why don't you just give me your number," I say, "and I'll call you to make plans." He smiles.

I was doing well, but I tricked myself into believing I could let him go. For a moment, I was convinced that asking for his number was to reject him, but a part of me really wanted to get my hands on it, because then he wouldn't be gone. Not like he was back then. At least this time I would have a way to reach him if I wanted to.

"That works fine," he says, his smile broadening. I'm disappointed with myself for my agreement, but it was the best I could do after my horror when I believed he'd gone. But here he is, about to go again. This is the moment.

He slips into his jeans and throws on his shirt. As he enters the bathroom, I assume to throw together some semblance of a look that doesn't scream "one-night stand," I hop out from the covers and toss on some clothes. Jeans, a blouse that's way too nice for jeans, and some flats. A glance in the floor mirror beside my closet reveals how ridiculous I look, but I shouldn't care. I'm never going to see him again. *Wait! What am I thinking?* If I want him to know what he's missing out on, I can't look like this. I throw off the blouse and kick off the shoes. I hurry to my dresser and put on a bra. He comes out as I'm buttoning it.

"Ooh la la," he says. I chuckle because he saw my full frontal just a few moments ago, so I doubt this is much of a sight. I head out of the room into the kitchen. I've decided to put on a kettle for tea, so I can be busy and not follow him around like I'm eager to spend what little time we have left together. I can at least have some self-respect. He follows me as I grab the kettle and take it to the sink, filling it with water. *Who's the desperate girl now?*

He stands there, gawking at me. "Really?" I ask, though I'm not all that bothered. I like that he wants it. It will make it even better when I never call him.

"Well," he says, "I guess I'm gonna head out."

"Sounds good," I say, setting the kettle on the stove and turning the heat up. He doesn't move, as if waiting for me to do something, but I can't figure out what. "Bye," I say. It's an empowering statement, one that's long overdue. I finally get to say goodbye.

It would have been nice if I'd had the opportunity to ditch him—walk out last night so he wouldn't see me go. Considering I brought him back to my place, it wasn't practical, but it would have been the ultimate "Fuck you!" While I can't have that moment, at least I have this opportunity to excuse him from my apartment, a gratifying moment in and of itself. He tucks his head close to his chest and heads out the door. "Bye, then," he says, sounding defeated.

As I hear the door click shut, I feel as good as I hoped. I did it! I reclaimed everything I wanted. Though I had plenty of moments that overpowered me, painful moments where I was afraid of him leaving again, now I feel incredible!

But his number? He was supposed to give it to me. Maybe I didn't win as much as I thought I had. Maybe he hurt me as much as he could have just by walking out on me like this.

It's amazing how fast a person can go from feeling totally empowered to feeling as if they've been stripped of everything, left as vulnerable as ever. Because I feel utterly defeated.

Just move on. That's what you do, Lana. You move on and you move forward, and you can do it again. You know you can. However, my words of encouragement do little right now. I brace myself against the edge of the stove. It's my only source of ease right now.

I have to get on with my day. I hurry to the cabinet and open it, scrambling for breakfast. As I reach for my box of Captain Crunch, I remember that it was on the counter the night before. However, a sticky note on the side assures me Jarek's the reason for its seemingly miraculous replacement. The note has a number and a winky face scribbled on it. Such a simple gesture fills me with hope. I don't understand why. Why would I feel hope when I'm never going to see him again? Is it just the victory, knowing I've affected him, that I could get his number from him? That at least this time he wants to be in touch with me?

I pull it off the box. I should rip it up, tear it apart just like I should rid him from my life forever. But I can't end it like this.

My heart won't let me.

I set my victory on the counter, beside the sink. Just don't call him. Don't text him. Keep it right there to remember that you could if you wanted to.

But I'm not sure how much this will help.

I survive the weekend without being so much as tempted by the sticky note. I wish I could say I've been as good about keeping Jarek out of my thoughts, but that's not true. It has been a constant struggle, but at least I've had work to keep me busy. Our preparations for the internal audit have been enough to keep my mind occupied, only occasionally drifting to thoughts about the man who shouldn't have re-entered my life.

I scan an invoice from a stack on the table behind me. I would have asked Stephanie's assistant Derren to do it, but Stephanie needed his help organizing a few boxes of receipts from the Merris Foundation event—the one we royally fucked up. Stephanie should have handled those receipts before the event, so I'm pissed that I even have to work on scanning these invoices. I was more than willing to do them when I first saw them in Stephanie's inbox, but she insisted she'd handle it. I guess if she meant she'd just give it to me months later, then she handled it.

"Lana." I turn to Stephanie, who stands in the doorway in a tight beige dress and ruby-red high heels that are tall enough that if she tripped, she'd surely break a leg. Her new highlighted extensions fall to her waist. I like this look far more than the bob with bangs she sported last week.

"Yes?" I ask. Her lips curl upward, assuring me, as they usually do in that position, that whatever she's about to say is good news.

"Guess who I just got a call from?"

"Who?"

"The Frenly Brothers' agent. They've agreed to appear at the fundraiser!"

I gasp. It's incredible news.

Farcon & Williams functions as a liaison between nonprofits and their fundraisers. Commissioned to pull off major events, we pull together designers, entertainment, and venues so the organizations do not have to manage these elements themselves. Since our work is to draw financial support to these organizations and because our own income comes from the success of these events, it's ever-important to find something that will draw people to the event. With fundraisers, entertainment is everything, especially with a cause like children with special needs, which, as my research has suggested, has not been a crowd-pleaser this year.

As the coordinator for this event, it was my responsibility to hire acts that could potentially draw the sort of clients we need in attendance so our hiring company can maximize their donations—and ultimately our profits.

While we have a huge folder archiving the various acts willing to work with us, I knew if I could nab someone bigger and better, I'd impress Stephen Farcon, the still-working partner of Farcon & Williams. Also, if this goes off without a hitch, I'll be assuring myself a position within the company.

With so much riding on the success of the event, the moment I was handed the account, I searched desperately for an act that could attract the money-makers in town. The Frenly Brothers, a duo of violinists who are considered very chic right now and grossed several million for their national tour last year, were at the top of my hit list. I'm baffled they agreed to participate just because of my little letter, but I can tell by the look in Stephanie's eyes that she's impressed.

"Are you kidding?" I ask.

"Keep up the good work." She starts to leave but swings back around and leans against the doorframe. "By the way, my date with Marcus was incredible." Marcus is a guy she met on eHarmony last week. She considers him very promising, as he's an attorney with some big-wig firm in Roswell. "You don't even know, Lana. We went out to eat, and then we went back to his place, which is fabulous. I'm talking a waterfall on the wall fabulous. This guy is five stars all the way, and I mean...all the way."

I had my own five star evening, thank you very much. "That sounds nice. So when are you seeing him again?"

"Not sure yet, but I have a feeling about this one." As she does about all of them.

When she heads out, I open the scanner and retrieve the first page of my scanned invoice. My phone vibrates. It's Kelsey, texting to see if I'd be interested in playing tennis after work. She knows I can't play, so it's interesting that she asked me. However, I'm fine if it's a chance to spend time with her. Despite the pileup, there's only so much I can do, and I would rather take some time off today than spend all my time trying to play catch up at work. Also, with my Frenly Brothers victory, I think I deserve to get off a little early as a treat.

When I arrive at the courts, Kelsey is looking adorable in an outfit she clearly purchased exclusively for playing tennis. In a small white skirt, blue blouse, and bright blue shoes, with her hair pulled back in a ponytail, she is the quintessential tennis player. I could see her playing professionally on ESPN. However, I know her skills, so I'm vividly aware that I could never actually see her playing professionally. Perhaps that's why she wanted to play with me, because I doubt she's concerned about trying to beat me. As for her look, I'm wondering if it is designed to ensnare some man at this country club she so kindly invited me to. I can't really judge her for her efforts. It's what she's always been good at, and considering the shorts and blouse I'm wearing with my five-year-old Nikes, it's no surprise I've been single for nearly three years.

We play a few rounds, shouting small talk about Mom and Janet before Kelsey reveals she's trying out a new gym where a lot of cute, wealthy men work out.

"Yeah—I was going to this one in Midtown!" she shouts as she returns the ball over the net. "I thought it was great because all the guys were so nice, but they were more interested in helping me pick out new clothes than going out with me, you know?" I chuckle.

"Not your type?" I shout back as I miss the ball. I chase after it as it rolls against the fence.

"Not *their* type. I would throw myself under of any of those hard-bodied gods." I grab the ball and whirl back around. She's checking her phone. "God, I should've stopped us sooner," she says. "I thought we'd said eight."

"What?"

"I'm supposed to meet Jarek at seven-thirty for dinner."

"Jarek?"

She approaches the net. "Yeah. Didn't I mention we were getting together later?"

"You mentioned plans, but you didn't specify." I can't help but feel like I'm in competition with her, even though we've never been in competition over any man.

It was just one night. He can hurry off and fuck her all he wants. Not my business. Isn't it, though? Don't I have a right to tell him, "Hands off my sis!"? Shouldn't I at least warn Kelsey about him—tell her how he left me and he could easily do the same with her? Of course, maybe he wouldn't leave her. Maybe I'm the only one he'd leave.

"That's okay with you, isn't it?" she asks.

I can tell by the look in her eyes that she doesn't care if I approve. "Why wouldn't it be?"

"I just remember how you two used to get on, and I didn't know if there might be something still...lingering." I scoff to demonstrate how that isn't the case at all, but my performance is obvious. If she knew me as well as Janet, she would know I'm full of shit, but she doesn't, so I doubt she'll catch my lie.

"No," I say. "It's fine. He's...he's nothing like he was back then."

"I know, right? Can you believe it? Did you ever think a guy like that would end up making so much money?"

"I never thought he needed to make money."

"Lana, don't be silly. You know what I mean. Don't make this about something ridiculous. He's just so different—so much more ambitious...and charming." She doesn't realize she's basically saying *rich* over and over again.

"You think he's boyfriend material?" I ask.

"Absolutely!"

"He doesn't even live here. If you hook up with him, you know he'll fly back to California and not give you another thought?" I'm probably projecting here.

She eyes me curiously. "Will I be the first girl to have a good time?"

"Do whatever you want. I'm just saying if you're looking for something serious, I'd consider someone else. There's a reason he's still single."

"I'm playing it by ear, you know?"

I imagine Jarek putting the same moves on her, caressing her the way as he caressed me the night before last, and it bothers me. But it shouldn't. I don't care about him. Although, if he ends up being my brother-in-law, I'll wind up in a straitjacket. That would be too much to handle.

"Be safe and have fun," I say, attempting to shield my true feelings.

Even though Kelsey is the last person who would understand my feelings around this.

Chapter Four

I stop by Mom's to drop off some of the dishes I cleaned at my place after the party. As I set them in the kitchen, I see her through the window over the sink, tending to her garden. I put the dishes up and head outside.

This is when I prefer to deal with Mom, when she's one with the earth. It's when she's happiest, when I know I won't badger so much. "How's it going?" I ask as I approach her.

Her hair is hidden beneath a shiny white hat that hardly matches the dirt-covered gloves and boots she wears. She tears through the ground with a shovel as she lays seed, then moves on to the next spot and goes through the same motions. "Geoffrey got snippy with me today," she says. Geoffrey Handler is the executor of Daddy's will. One of Daddy's buddies in college, he was never Mom's biggest fan.

"Oh, really?" I ask.

"I was trying to pull from that trust...just a little more to buy a little something."

"Why would you need to pull from it?"

"A little facelift that I was hoping—"

"A facelift?"

"Lana, I don't like how it all looks. It's been bothering me for a while, and I want to get a little nip/tuck. Is that so awful?" She grabs the skin beneath her chin and wiggles it back and forth. "Look at this. Just look at it. I have to take my anxiety medication every time I look in the mirror." This won't be her first facelift, but considering her last was three years ago, I feel this might be premature.

"I guess not," I say. "But why do you need to pull from the trust?"

"It's our money, isn't it? We shouldn't have to rely on Mike's lack of foresight about the economy to make our financial decisions."

When Daddy passed, he'd given so much of his money to charities there wasn't much left. We made it for a few more years, but we knew the money was dwindling until Geoffrey discovered, through some of Daddy's paperwork, a Swiss account that held a substantial amount of money. Geoffrey explained Daddy had created this account as a sort of nest egg, and it's whereabouts had only been uncovered when he found the paperwork in an old lot box Geoffrey had neglected to check after Daddy's passing. With these documents were instructions from Daddy that each of us be granted a monthly allowance. While the amount was more than generous, Mom never liked the limitation. She insisted we contest the will, a prospect Janet and I fought violently against. We saw it as a sort of affront to our deceased father—an insult to argue with a man who could no longer justify his actions, ones he certainly didn't need to justify since the account provided us with more than enough to live on.

"Can't you save up when you get your monthly stipend?" I ask.

She groans and wipes her arm across her forehead. "I knew you wouldn't understand. I don't know why I even talk to you about these things. Your sister never has a problem understanding why I need these things."

"Because she'd probably do the same thing. I'm not Kelsey, though. And I'm sure Janet would see it the same way I do."

"If your father were alive, he'd be fine with me having my little tuck and nip or clip and whatever else I wanted. He'd want me to be happy. God knows if he'd wanted something, he wouldn't have hesitated to nab it. If he'd been better with money those last few years, we'd be set for two lifetimes each. Now we might as well be standing in line at the food bank."

"That's a bit of an exaggeration."

"You don't remember how much there was to begin with—how much he blew through. It'd kill you if you knew how much of our money that man wasted." I want to explain that it was *his* money to do what he wanted with, but this is one of those times where it's best to bite my tongue. "I know, I know," she continues. "Defend him all you want. I understand why you love him. You and everyone else did."

"And *you*," I stress, reminding her that we're talking about her deceased husband and my father.

"Of course, but I saw his faults. Most didn't. He had a way with people that you don't see in too many. He could flash a smile, and you just felt like everything was going to be all right. It was so disarming."

I remember when he would come home wearing that smile and wrap his arms around me and tell me that he was going to take us out to get ice cream. Funny how the prospect of such a simple outing made me the happiest girl in the world. Seems like it should have taken more to excite me, but just receiving that loving gaze and the simplest of treats was all it took. Daddy knew how to make all of us smile, even Mom. Though she held onto her moods frequently, he knew how to crack her. I always thought that was why they ended up together, because she needed him for those moments of release, and he must've enjoyed seeing her light up when she finally caved.

"I guess all things must come to an end," she says as she uproots a long vine that's in the way of her new seedling hole. She tosses it aside. It's sad hearing Mom say that about Daddy, and the apparent symbolism of her tossing the weed aside disturbs me. Surely it was unintentional, but it bothers me to think she could so easily discard her recollection of my father and trade it in for a new face.

The week passes quickly.

I'm still scrambling around the office. And while everyone prepares for this internal audit, there are moments where I feel like I'm the only one doing anything. Derren sits, playing some app version of Scrabble—one he's always talking about. He's not even trying to hide it. Every time he amasses more points, he proudly announces it, ignoring my repeated reminders about the various tasks I need him to perform.

Seeing that he won't be working today, I've started handling the tasks I passed along to him, despite my efforts to catch up with the scanning Stephanie should have completed months ago. But I can't be that mad at Stephanie today, because she's running around, too, though hers is because she's trying to cover her bases and appear as if she hasn't neglected a major account.

I finish some emails, playing catch up with my regular routine— those responsibilities I have to complete while simultaneously prepping for this audit, including preparations for the fundraiser I'm supposed to have totally organized in two weeks.

I check the time on the computer. 2:35 PM. One thing I'm sure of is that I will take a break. I won't spend the entire day working my ass off and neglecting it the way I usually do. Even if I just take thirty minutes, I'm getting out of this office. If Derren can sit on his ass and not give a shit for the whole day, I certainly deserve an hour.

Once I've finished checking my emails, I start down the stairs. On my way out of the office, I run into anyone and everyone who could have something for me—some task or responsibility they want to add to my already drawn out to-do list. They hand me paperwork and tell me about emails I'm still working on addressing. Days like these, I feel as if I need a Xanax. Knowing how easy it would be to ask Mom for one, it's always tempting, but I've never caved to the temptation—if only because I don't want to her to get excited that I may have inherited her anxiety.

As I round the corner at the main entrance, feeling as if I'm finally too far for anyone to accost me, I see...*No. It can't be!*

Jarek stands on the other side of the glass wall before the lobby. He leans against the reception desk, gazing down at Victoria, a dark-haired, blue-eyed angel whose eyes are lit up, suggesting she's submitted to his magnanimous presence.

I'm too stressed to deal with this at the moment. I start to turn back around when his gaze catches mine. I make like I just saw him, fake a smile, and do an awkward wave that I try to take back, but it just turns into this weird half-wave, half-muscle-spasm-looking-thing that I regret.

He laughs, surely enjoying what an idiot I've made of myself. I make a goofy face, the way I used to when we were kids and he caught me in some precarious situation. His smile settles and he gazes at me softly so that I feel the heat rush to my face. Once again, my body betraying me. I can't blame Victoria for how she's fallen for him in their brief exchange. It's just his way. But what is he doing here?

I open the glass door to the lobby. "Hey," I say as casually as possible as I approach him. "What brings you here today?"

"I thought I'd stop by to see if you wanted to go to lunch." He looks just as stunning as he did the other night, in a striking gray suit with a navy blue tie. His hair is gelled up in the front, fashionably tousled in a way I imagine he learned from a hair stylist. It seems too meticulous for Jarek.

"I'm actually running an errand," I say. "And my lunch isn't for another hour. My boss is on lunch right now." I'm such a liar.

"Stephanie got back twenty minutes ago," Victoria says. "If you want, I can check to make sure she's fine with you leaving."

Her intervention puts me in an awkward position, so I go with it. "That'd be perfect. Thank you so much."

She calls and Stephanie is, of course, fine with me going on lunch, so Jarek and I head across the street to a diner where I frequently grab lunch. I create my lettuce heaven at the salad bar and meet him in a booth he's found for us. He has a full plate with a burger and fries, which seems unfair considering I couldn't eat like that without serious physical consequences. Obviously, his abs aren't the product of a carefully managed diet. Just another reason I hate him.

"I see you can still eat anything you want," I say bitterly, as I used to when I was sixteen and saw him devour pasta while flaunting those flawless six-pack abs, the very ones I'd tried to convince myself for some time I wasn't at all attracted to.

"Yeah...guess you've acquired a rabbit's taste buds."

"Unfortunately not, but the metabolism's the same as ever, so I do what I must." He chuckles, and the friendly exchange lightens my tension about this lunch. "What brings you out here today?" I ask, more than a little curious. I don't imagine he was right next to my building.

"I had a meeting at the W, and I was thinking that since I was so close, I'd drop in. That so weird?"

"I guess not." Maybe a little, but if any other friend had done that, I wouldn't really question it. However, he isn't a friend. He's someone I hooked up with the other night. Considering our history, he's more than that, and had I actually expressed how furious I really was with him, he'd know why this is totally inappropriate. However, since I didn't, I'm stuck having to act like I'm not still reeling from the emotions of that day.

"How was your date with Kelsey?" I ask. I want it to come across as nonchalant, but I'm not that good at hiding how I feel, and I can feel the jealousy slip past my lips. It's too late to take it back, though. I hope he didn't catch it, or didn't take it as seriously as I feel I delivered it.

He smirks. "I don't know if I'd call that a date."

"Oh, just trying to tend to all the Raeven girls' needs while you're in town?" Another dig. This one feels warranted, considering he plowed both me and my sister. While I wish I could act totally cool about it, if he says he did something with her, I'm liable to leap across the table and stab him in the jugular with my fork.

His smirk expands. "Jealous much?" Since he didn't outright say no or laugh at my suggestion, I assume he's playing coy.

"There's nothing to be jealous of. It's your life and you can choose to see whomever you want. Even my sister." *I hate you! I hate you! I hate you!*

"You can say you're not jealous all you want, but I've known you since you were fourteen, and I know when you're annoyed."

"It's been a long time, Jarek. I'm not sure you know me as well as you think." *Like you clearly don't know how fucking mad I am at you for what you did!*

"Oh, really? Is that a challenge? Let's see if I can have a crack at it. You're not eating that much because you still feel like a chubby girl next to Kelsey. You dye your hair a shade darker than it really is because you think it doesn't make you look as plain as *you* think you normally look. You don't wear designer clothes because you don't like people who try to act better than they are. Yet you don't dress like a frumpy convenience store clerk because you know you have to do a little something to get by in this world. Your favorite food isn't salad. It's a grilled cheese sandwich, and if you were given the choice between that and strawberry shake, which you also love, you'd take the sandwich. And I bet you probably still sit around on Friday nights watching black-and-white slapstick comedies that you've seen a hundred times."

I don't know how to play cool when I feel like I've just been insulted with a dose of the truth. He doesn't deserve the victory. "I don't watch those movies anymore," I say.

He eyes me skeptically, and he has a good reason to, since I'm a liar. "Oh, really?"

"Not even one."

"So all those VHSs on your bookshelf are just...keepsakes?"

I nod repeatedly like a crazy person, trying to stifle every impulse that urges me to lash out at him. If he wants to pick at me, there are a few things I want to pick at him about.

"Two can play at this game," I say. "You wear your designer suits because you despise where you came from, which is delinquency. You got your fancy job because you grew accustomed to the lifestyle my father enabled you to become accustomed to. You probably wouldn't be the one to fix your car even in a life-or-death situation because it'd be so beneath you now. And I'm guessing that your last major relationship was with a girl named Tiffany or Jessica or some equally generic name." His expression transforms from skepticism to hurt, and as cruel as some of my jabs were, I can't say I feel all that bad about it, since it's the truth.

"Is that how you think of me now?" He sets his burger down and rises from the booth. He's only taken one bite out of his burger.

"Am I wrong?"

He stands there for a moment, as if trying to think of what to say. "I guess *I* was," he says finally.

"Was what?"

"Wrong about you. Thanks for having lunch with me, Lana. It was nice seeing you again."

"You too," I say curtly. He turns and leaves, and though it isn't easy, because it feels so similar to the last time this happened, it feels better knowing I did something to make it happen, that he left because I was a jerk to him.

Does he think he has a right to be mad at me? After what he did, he doesn't have a right to be mad. He never has a right to be mad, though the longer I sit here with his hardly touched tray of food, the guiltier I feel about the severity of my attack. But what was I supposed to say after he assaulted me with all those things he didn't deserve to know about me? Was I even that far off about who he's become?

I doubt it. If he can't take it, he shouldn't dish it out.

Chapter Five

Friday night, Kelsey texts to see if I want to meet her at a bar in Buckhead. Considering the week I've had, Jarek's visit included, I'm eager for an escape. I need a drink—a few, even. I just want to forget that Jarek even came to town...that I ever set eyes on him again.

I slip into the bar and lower my jacket, which I used to cover my head from the rain as I dashed through the parking lot. I look my jacket over to see how much rain has collected on it, but it's not too bad.

I scan the packed venue and spot Kelsey seated in a stool behind the bar. She sips from what I assume is a glass of vodka and Redbull. Her favorite. I can't stand the stuff.

"Hey, sis," she says as she spots me. Her hair rests behind either shoulder, looking flawless, as if she's stepped out of an Herbal Essence commercial. She wears a dress that I'm sure is designer and a set of pearls that are probably real.

"Is Janet here yet?" I ask.

"She's here all right." She glances at the dance floor. Janet, in a black skirt and a long-sleeve maroon jacket, is shaking her ass against Jarek's crotch!

A massive crowd fills the dance floor, but despite how busy it is, Janet and Jarek catch the judgmental gazes of more than a few patrons. Jarek laughs as he indulges Janet with the dance. In a periwinkle button-up with sleeves rolled up and a few buttons undone, it's clear he's not trying to appear more laid back than the last few times I've seen him. "What's he doing here?" I ask severely.

"I invited him," Kelsey replies, eyeing me as if she's suspicious about why I asked that—and with such a harsh tone. "Is that an issue?"

"No, no. I was just surprised to see him." I sit on the stool beside her. As the bartender approaches, I order a ginger ale. I'd rather order straight liquor, but if Janet's drinking, I assume I might be the only one who can drive her home. I don't look back at the dance floor. I don't want to deal with him again, especially after our last encounter, but I know I'll have to.

The song fades into another before I hear, "Lana!" Arms wrap around me, and when I turn, I see the glazed-over look in Janet's eyes. *Dammit, Janet. Get it together!*

Dammit Janet was her nickname in college, given to her by her friends. When I was a senior and she was a freshman, I'd meet her out with her sorority sisters, and they used the name with affection and humor. Still, Dammit Janet was a notorious drunk. Though I'd experimented with some of my dorm-mates when I first started attending classes at the University of Georgia, a few nights of vomiting and some nasty hangovers during tests prevented me from investing too much time in partying. "Janet, don't you think you should be taking it easy?"

"I've been trying to get her to stop," Jarek says, stepping up beside her, "but the clever girl's managed to sneak drinks for the past thirty minutes."

"It's my fault," Kelsey says, something I don't doubt for a moment. "I keep letting her too close to mine."

"Oh, no!" Janet cries as she stares at a clock on the wall behind the bar. "It's almost eleven! Kirk's going to kill me if I don't call him!" *What is he, her babysitter?* She snatches her purse off the counter and starts off, riffling through her purse as she heads for the front door. I rise to follow her, to make sure she doesn't get into any trouble.

"Don't worry," Kelsey says, "I've got this one." She takes her drink. "We'll go together!" she exclaims with false sincerity. She turns to Jarek. "You mind? It'll be real quick."

"Not a problem," he says. The jealous fire within me burns at my cheeks. Kelsey follows behind Janet. Whatever cruel power reigns over this universe clearly just wants to make my life miserable.

As they head off, Jarek orders a shot of Tequila. He doesn't look at me. I guess he's as eager to see me as I am him, especially considering what a bitch I was the other day. A part of me feels I should apologize, yet I'm owed a bigger apology than he's offered or could offer.

"Good day at work?" he asks.

"It was fine," I say curtly. "How goes your business here?"

"Not as good as I was hoping, but I'll know for sure in the next few days."

"On another date with Kelsey, I see."

"What's it to you?"

"Just an observation."

"Did you have anything else you wanted to lay on me while I'm still in town?"

"Nope. I've covered everything."

He gazes at me as if he's furious, and I'm glad he's mad. It's nice knowing that after all these years, I can still get to him. "Did I say something? Do something the other night?" he asks. "Is that what this is about? 'Cause I was really looking forward to getting together again."

"You mean fucking again? Is that what you wanted?"

He looks around, baffled. "Seriously, what do you think has happened to me? Do I really seem all that different?"

I study his look. Though he appears more casual than the last time I saw him, with his button-up loose against his khakis and the rolled-up sleeves, it's still nicer than he would have worn back in the day. And that hair is just as flawless as it looked that night at Mom's Women's Charity event. "You look a lot different," I say.

"It's interesting that a girl who's always had money thinks she can judge me now that I have a little."

"You have more than a little. And what makes you think I've always had money? We've had a lot of years where we've had to fight and scrape just to get by, same as everyone else."

"According to your Mom, that's not a big problem right now, so it's not like we're on totally different planes of existence." *Why are we still talking?* "And who are you to judge me for being different now?" he continues. "You don't even watch those damn movies you loved so much."

"Of course I watch those movies."

"So you lied?"

"Yes, I lied. You thought you were so clever because I haven't changed *at all,* evidently. You think you can come back here after all these years and read me like a book. I'm sorry if you don't like my attitude now, but I've had a lot of life to live while you were gone, and it's made me this way, so sorry if it doesn't fit the fragile mold you remember." He smirks. "What?"

"You still watch those movies."

"Oh my God." I hop off the stool and start to leave.

"Where are you going?"

"I'm going to find Janet and Kelsey."

"No, please. Wait a minute."

"Yeah?" I ask, turning back to him.

"I'm not any different than I was back then. I'm still a goofball. I wear these clothes because, like you, I'm expected to look a certain way for my job. I don't even pick the shit out. I have a designer who coordinates it all. Hell, she has to match outfits for the week because I'm liable to grab mismatched socks if she doesn't handle everything. I still fix my own car, and I still have the same fucking cassette tapes that we used to listen to in the truck together." That's adorable, and I wish he hadn't said it because it sets me at ease about him, and I don't want to be at ease. I want to hate him! I want to hate everything about him!

"It's still me, Lana." It's too bad he doesn't understand that that's what I'm mad about. He's still the guy who walked out on me. He's still the guy who left my family in our time of need. And for that, I can never forgive him.

He shifts his gaze to the end of the bar. "Oh, shit," he says. I turn to see Janet gulping down a shot. She sets the glass next to two others.

"Dammit Janet."

I dash across the bar. When she spots me, she giggles. "Hee hee. Am I bad?"

I roll my eyes. "You're just a mess. Where is Kelsey?" I'd forgotten how irresponsible she could be. She keeps it checked when she's around Kirk, and since I've rarely seen them apart, I didn't realize she could still achieve sorority-girl sloppiness until now.

She shrugs, turns to Jarek, and smiles. "Hey, Jarek," she says in her most flirty tone possible.

Do all the Raeven girls have a thing for him? I grab Janet and start my quest to find Kelsey, who I catch stepping out of the bathroom. "You said you'd watch her!"

"I brought her back in. We were just at the other end of the bar. I didn't think it'd be an issue."

"Great. Just great. Please tell me you drove her." She shakes her head.

"I drove myself, silly," Janet says.

"Well, you're going to stay at my place tonight, I guess." *Thank you,* Kelsey mouths.

I don't want to deal with her right now. This is all her fault. I mean, it's Janet's fault, but Kelsey could have done a better job discouraging her up to this point. Kelsey knows just as well as I do how she can get. Although I'm sure neither of us expected her to act like this.

Jarek helps me drag Dammit Janet to the car. The rain has settled down to a light sprinkle, which makes it easier for us to transport her. "Thank you," I say, setting her inside. He walks around the car and gets in the passenger's side. As I slide into the driver's seat, I ask, "Did you drive here?"

"Took a car."

"Oh, did you want a ride?" I ask, thinking this is an odd time for me to drive him back.

He eyes me like he thinks I'm a bitch for thinking he's trying to mooch a ride off me. "I was going to help you get her back and then get another car. Considering you live on the third floor, I thought you could use the assistance."

"Oh, thank you." *That's incredibly thoughtful.*

"Are you guys going to pork?" Janet asks like a goofy teen.

"Shut up, Janet," I say, as if I'm also a teenager.

She giggles. "Don't tell me to shut up. Always thinking you're my parent. You're not, Lana. You're not Daddy. And you sure as hell aren't Mom, but for different reasons." She laughs at that, too. Jarek gazes at me, as if he's amused by her remarks. I start the car and head back to my apartment.

The car is silent for a while, except for the sound of raindrops hitting the windshield and the wipers swishing back and forth. I turn the music up.

"Oh, God, it sounds like *The Exorcist* in here!" Janet squeals from the back. I turn it back down.

"I would have thought you could hold your liquor a little better than you did in college," I say.

"I would have thought you would have a better sense of humor by now," she snarks. "And it's all down. That's what matters, right?" Jarek chuckles.

"Don't encourage her," I insist. But he keeps laughing.

"Jarek thinks I'm funny," Janet says. "Do you like funny girls, Jarek?" Through the rear view mirror I catch her winking at him, a playful wink, a wink Janet would only give a man she wasn't seriously pursuing, because in my experience, when she's actually interested in a guy, she's the least flirtatious person in the world.

She takes her seat-belt off and leans over the console between Jarek and me. "Please put your seat-belt back on," I say.

"Don't tell me what to do. I'm just trying to talk to you." She turns to Jarek. "Hey," she whispers, "you mind telling me something?"

"What?" he whispers back.

"Did you and Lana ever...?"

"Okay, Janet," I say, throwing my arm back and shoving her.

"You did, didn't you?" Her eyes light up as if she just unearthed some great secret.

"It's none of your business. Now just sit back there."

"You totally did. Was it good?" *I hate you so much right now. I wish I could pull the car over and punch you in the face.* Through the rear view mirror, I see her beaming at me. "It's huge, isn't it?" I'm glad it's dark in here because I don't want either of them to catch the change in my skin tone.

Jarek presses his lips together, like he's not willing to offer anything about this, which is a damn good idea, because anything he says right now is likely to piss me off.

"I can see it in your pants," she continues. "It's practically a billboard you're walking around with. You'd think you tailored them just to show it off..."

"Janet, please..." I say, hoping to get her off this subject. Dammit Janet finds this hilarious, but I know Sober Janet won't be nearly as amused about what she's talking about. And I doubt Kirk would be either.

"What?" she asks, but her attention returns to Jarek. "My friends and I used to sneak around to the garage, when you were working on your truck. We'd see it just poking out in those jeans. First time my friend Marla pointed it out to me, I thought it was hard as a stone, but nope, that's just how it always is, dangling around. It must be a fucking weapon. Is it a weapon, Lana?"

"Janet, you're going to feel so stupid tomorrow!"

"I feel stupid right now. And every day, so what's changing? Just let me talk about this. It's always been on my mind, and I want to talk about it. Kirk's got an itty bitty baby dick. It's like if a baby carrot had a premie."

"*Janet!*"

"It is! Obviously that's a ridiculous exaggeration, but you know what I mean. You don't feel that." She cringes and shakes her head. "You should have taken your shirt off more," she says to Jarek. "Seriously, you had a real good body when we were younger..." *He has a better body now.* "...and my friends always liked it when you did things around the house shirtless. I think our house would have been the place to hang if you'd just been our own little Magic Mike. I mean, *huge* Magic Mike. 'Scuse me, Mr. Man." *Mr. Man? Did she learn how to flirt from a thirteen-year-old girl?*

"Why don't you already have a wife?" she continues. "How old are you? You're too old not to be married. Lana's getting there. Twenty-seven."

"Not for three months, thank you very much."

"Close enough. But there's still time...if she'd learn how to keep a man. Pfft. Fat chance of that happening." I'm done interfering with her rambling. "I guess it's good that you're not married, though," she says. "Don't listen to the others."

"Others?" Jarek pipes up.

"The liars. The ones who tell you how amazing it is to be married. Oh, God. You never get to do anything. You're always waiting to see if the partner approves...see if you can go out...see if you have to stay in again. We always stay in. That's no fun. I want to party."

She quiets. As relieved as I am that it's stopped, I'm a little sad to hear that she's unhappy in her marriage. Maybe she's just having a difficult time right now since Kirk is gone. I doubt she feels this way normally.

"It's okay that you're not married," she says. "You just haven't found the right one yet." I see his eyes on me in my periphery. *Why is he looking at me? Is he acknowledging I'm not the one? Is he regretting what he did?* I want to turn and look at him, to see what he thinks about that, but I don't want him to interpret my looking as some sort of desperate longing for him...I mean, clearly there's desperate longing going on, but he doesn't have to know that!

"Janet, seriously?"

I battle her limbs as I pull her from the car, but she fights. I don't know why. Where does she think she is going? "I can do this myself!" she screams.

"Okay, come on," Jarek says.

She bats her eyes at him. "Anything for you, babe."

Kirk would love to hear that, I'm sure. I lead her into the guest bedroom and she throws herself onto the bed. She stirs. "Lana...Lana..." she says, her eyes shut, her arms laying limp over her head as she lays flat on the bed, her skirt hiked up so far that a few more inches would be revealing more about her choice in underwear than I care to know. I pull her back to her feet and pull the sheets back, helping her under the covers. I tuck her in. "Lana!"

I don't acknowledge her rambling. As I'm about to start out into the living room, where I left Jarek while I prepared her for bed, she grabs my wrist. I turn back to her.

"Are you happy, Lana?" she asks, reopening her eyes which glisten with water.

"Yes."

"No, you're not."

"Why do you say that?" I ask, wondering if her state might evoke an honest reply. She appears as if she's suddenly sobered up.

"Because I look into your eyes, and I see how sad you are," she says with a slur. "How do you do it? It hurts so much, and you just find a way."

"What hurts so much?"

The water in her eyes stirs about. "Life."

Though I understand her sentiment, it saddens me to hear my little sis sound so unhappy. I try to convince myself it's just the liquor talking, but I know better. I sit on the edge of the bed and scoot closer to her. "What can I do?" I ask.

"To be happy?"

"To help you."

A tear runs down her cheek. "I don't think I can be happy. It's too late for me. But you were always so happy, so full of life, and now when I look at you, it seems like every day, you lose a little more of that life you had. And I just keep thinking, what if Dad were here to see you?"

Her words jab at that memory of Daddy, make me fear the notion of looking at my life now— how restless I feel, how sad I've become. I know Janet didn't mean to stir this feeling, but since it's about Daddy, I can't help but feel saddened by it. And what would he think if he saw Janet in this state? Would he be angry with me for not doing more to keep her in my life? It feels like every time I inquire about her life, she just pushes me further away, so I don't know what to do.

"Lana, don't be sad. You don't need to be sad anymore. Why can't you just be happy with Jarek?"

I'm horrified. Why did she say that? Am I so transparent?

"You guys were so happy back then. I remember being jealous because I thought you would grow up and get married and have kids."

"There was nothing between us."

"Yes, there was. Everyone knew it. And we were all waiting for you to wake up and see it. What happened? Why did you push him away?"

Push him away? I want to object, but Jarek is in the living room, and I don't want him to hear us talking about him. "You're so drunk," I say.

"But I'm saying things that are truer than anything most are willing to say. I'm telling you what you already know. I believed in magic back then, Lana. I believed that good things could happen to good people and that everything would work out in the end. But I'm not sure anymore. Why do they lie to us? Why do they tell us that we're going to grow up and everything's going to work out for the best?"

I don't know, Janet. I don't know. But I can't respond to her while she's like this. "Just get to bed," I insist. I rise and start for the door.

"Lana," she whispers. As I reach the doorway, I reluctantly turn to her. I fear what she might say. Her words have been more personal than anything I'm used to hearing from her.

"Yes, Jan?" I ask, working to fight back the emotions she's stirred.

"Please be happy again. Please laugh again...the way you used to. Or just smile. It doesn't hurt to smile every once and a while. Daddy might see you, wherever he is."

I almost lose it, so I just nod and step out the door, bracing myself against the wall, because all I want to do is drop to my knees and cry.

If only Daddy could see me...if only he knew how unhappy I am right now, how alone I feel every day.

"She okay?" comes from the entry to the hallway.

Keep yourself together, Janet. Just keep yourself together.

I gaze at him from the side, tilting my head to allow a tear to rush down the cheek he can't see. I remind myself of the asshole he was to me, of how responsible he was for all the misery I've felt for so long. If there was one person who had the power to pull me from my misery, it was Jarek, but now there's no hope. The very man who could have brought me so much pleasure now evokes such contradictory, painful sensations that it's only in fleeting moments, like that night together, that I'm able to exile all those cruel thoughts from my awareness.

"I guess I'll drive you home," I say. I slip past him and head toward the door.

Nice as it was that he helped me with Janet, her words have reminded me about the horrible state he's put me in. I'm furious for what he's doing to me by being back. Furious for how stupid he must be to fall for Kelsey's act. I shouldn't be mad at him over that. After all, I have plenty more valid reasons for being pissed at him, but right now, this one bothers me the most.

"I can get a car," Jarek insists.

"No, I owe you for this."

"She going to be okay if we leave?"

"Only if she has a problem finding the bathroom." As I reach for the doorknob, I feel his hand on my arm. I spin back to him.

"Lana, Lana," he says. I look into his eyes—a big mistake, because how am I not supposed to get lost in those beautiful eyes? *Please, body. Just get out of this place.*

"If I said something the other day at lunch, something that provoked you, I'm sorry." *You have so many other things to be sorry about.*

A crash of thunder precedes the trembling of the floor beneath our feet. "We'd better get out of here before it starts pouring," I say. I turn from him but he grabs me again. "You can stop grabbing me anytime," I say, shoving his hand off mine. He gazes at me, startled.

"Sorry, I didn't mean to—"

"I'm sure. Can we go?"

"Are you mad at me?" *Aren't I always?*

"Don't you need to be getting back to Kelsey?"

"There's nothing going on between me and Kelsey."

That's what you think. "Yeah, okay," I say.

"Why are you acting like this?"

I want to yell at him about that morning—that day I waited for him in agony, trying to assure myself that he'd return. I want to yell at him about so many things right now, but he's been so helpful, and being this close to him makes it hard for me to express my fury. It makes me feel weak, vulnerable. *Damn you, Jarek Dean! Why do you do this to me?*

"Lana, I thought we were starting to get along. I thought maybe we could—"

I know where this is going, and I won't stand for it. "You thought we were going to start dating or something? Really? Come on, Jarek. Don't be ridiculous. You think you can walk in here, years later, and pick up where we left off. I don't see you like that, and I'll never see you like that. What we had when we were young was a stupid mistake, and the night we had— that was just for fun, but that's all. Don't you get that? Tell me you're not so childish that you actually believed anything more could come of this."

His gaze sinks, and I can tell he's hurt. He should be hurt, because everything I said is what I've been yelling at myself all these years. It's nice that he should share in some of that shame. *No, Jarek, I won't be opening up my heart to you so you can crush it into a thousand pieces again.*

"You should go," I mutter. Everything in me is telling me to console him, to apologize for the cruelty, but I don't have to, and I shouldn't have to. *He's the asshole. Why do I have to keep reminding myself of that?*

"I thought you were going to drive me back," he says.

"I can get a car for you if you want."

He gazes at the window. Droplets slide down the glass, obscuring the view outside. "Don't bother," he says. He hurries out.

I approach the door and rest my hand on the knob. The little girl in me wants him to return, to storm back in and beg me for forgiveness. She wants him to wrap his arms around me and whisper how much he's always loved me and needed me. She imagines us reconciling and moving on, together.

I hurry to the window and glance out to see his exit, to watch him leave me once again. It's raining harder than before so the sound of the drops fills the apartment. He runs out from beneath the foliage of the trees before my building and rushes across the street, ducking his head and tucking it beneath his jacket just as I'd done when heading into the bar tonight. He moves quickly, right toward the dead streetlight across the street. He looks like he might run into it, but surely he'll notice it as he gets closer.

I consider opening the window to call out to him, but he can run into it for all I care. Time slows for a moment as he makes contact with the pole and collapses onto the street. I gasp, and without wasting a moment, I hurry out the door and rush down the stairwell.

He's fine, I try to convince myself. But it looked like a serious collision. I scold myself for not opening the window. I should have warned him. But it was his fault for rushing across the street so recklessly. I told him there was a bad light the first time he drove me back to my place.

I race into the rain, feeling the drops hit my shoulders and hearing the splash of water from puddles I run through. It's hard to see in front of me, and I can tell by how dark the opposite side of the street looks why Jarek made his way so boldly forward. I cross the street and approach his body, lying limp beside the curb.

I fall to my knees and pull his jacket back, revealing his face. Blood rushes from a wound on his forehead. The rain clicks against his jacket. Since I didn't think to put on a jacket before I came outside, I'm shivering from a brisk wind that rushes by. "Jarek...Jarek..." I say, pushing him, hoping he'll stir to life. I pat my jeans for my phone, but I set it on the counter when we got back. I look around, desperate for help. I'm not just going to leave him out here like this.

A groan. He stirs. "Jarek, come on. Get up. We have to get inside."

This is my fault. If I hadn't had that outburst, if I'd driven him home, this never would have happened. If I had warned him about the streetlamp, he wouldn't have run right into it.

He glances around, disoriented.

"Come on. It's okay."

"Lana?" he asks.

"I've got you. Let's get you up. You'll freeze to death out here." I help him to his feet, wrap his arm around me, and guide him back into the building. It's a slow process and we're shivering together as we make it back into my apartment. I escort him into my bedroom. "Come on, we need to get you out of these clothes," I say, hardly caring that I'm as wet as he is. I fish through the drawers in my dresser. I don't know what I'll give

him to wear. I have a few tees that'll work for a guy, but no options for
pants or underwear.

He quickly sheds his pants and shirt so he's just in a soaked pair of
boxers. He's shivering like he's in shock, his muscles trembling seemingly
independently from the rest of him. The blood rushing from the wound on
his head captures my attention. I hurry into the bathroom and snatch a wad
of toilet paper from the holder against the wall before sifting through the
cabinet for a bottle of peroxide. I head back to my patient and lead him to
the bed. "Get out of those boxers," I insist. He hesitates, as if he doesn't
want to be rude. "Seriously? I've seen you naked." I yank them down for
him, and he lifts his feet as I remove them. "Now sit down." He obeys,
and I sit beside him, preparing the peroxide and tissue before dabbing the
wad across his forehead. "You clumsy bastard," I mutter.

His gaze meets mine, but I'm too busy cleaning his wound to notice
his expression. As I complete my task, relieved to see that it's not too
serious, I look at him. He looks sheepish. It's disarming, and suddenly my
awareness is fixated on his beautiful physique...in my bed. Heat fills my
cheeks.

I start to turn away so I can shield my emotion from him, but he
captures the back of my head in his grip and pulls me close, forcing a kiss
that I relax into, because despite every desire in me to resist, I can't.
Seeing him lying on the ground beside the curb terrified me. I couldn't
lose him...this man who wasn't even mine. It tore into my soul, stirring
those painful memories of Daddy.

His touch is cool, since he's still freezing from the rain he's soaked in.
As he wrestles me out of my blouse, I kick my shoes off, and he forces my
jeans to the floor. A powerful heat radiates all around me. Everything's a
haze, and I feel like I'm in a wonderful dream as he wraps his arm around
me and lays me across the bed, tenderly kissing his way down my neck.
His cheeks are warm, but the chill at the tip of his nose bites at my flesh,
as does the water that drips from his damp hair. The sensations battle for

attention, confusing my nerves nearly as much as these conflicting thoughts confuse my mind. I shouldn't do this. I should fight him. I should tell him to leave. But that look in his eyes, so weak, so vulnerable, has left me wanting nothing more than to bring him ease. Not just for him, but to ease this pain within me—this burning lust I've felt since he's returned to my life.

I think about Kelsey—about how she wants to win him. She doesn't care about him. She never cared about him until he had money. I'm the foolish girl who's always cared about him, and my hate only stems from these deep, powerful feelings that I fear can never leave me—the feelings that will haunt me until the day I die.

If this is what I'm cursed with, then why shouldn't he take me? Why shouldn't he claim my body for tonight? It's a temporary relief from a deeper longing that can never be sated, but it's still relief...and I want it so badly.

He unfastens my bra and tosses it aside, freeing me as he unleashes tender kisses across my breasts. Swirls of delight ripple across my body, the sort of ripples no man or stroke of my finger has granted me. This is a sensation only evoked by Jarek.

He trails his nose down my belly, to my navel, his fingers kneading either side of my hip. I roll my head across my pillow as I revel in delight. He kisses down my stomach and farther, until he's reached his destination. A rush of energy flies up my spine to the front of my head, like waves of energy shooting through me.

With each tease of his tongue, each touch of his lip, my thoughts move further and further from all those moments before. I'm lost in this experience, gasping, moaning with desire and longing for him to never let it end. When his lips abandon me, I'm reminded that it must. However, it's only a moment that I'm without them before they return, kissing my lips. Spreading his legs across the mattress, he pushes my legs open.

Condoms! I scoot back, twist onto my side, and crawl to the nightstand, where I retrieve the condoms and lube. He wraps his arms around me, and I can feel his torso pressing against my back. He takes the condom and lube and pulls me back so my shoulder blades rest against his firm chest. He nestles his nose against my neck and his warm breath rushes down my flesh, toward my chest. His nose has lost the chill it began with. I suppose my body has helped bring it back to its usual temperature.

His free hand strokes up my side, caressing my obliques as his fingers skillfully make their way up my abdomen. He kisses my neck once more before trailing kisses up to my ear. His teeth massage my lobe before offering a gentle tug. As his warm breath hits the inside of my ear, a surge of energy rushes down my body, stirring powerful desire deep inside me, leaving me wanting him to invade the same place. Not in a few moments. Not when he's ready. Just now. I want him pushing into me, filling me with that intoxicating pressure...that pressure that assures me he's so close, the raise of his shoulders, the twist of his expression letting me know it's time.

But we're so far from that moment. We're just beginning. The hand that strokes me settles on my breast, and Jarek rubs it across my nipple. I push my hips back so that my ass presses against him. I feel the girth, the length, the power of his pelvis as he pushes forward, allowing his cock to slide vertically between my buttocks.

With one arm around my body and the other sliding around my legs, he scoops me up, lays me on my back across the bed, and kisses me again. The sensations run through my body as if the cells in my nerves are gossiping to one another, expressing their excitement about what is about to happen. His kisses continue, paralyzing me, keeping my thoughts still and my body quivering in uncontrolled fits of excitement.

He pulls away and his hand lowers. As I inspect his work, I see he already has the condom on. A skillful move I didn't see. Nice work, Jarek.

He maneuvers himself into me. There's that pressure, that force my body needs right now. I like to believe it will be easier since I had him so recently, but he is hardly in and I can already feel that, though it's easier, it's still a struggle. I bite my tongue, suppressing a groan, but another thrust forward is too much for me to keep in. I sing out my pain.

He halts. I take a deep breath, preparing myself for what must come next. He wraps one hand around my leg and sets another on my belly, gently rubbing, as if to sooth me as he continues to enter. I throw my head back so it hits the edge of the mattress.

He strokes his hand up and down my abdomen as he continues filling me, possessing me with his cock. As he begins his thrusts and we catch our stride, he leans down and whispers, "Put your arms around me." I do, and he wraps his arms around me and hoists me into the air. His biceps bulge as he holds me midair, while he's still filling me. He looks into my eyes as if he wants to see my excitement, and I don't think I disappoint him. He steps off the bed, carrying me until I'm up against the wall. I don't have control of my body anymore. He's in control of that, which is fine with me. I trust his strength and competence with his skill.

He kisses down my chest, his lips massaging my breasts as he thrusts more. I wrap my legs around him, clinging on as he maneuvers back and forth, touching those places inside me that desperately wanted to feel him before. I throw my head back against the wall and groan even louder. I hope Janet can't hear me, but a part of me doesn't care because I can't control myself right now. I just want him in me, as deep as he can go, as hard as he can go. *Wreck me, Jarek. Claim me!*

His lips return to mine and I feel his sweat, surely from holding me up this long, trickle onto my face. I know I can't weigh an incredible amount, but it's impressive that he can keep me up this long. As he thrusts, I feel as if he's filling me more than ever before and deeper than he managed to get the last time we fucked.

He whirls around and lays me back on the bed, never exiting, only ceasing his pelvic-assaults on his way to the bed, but as he releases me, he kneels on the mattress, leaning back as he penetrates me.

His muscles are tense and red, nearly matching the wound on his forehead. His biceps bulge with veins—I assume from holding me up. That was just showing off. He didn't need to do any of that. But I'm glad he did because it was so erotic.

He continues to touch that delicious spot within me, that place that sends my muscles into fits and spasms, while trailing his hands around my body as if he just wants to pleasure himself with the feel of it, as if he's trying to feel his way around so he can remember every bit of it. I love the idea that he wants to forever have this experience embedded in his memory.

He wraps his arms around my legs, helping them stay in place as he continues, now moving much faster than before, and the speed stimulates my g-spot in a way that makes me toss my head to either side. I must look so ridiculous right now, but considering how good it feels, it's not something I'm willing to interrupt or control. I deserve to feel this good with him. I've had to endure the pain, so shouldn't I get the pleasure?

He grunts through his teeth, his eyes locked in a grimace as if he's in pain, as if all he wants is to fill me with his come, and that's what I want. *Fill me, Jarek. Fill me up!*

He leans over me and looks into my eyes, and I look into his. As his movements become more consistent, more rapid, I know I'm about to succeed in pleasing him. His legs shake and his shoulders arch back. *Here it is!*

He jerks forward, as if someone has pushed him from behind. A war-cry strains from his mouth, sounding as if all he's wanted was to get this out...as if he's been blue-balling and just needs that release.

He pants, perspiration covering his forehead along with a bit of blood that's started drying where he hit the streetlamp.

Despite how erotic the experience was, I'm satisfied without being taken all the way. I wouldn't have changed a moment of the experience for anything, and the pleasure I felt in his satisfaction was inexplicable.

I feel something on my clitoris. It's his thumb, which he's using to stimulate me, as he's so cleverly done before. He smiles a devilish smile, and I can't believe what he's doing. He restarts his thrusts, stimulating me with a slick, calculated circular motion of his thumb, one that teases as it comes and goes with unpredictable maneuvers. Even better, his cock is still hitting that spot inside me, and between that and this massage, it's too much for me. Goosebumps rush up my body before I toss my head back. I'm forced to obey my muscles as they lock and I feel as if something has just exploded inside me. Then I remember— something has.

While I recover, he leans down so we're panting in each other's faces. He smiles again before planting a kiss on my lips. It feels so good to have him on me like this. As a bead of sweat drips from his brow and falls on my chest, I love knowing I have him on me. I hope he's stained me with his scent, if only so it'll linger for a few minutes after this.

Chapter Six

I wake, expecting to see Jarek lying beside me, but he's gone.

Of course he is. And though I should have expected as much, it evokes the same feelings I had back then. This is what it's like to be abandoned over and over and over again. I rise from the bed and throw on my robe.

What felt like such an incredible, beautiful experience last night has left me feeling guilty, ashamed. I know better, and still I can't resist. What happened is my own fault, and I must accept that. I head to the guest bedroom to check on Janet, but when I sneak a glance inside, it's empty. All alone...again.

I hear stirring in the kitchen. She must be making herself some breakfast. As I make my way out of the hallway, I see a shirtless Jarek standing before the stove. He holds the handle of a frying pan on the burner in one hand and a spatula in the other. He shakes the pan, and as he flips its contents in the air, I realize what he's making. "Omelet?" I ask.

It lands in the pan, and he shifts his gaze to me. His eyes light up and he smiles. "Of course."

When we were younger, he made me cheese, ham, and jalapeño omelets. After church, Daddy took us to IHOP, where I'd order an omelet for breakfast. On weekends, sometimes Jarek would recreate the omelet. He wasn't good at it, but I appreciated his efforts and always expressed my gratitude for the attempt. Here he is again, years later, bringing back that same memory. But what's the point?

I approach the kitchen island and sit in a stool. "Coffee?" he asks.

"Yes, please." I study the wound on his head. It doesn't look as bad as it appeared last night. Just a few scratches. He must have removed the Band-Aid I placed there after we fucked.

He pours a collection of cheese and jalapeños onto the egg and pulls a mug from the cabinet. He's clearly made himself at home, as indicated by his familiarity with my kitchenware. He heads to the coffee machine and presses a button, releasing the coffee into the mug.

"Someone was on top of this morning," I say, impressed with everything already being made. And I'm glad. Considering last night, I'm really not in the mood to get ready for the day.

"Sugar or cream?" he asks.

"Black." He eyes me curiously. "Can't afford the calories," I say.

He shakes his head. "You're ridiculous." He hands me the mug and walks back to the pan, his ass shifting in his jeans, stirring a similar sensation in my lady parts as the night before. *Yummy.*

I feel like I should do something to put a stop to this moment, like there's something wrong with him being here like this, but I'm too tired to do anything but let him get on with what he's doing. He removes the omelet from the pan with the spatula, sets it on a plate, retrieves a fork from the silverware drawer, and sets the plate down before me. "Enjoy," he says. He turns off the stove and heads to the dishwasher, where he washes the dishes he used to create breakfast for me.

"Aren't you going to eat?" I ask.

"Did while you were sleeping."

I cut the omelet with my fork and have a bite. The cheese and jalapeño goodness explodes in my mouth. "Oh my God," I say, my mouth full of the incredible concoction. I chew and swallow. "This is really good!"

As I finish the omelet, he's still doing dishes. I notice he's also done the ones I've neglected for the past few days, and I'm embarrassed. "You didn't have to do all of them," I say as I pass him and scrape what remains of the food residue into the garbage disposal.

"It wasn't an issue," he says.

I set the plate and fork in the dishwasher. "Well, thank you." I start to head back to my chair to enjoy my coffee when he steps around me and presses his lips against my cheek. I permit myself this moment because I'm still trapped in the ecstasy of the night before and knowing he's still here. I roll my head back as he kisses down my neck. He unties my robe and pulls it open. He fondles up and down my sides, massaging his fingers against my hips.

He pulls the robe off and drops it so that it pools at my feet. I spin around, feeling vulnerable, exposed, but excited all at once. He kneels slightly, cups his hands under my butt, lifts me in the air, and spins me around. As he sets me on the island, I now realize it's the perfect height. Glad I didn't get the bar height island.

He retrieves a condom and the bottle of lube, which he must have lifted from my room. He has a wicked smirk on his face, as if he's so pleased with his forethought. He sets them beside me on the island. He kneels slightly so his torso touches mine, the metal button of his jeans rubbing against my clitoris.

I gaze into his eyes, those loving eyes I remember feeling so safe with, and I feel safe with them now, even though I shouldn't—even though I should know better.

He thrusts his pelvis against mine. I want him in me—*need* him in me so badly. If he knew how much I craved him...if he felt for me a fraction of what I feel for him, how could he ever walk away from something so powerful, something so life-giving?

He kisses between my breasts. Each soft peck evokes a powerful sensation, making the spots he pays attention to radiate energy, life. Swirling sensations collide in my head, relieving what feels like years of ignored tension. As his lips near my nipple, I feel eager anticipation for his expert touch. The touch of his lips softens and the subtle sensation he leaves stirs a deep hunger within me. *Why is he still wearing those jeans? Those damn jeans that look so good on him.*

And I can't bear it. I lean up and push him off me. He looks bewildered as I undo the button of his jeans and force them to his knees. As he realizes what I'm doing, he smiles. But I'm so busy ripping the condom from the wrapper to pay much attention to him. I hurriedly roll it on and massage a wad of lube over it. All I can think about—all that consumes me is how much I need him inside me, how much I need him to invade my body again, to touch all those nerves that right now are begging for satisfaction, not just by anything, but by his erotic touch.

As I lean back, waiting for him to enter, he gazes at me, still smirking, as if he's so proud of himself for filling me with this unbearable desire. I want to just scream, "Get in me!" But I hold back, trusting he'll satisfy me, as he always has. He wraps his hand around my neck and clings tightly as he uses his other to guide himself into me, slowly, so that I can feel the pressure, the soothing of those pining nerves. I toss my head back and he forces himself fully in, evoking a moan.

He grunts as he pushes in and pulls slightly out before returning to his work, his efforts at arousing himself sending sensations rushing across my body. He pushes me back so that I lie across the island. I hear him groan as he forces himself deeper within me. I groan from the sheer ecstasy of it all.

He speeds his thrusts and wraps his arm around my leg to keep me from sliding, as he did to keep me from sliding on the bed the night before. Admittedly, the kitchen island isn't the most comfortable place in the world, but that sensation of discomfort is far surpassed by the pleasurable emotions that jet through me in waves.

If only there was a way I could have him all over me, every part of him touching every nerve across my body. If only I could have his lips tending to every bit of flesh—then I could be happy forever. He captures my other leg in his arm and uses the leverage to push even farther into me. He stops.

Why did he stop? It's not enough. I need so much more.

I gaze at him. Here I am, lying before him, desperate, needful. He releases one of my thighs and rubs his hand against my belly, scanning my body.

I don't know that I would normally like this kind of scrutiny, but the look in his eyes assures me he's only appreciating everything he beholds, so I don't interrupt. "You're so beautiful, Lana," he whispers as he teases my body with subtle movements. I turn to avoid his gaze, and he grabs my chin and turns my face so I'm forced to look at him. He appears as if he's about to say something else. I wonder what, but instead, he forces himself in me again. I'm relieved, because I don't know if I could handle any words from him in this moment. They would slay me.

He pushes in even deeper and I scream out, but not from pain. The feelings are just so sharp, so intoxicating, and coming so fast I can't help it. Jarek's expression is rife with concern, but I reach my arm around and grip his ass, tugging to let him know that he has to keep going. I need this. It feels like I need it more than I've ever needed anything. I find myself moving my hips instinctively, like my body is desperately trying to put an end to the agonizing emptiness within me.

I want to see that look in his eyes, as I saw the night before, that look of arousal, of satisfaction, of eagerness, of excitement. I want to see his release. I look for it, searching for him to be close, because I know I am, and I don't know that I can keep from climaxing soon.

He leans back farther. *What is he doing?*

He feels his way to my clitoris, which he massages with his thumb once again.

No. This is too much. Way too much, and as he provides me another push and massages me in just the right way, I throw my head back. My face contorts and twists in what I imagine is the most unpleasant of expressions as I'm lost in an abyss of vacillating emotions.

My thoughts dwell on the sensations so that I can't even focus on my surroundings until I see Jarek cringing as his pelvis jerks powerfully against me. He groans through ground teeth, his expression like one I imagine he'd make amidst a heated argument. Then he collapses on top of me, his warm chest against mine. It feels as if he's caught me from the fall I experience as I rapidly descend from my miraculous high.

He lies against me and we breathe together, intensely, allowing ourselves to recover from the cardio workout. He's still inside me as he places his arms on either side of me and props himself up.

He gazes into my eyes. I'm tearing up, a product of the sheer pleasure I experienced. I hope he doesn't interpret it as anything else. Although I can't be sure it's not from a part of me that deeply wishes I could have had this every day from those early years to now. *How many women have been lucky enough to experience this pleasure with Jarek? How many have been equally disappointed when he's moved on without them?* At the very least, I have the satisfaction of knowing it was good enough for him to return once more.

He smiles cockily, as if he's proud of what he's done to me. And he should be. "I don't want to leave," he says.

I eye him curiously. The statement evokes my memories about that morning, making the crash from the erotic high even more depressing. In a moment, I went from feeling so aroused and lifted to feeling ashamed and embarrassed. I'm totally vulnerable beneath him. "You can stay for a while."

His smile broadens. A wicked glint sparkles in his eyes. "I don't think we're talking about the same thing." As I catch his true meaning, I can't help but laugh, relieved of all that accumulated guilt. He seems so happy, as if we're more than a hookup. However, I imagine that's the way he always is with girls. He must convince all his tricks they're more than just a night, that they're his future girlfriends. We've all been duped by his charm, charisma, and erotic power. Vulnerable and exposed as I feel beneath him, dwelling on how I'm nothing but a toy to him, one he can so easily dispose of, I can't help but feel I would rather be his toy than nothing at all.

He rises and pulls out of me, leaving my body to chill in the cool sting of the air. I want to throw myself at the floor and toss my robe back on. I at least want to conceal my breasts, but I don't want to seem insecure. I want to appear in control.

He turns, opens the pantry cabinet, and disposes of the condom in the trash can inside. I get a good view of his beautiful ass. He kneels down farther, grabs his jeans at his ankles, and pulls them up, covering some of my favorite parts. He turns back to me, his expression more serious than before.

"What's wrong?" I ask.

"I have a virtual meeting I need to take care of in about an hour."

This was it? This was all we had? "On a Saturday?" I ask.

"The life of a billionaire," he says in an adorably self-indulgent way.

"I should punch you in the face for that. Some of us have to work our asses off just to get by."

"Whatever makes your ass look that good is a positive in my book."

"Oh, really? You like my ass?" I ask. He nods.

"Then watch it walk away from your conceited self." I hop up from the island, scoop my robe off the floor, and head to the bedroom.

I hear him laugh behind me and I'm pretty proud of myself for my quip. "We should do lunch," he says. I feel it would be best for me to deny him. I could say I have plans. I could make up some extraordinary story about how busy I am so I don't have time for him, but I can't help myself. I head towards the hallway and turn back to him. He's ogling me, and I can tell by the gleam in his eyes that he likes what he sees.

"That sounds good to me," I reply.

"I hope this is all right," I say as we sit in a booth in the local pizzeria I suggested for our lunch date. "Sorry if it's not as fancy as you're accustomed to." I'm teasing, but he must know some part of me is concerned he's judging my tastes.

"Will this meet your caloric needs for the day?" he asks. *Touché*. I chuckle. "Today can be my bad day."

"From what I've seen so far, it is," he quips. As I laugh, his expression turns serious. "Do you really think I've changed that much?" he asks, as if he's hurt by my constant reminders that he's so different. "You know it's still me. Bumbling, ridiculous me."

"What part of you was ever bumbling or ridiculous?" I reflect on him standing before his truck, black oil soiling his shirt, which glistened in the afternoon light—beaming nearly as much as the twinkle in his eye as he gazed at me beside him. I acted out the day I had with my friends, as I usually did when I got home from school. He swooped down and grabbed a wrench from his toolbox. As he stood back up, he hit his head against the hood. I laughed so hard, I practically shrieked. He blushed, and as he turned to me, he wiped his hand across his forehead, adding a black smear to his already dirtied face. Even then, looking filthy as ever, he was adorable. Bumbling as he may have been, it was hard to appear that way when he was so attractive and charming.

"Whatever," he says. I detect a hint of false modesty.

When the waitress arrives, we order and then he asks, "So what has Lana been up to all these years?"

"I've told you everything that's important."

"No, you haven't. You've told me just enough so that you thought I'd stop asking questions."

"You haven't exactly been eager to tell me what you've been up to. Are there bodies lining the West Coast that I need to alert the authorities about?"

"You'd alert authorities? Oh, I thought you were someone I'd be able to call. No, but seriously. Where do I even start?"

"Any part where you explain how you became a billionaire will be intriguing, I promise."

"That old story," he says, throwing it away as if it's nothing, though I can tell by the look in his eye he knows it's far from nothing. "I started taking classes at a community college in Glendale, where I met a friend of one of my professors who taught at USC. He asked me to help him with an engineering project and encouraged me to apply for a scholarship to MIT. When I finished up with school, I went to work with a company in Seattle that sells a few packaging components to various companies. I came up with the idea to design machines that we could sell to these companies that did the same thing, which would save these companies tons of money. Big corps like cheaper, so I found I had a lot of interest early on. Started my own business with money I got some of my peers to invest. It's really not all that glamorous, but it happened to take off. I got a bunch of heavyweight clients very early on through some great connections that I was fortunate enough to have."

"I imagine you earned those connections," I say, because I'm sure his personality has led to him making a lot of friends along the way. "But why start your own company?" I ask. "When did you become so entrepreneurial?" This wasn't the Jarek I knew. He wasn't entrepreneurial, and that wasn't a fault. He just didn't have extravagant dreams. He was simple, and as Mom noted, he would have been perfectly happy being a mechanic for the rest of his life. I remember his dreams of a double wide trailer and a few cats. Hardly glamorous, yet it was the only dream I needed him to have.

"I wanted to be successful. If your father taught me anything, it was about being a businessman."

"Good on you," I say, trying to brush off the subject of my father. "So what about the women? There must be a lot of girls out west who you've been in relationships with."

"There have been girls, but no one serious. Not really."

"No girlfriends? No fiancées? Really? I remember you in college, and you didn't really avoid girlfriends."

"I don't know if you could call them girlfriends." I blush like I would have back when he first began talking to me about girls he was interested in—girls at the time I assumed he was having sex with. Being older and wiser, I'm certain he was having sex with them.

"What makes you think I've gotten engaged?" he asks. "Have you gotten engaged a bunch since I've been gone?" His gaze suggests he really wants to know the answer.

"Not engaged, but I've had boyfriends. Todd Jedder, Ryan Karson, Jedd Spears." He appears viscerally uncomfortable by the mention of the names. "Do you know one of them?" I ask.

"No, no. These were guys you were in serious relationships with?"

"Todd and I dated for two years. He was probably the most serious." His face is stern, as if he's angry. I almost think he's jealous, but considering our history and our current situation, I know that can't be true.

"How serious was that?" he asks. I'm wondering by his look if he really wants me to tell him. I'm not sure if I should say.

"We talked about getting married. I'd say that's pretty serious." I notice his fingers pressed against the tabletop. *Why is he reacting like this?*

"But it didn't work out," I say.

"Why not?"

Because no one could ever impress me more than you. I'm not going to tell him that, but it's the truth. "Because I would have been settling for him. We had a lot of fun, and I enjoyed being with him, but at the end of the day, there wasn't any magic. Never was, and he knew that. He had a hard time when we broke up, but I know it was for the best."

"And the other guys?"

"Just passed the time."

"When was your last...for lack of a better word...more serious relationship?"

This seems like an awful lot of focus on my boyfriends. I would never ask him this much about his girlfriends. It'd just piss me off. Of course, that's what this seems to be doing to him, though it shouldn't be. "The last guy I dated—like, seriously dated—was last year. I haven't been serious about a guy—"

"But you've been with them?"

"Yes. A few." *Enough.*

He tenses his jaw. *Does he think I've been a slut?* I'm twenty-six, and I feel like my love life has been fairly tame for a girl my age, but his reaction is making me second-guess myself.

He nods repeatedly. "Good, good, good."

"So you haven't had anyone serious? Really? Come on. I don't believe that."

"No one," he says in a tone so severe I don't doubt him. *Why does he sound angry?* If he thinks he can pry into my love life, I have just as much right to pry into his. Although perhaps his mood comes from never having met anyone special. Definitely not me.

As I reflect on that sad thought, I realize this discourse about our pasts is a terrible idea. *Who even started it?* I think it was me, but I shouldn't have. I'd rather talk about something else—anything else. However, I'm struggling to think of a new direction for the conversation. The first things that come to mind are, "Why did you leave? Why didn't you call? Why didn't you talk to me?" I settle for, "What does your job entail?"

He appears to relax. "Meetings. Lots and lots of meetings. I've never done less manual labor in my life, and it kills me."

"I bet," I say, recalling those afternoons with his truck and some of Daddy's projects around the house. He completely redid our front porch and the patio out back. He loved the work. I think he liked doing it because he saw it as his way of repaying Daddy for giving him such a different life.

"I didn't think being rich was just about having fights all the time," he continues. "Sometimes I feel like I'm not doing anything. So I'm a workout-aholic. Hit the gym as much as possible just so that I can give my body something to do."

"It shows."

"You obviously take care of yourself, too."

"You mean starve myself?" I ask. He looks at me, his look asking if he should be concerned. "Don't worry. I eat plenty. I just try to keep a lid on it day to day. I'm sure you can remember I wasn't exactly the most health-conscious girl."

He chuckles. "No, you weren't. When I think about how much Captain Crunch you ate, I worry about what's streaming through your veins."

"That's what happens when I don't have a guy here to make me omelets every morning, so...you know..."

"As you probably could tell, I've perfected my omelet-making over the years."

"Yes, you have."

"So what about your job?" he asks. "Are you happy?"

I shrug. "As happy as I guess I can be."

"Which means?"

"I'm a little frustrated. There's a lot of pressure with this job that I'm working on right now. But it's a little disappointing. When I signed up to help people, I didn't think that would mean I just got to sit around a desk all day and stress about deadlines and invoices. I guess it's kind of like what you were saying about being a CEO. When I'm behind the scenes, I don't really get to work on a lot of projects that I'd be really passionate about. I don't feel like I'm really helping anyone."

"Not exactly Hearts & Hugs," he says, referring to an organization we used to volunteer for when we were in high school. Hearts & Hugs used to set up a stand downtown to serve impoverished families. I usually handed out food while Jarek manned the barbecue. I don't imagine they even do that anymore.

"Nope," I say. "Just orchestrating money-making endeavors."

"That go on to help people."

"Yes, but it doesn't feel very personal. You don't see any of the people that you're helping, and I think that makes a difference. When we helped at Hearts & Hugs, we got to see the people who benefited from the charity. We knew we were doing something that mattered. I don't know. Sometimes I think making a connection with someone is valuable. Maybe not as valuable as paying for them to have a good education, but I think it matters." His expression softens. He appears impressed, though I'm not sure why. "What? I'm not like Mother Theresa. I just want to do a little here and there, where I can. And I don't feel like I've had the time ever since I got this job."

"That's really thoughtful. So how much do I need to make out to this fundraiser?"

"Oh, no. I couldn't—"

"I have all this money. Why shouldn't I give some of it to help these kids?" *Why is he being so nice to me? Where was this cordial nature back then?* I'm not saying he wasn't generous or kind, but I can't imagine anyone eagerly throwing money at me. Isn't raising money all about guilting people into giving it? That's how Mom always works it.

"I can't really fight you on that."

"When is it? I'll put it in my calendar."

"I doubt you'll even be here. It's not until next Saturday."

"With the way this project is going down, it looks like I could be here longer."

"Really?" I ask a bit too hopefully. I wish I could go back in time and retract the statement. I shouldn't be excited that he will still be here. I should be furious that he thinks he can waltz in here and hand me some cash for a fundraiser and think I'll be okay. I have no reason to be okay. But I can't help but feel like I want to spend more time with him. *Jarek, you've lured me in again.*

"Yeah, really," he says. "But that doesn't have to be such a bad thing, I'm learning."

Perhaps I've given it up enough that he's expecting me to hand it right over to him, and maybe that's not such a bad idea. I've enjoyed our experiences. What am I talking about? I haven't just enjoyed them. I've reveled in them. I've delighted in his touch, savored the sensation of his breath crawling across my flesh. I've allowed myself to become intoxicated with him all over again. Isn't that a terrible thing? Shouldn't I be telling him to leave me alone? Shouldn't I deny him entry just for the sake of the girl who never would have been so willing to let him in?

As much as I wish I could put up a cold, guarded front, I'm convinced I have to give this to myself. However, I know how painful it can be—how much it will hurt the day he leaves. That will be hard...so painfully hard.

A series of thoughts rush through my head, making me feel like a crazy person:

Voice 1: No, you don't want to do that. He'll just leave again.
Voice 2: But this time, you know that...and he won't be able to hurt you.
Voice 1: What are you talking about? You're already head over heels. Get out! Get out!
Voice 2: Shut up, bitch.

Considering the details about my past and how quickly I've thrown myself at him since he arrived, he must think I'm a whore, but what do I care what he thinks about me anymore?

"What are you doing tonight?" he asks.

"Really? You think I don't have any plans?"

"I'm sorry. Your dance card is already full?"

"Maybe I just don't want to do anything with you," I say, teasing him the way I would have when we were younger.

"What if I insisted?"

"Insist all you want. Doesn't mean it will happen."

"I promise it'll be worth your while." A powerful sensation radiates from the part of me that's most excited about this erotic promise. I wish I could leap over the table, rip off his clothes, and make him fuck me right here. This chemistry I feel toward him, especially after years with other boys, amazes me. Before he came back into my life, I could explain away that chemistry as the product of him being my first, but now I can tell that the attraction is deep, profound. It must be whatever pheromones he exudes. Whatever it is, it's overwhelming, and I'm appreciative that I have the appropriate restraint to keep me from making a spectacle out of myself.

He finishes chewing his slice of pizza and wipes his napkin across his face. "Maybe we should have a sleepover," he says. "Put on an old movie...see what happens." He knows me too well for someone who hasn't seen me in forever. The only guy who'd ever watch those old classic movies with me was Todd, and only because he knew I would watch them with or without him.

"That's fine," I say, "But I think we should set some ground rules." He eyes me curiously. "We're both adults. We know what we're doing, and we know that once you go back to California, that's the end of it. Let's not pretend this is something it's not. Fair enough?"

He smiles. It seems that's what he wanted to hear, and I'm disappointed. The only reason I said it like that was to prove I'm not the eager girl I was at seventeen. I won't beg him to be my boyfriend. I'll enjoy the parts of him that are worth enjoying—the ones I can't enjoy after his departure. But I still wish my statement had evoked disappointment—that he would have said something that suggested he thought there would be more. Again, I'm reminded I'm the only one who ever wanted something more.

Fuck me.

And I guess that's exactly what he's going to do.

Chapter Seven

I've tried on nearly half the blouses in my closet, and because he's only seen my archaic underwear—underwear I've owned since I was dating Todd—I ran by Victoria's Secret and grabbed matching ones for a change. I don't plan on being the lay he remembers because she always looks like a homeless person in her undergarments.

I try on another blouse, buttoning it over the blue bra that I'm so proud of myself for picking out. When the doorbell rings, I hurry out of my room, working to calm myself.

He doesn't know what you felt back then. He doesn't know what you're feeling now. Just play like he matters to you as much as you mattered to him back then. Be strong. You can do it.

From these last experiences, I know regardless of my feelings for him, as soon as we hit the sheets, I can forget what transpired between us...or at least enjoy it regardless of the inner turmoil that rages while I'm working to enjoy myself.

I open the door. He's wearing a navy blue button-up with the top two buttons undone and a pair of gray slacks. It's an attractive combination that I imagine his designer arranged for him, because the old Jarek never would have thrown together such a sexy look. I can't help but wonder if this designer of his is attractive. They've probably done it a few times. Jealousy intensifies within me, which I know is ridiculous because I have no reason to hate what, for all intents and purposes, is a figment of my imagination, not even a real person.

"Hey," I say, my tone making me sound as if I'm surprised he's here, which is odd, considering I was going for super-cool and slick. *Epic fail.*

He smiles broadly, probably because he knows he's getting some tonight. But so am I, mister.

"Hey," he says.

I eye a strap that stretches across his button-up, leading to a leather bag that hangs at his side. "Did you bring homework?" I ask.

"Just things for tomorrow morning."

"Of course. Come on in." He follows me inside and closes the door.

"Any pressing news on the business front?" I ask.

He shakes his head. "Not particularly."

I'm waiting for him to assault me, because that's what he really wants, isn't it? The pretense of the movie was just a way to get back inside my place...and, well, inside me.

He sets his bag behind the couch and steps around, into the living area. He kneels before a shelf beside the TV, where I keep my VHSs. I step around the couch and join him. *Is this pretense, or does he really want to watch a movie with me?*

He cringes, like he's not finding what he's searching for. "Where's *Bringing Up Baby?*" he asks.

My thoughts return to nights where we lay on the couch, our heads on either side, lounging on pillows as we enjoyed the slapstick comedy. It was one of my personal favorites, and while when he first started staying with us, he didn't understand my affection for classic movies, he eventually came around. Some nights, he would sneak into my bedroom and watch them with me. Looking back, it probably wasn't the smartest idea for a young girl to let an older guy into her bedroom to watch movies, considering all the things that could have transpired, but at the time, I felt so safe with him, and he never did anything that would have made me think he would have been inappropriate. A perfect gentlemen. Although, after a while, I wished he wouldn't have been a gentleman.

"I had to throw it out," I explain. "I played it one too many times and the tape tore."

"And you didn't buy a new one?"

"I never really had time."

"To go online and order a VHS? Or a fucking DVD?" he says, looking at me as if I'm the laziest girl on the planet.

"Are you seriously judging me for not having that movie?"

"We used to watch it together." I want to fuss at him, remind him that I've had nine years without him where I didn't imagine he'd just pop back into my life and want me to have the movies he'd prefer. However, I know better than to go there.

"What is this?" I ask. "A trip down memory lane?" On top of my frustration about his pestering about a movie he thinks I should have, I wonder why he would want to watch a movie that reminds him of our past. "*The Philadelphia Story* is down there if you want to watch that instead. For a while, you couldn't tell the two apart anyway."

"Oh, no, no, no," he says, retrieving a VHS from the shelf. He flashes the cover. *It Happened One Night.*

"Works for me." *Does he not remember how much he despised that movie?* He thought it was so stupid, so much so that I eventually gave up watching it around him—unless I wanted to in spite of him.

I go along with this ruse because I know movie-viewing will probably last for a few minutes before we get to the fun stuff, the reason he's here. Then it's bye-bye movie.

"Mind if I put some popcorn on?"

"I'm not sure I have any."

"Sure you do. I saw it when I was making that omelet."

It's official. He knows my kitchen better than I do. "Go for it."

He dashes past me and heads into the kitchen. He rummages through the cabinet and retrieves a bag, which he places in the microwave. As the buzz of the microwave sounds, he heads back into the living area and grabs his bag. "Mind if I change real quick?"

Change? "By all means," I say, curious to see what he's about to put on. He heads into the bathroom. A few moments pass. I turn on the TV and start the movie. As the sound of popping fills the air, I press pause to wait for him.

Jarek fixing popcorn reminds me when we were kids. Daddy was always the one to make dinner, so if he was out for a business function or benefit, Jarek would pick up frozen ravioli and garlic bread, which I'd heat up. Then he, Janet, and I would watch a movie together. It was a silly ritual, and I'm amazed we didn't get sick and tired of the simple meal, but it was something we actually looked forward to.

When he comes out of the bathroom, he's in periwinkle pajama bottoms with green pinstripes and a white tee that shapes his fit form, as if it's just as tailored as the outfits he wears. His shirts always seemed to fit as if they were designed just for his physique. I remember when he would scamper around the house in a white tee and pajama bottoms. He'd steal my homework and I'd chase him around the halls until I managed to catch him. Then he'd raise it over his head to keep it out of my reach, and when I'd ask him what I needed to do to get it back, he'd say I could only have it if I called him the most amazing man in the world. I would say it as sarcastically as possible. However, it wasn't that easy to satisfy the homework tormentor, because he would make me say it until he believed I was sincere. I can't say I was innocent in that game, because I could have easily attempted to keep snatching it, and I only dragged it out because I enjoyed the sport.

Some nights were less dramatic. I remember studying for the SAT one evening after I finished my homework. I sat at the kitchen table, weary and wanting to go to bed, but knowing I needed to get my practice in or I wouldn't do it. Jarek peered over my shoulder, curious about the problems I worked on. As I showed him how to work them, I discovered I actually improved my own performance. I wonder if those moments helped him with his college career. Surely my brief tutelage was of some benefit, but I can't take much credit considering how quickly he picked up on things. And I benefited just as much from the experience. Still, it bothers me that my assistance might have in some way been responsible for his success. I wish I could go back in time and refuse to show him anything. Although that isn't true, because as much as I hate him for what he did, I can't help but be proud of all that he's accomplished. It doesn't make me mad that he's so successful. It makes me sad, because I couldn't share in those victories with him.

My attention returns to the present, with this gorgeous man, who retrieves popcorn from the microwave and fixes himself a glass of water. I join him and pour myself a glass of ice tea.

Maybe I should enjoy tonight the way I do our sex. Just let go...if only for a few moments, so that I can appreciate this time with him.

Once we're finished gathering our concessions, we head into the living room. I pick up the remote from the coffee table and press play while he lounges across the couch.

"Am I just going to stand?" I ask, looking at how he monopolized the couch. He looks at the space between him and the edge of the cushion.

"There's room right here," he says. I finally understand. He's playing like he wants to watch this movie so he can get all touchy-feely. This makes much more sense than us watching a movie I know for a fact he doesn't like. I'm game for whatever puts him in the mood.

I lay before him and he wraps his arm around me. The bulk of his biceps presses against my side, and as I gaze at them, I'm amazed by how wide they are. I've seen them plenty, but resting against me, they've expanded to twice their usual size. He squeezes, as if to make sure I'm still there. It reminds me of the way Todd used to hold me in bed sometimes. It's an affectionate hold. I'm not comfortable with what it suggests, since I still hate Jarek's guts, but that masochistic part of me doesn't mind. She revels in this moment.

As the movie begins, he offers a joke about the funny way the people talk in these old movies, doing a terrible impersonation of Clark Gable that I can't help but laugh at. We share popcorn throughout until it becomes so scarce we're battling each other's fingers. It's a fun game that transports me back to a time before he hurt me. The movie flies by and when the credits roll, I feel awkward about what has just transpired. *Did I really enjoy a movie with him?* That wasn't the plan. We were supposed to fuck. Now I feel like I'm falling into some sort of trap—like he needs me to fall for him so he can break my heart. Surely he's not that devious or manipulative, but do I know him? I want to believe I do, but I know better than to trust my feelings, because clearly they aren't as accurate as I once believed.

He offers a gentle kiss—the sort of kiss I'd expect from someone like Todd after we've dated for a while. Sweet, affectionate, loving. Not the sort of kiss two people should have when they're hooking up. I don't know how to interpret it. It's hard for me to say we're just hooking up after watching *It Happened One Night* together.

What am I doing?

I return his kiss with a stronger one, making my intent clear. He needs to fuck me right now so that we can abandon this date-like rendezvous, so I can remind myself what this is really about. Fortunately, my kiss leads to him stroking his hand up and down my side. He kisses me harder and rolls on top of me, pressing his body against mine. He leans back and unbuttons my shirt. Exposing my belly, he leans down and kisses it as he continues undoing my shirt. Once my buttons are undone, he beelines to my breasts. He stops and studies my bra.

"Well, this is nice," he says. I'm flattered, and at the same time disturbed knowing he must have noticed how shitty I looked in my other bras. However, I don't have much time to focus on this, because soon, he's kissing under my bra, his fingers trailing around to my back. I lean up so he has access, and he unbuttons and removes it so that soon he's kissing and kneading at his object of desire.

This is much better. This is what I need this to be.

As he caresses one hand down my chest, to my jeans, the nerves he touches prick and tingle as a rush of delight runs from the base of my spine to the back of my head. His kisses across my breasts are wide, as if working to get as much of my flesh in his lips' scope. He offers the faintest of kisses, leaving me uncertain of what his kiss will bring next. Then he kisses to my nipple, his tongue and lips moving in an unpredictable rhythm, using just enough pressure to arouse me further. My hips thrust about as a deep hunger overtakes me, longing for him to be inside of me.

He ceases his oral affection, and as I look at him, he's gazing up at me, clearly pleased at his ability to arouse me this much. He should be proud, because he's doing a damn good job. "I should get a condom," he says, his breath rushing across my flesh, sending a tickling sensation rushing up my back.

We head to the bedroom, where I remove my blouse, toss it to the floor, and grab a condom and lube from the nightstand. A burst of inspiration sends me to the drawer just beneath it. I retrieve a long, black handkerchief. It's a little toy I purchased when I was with Todd, one we'd used to stimulate interest when our sex life started to feel mundane. Todd would tie it around my face, and I'd enjoy not knowing where he was about to touch me, kiss me. The piece has given me an idea.

Jarek starts to remove his shirt. "Uh-uh," I say. "Did I say you could take that off?"

He stops, his gaze shifting to me, filled with eagerness and surprise, and I know I have him under my control. "No, you didn't," he replies, releasing the hem of his shirt and letting his arms fall to the side. I toss the lube and condoms on the bed and step before him again, allowing him to gaze at my exposed breasts as I scan his fully-clothed body over. I step around him and sit on the bed, spreading my legs.

He starts to turn. "I didn't say you could turn around, either." He stops and faces the wall behind him.

I don't know why I'm in such a playful mood, but I like this control. I like knowing I can get him to do my bidding. I want him to be my puppet, doing exactly as I desire. I stand and tie the handkerchief around his face so that it covers his eyes.

"Oh, really?" he asks.

"I don't believe I said you could talk, either." He stiffens, as if he's being cautious not to make any moves that I could scold him for. As I finish tying my knot, I sit back on the bed. "Turn around," I instruct. He obeys. "You can remove your shirt," I say. He grabs the hem and pulls it off, just as he was about to do before I interrupted. His abs and that massive chest, beautiful products of his working out, are exposed for my pleasure. I enjoy the divots between his muscles, the grooves that dip from his chest around his bulbous pecs. I enjoy the fine lines between the muscles in his six-pack.

I catch the upward curl on his lip; he's surely impressed with himself because he must know how good he looks and how much I'm enjoying it. I wish I could just slap that right off his face. *Conceited bastard!* But he should know how good he looks, because he's worked hard for it.

"Walk toward me," I say. He does, but he apparently overestimates the distance between himself and the bed because he slightly fumbles forward as his knee hits the mattress. I chuckle. "There's that bumbling, ridiculous boy," I joke. He opens his mouth like he's about to make a joke about his mistake, but he quickly presses his lips together. "Good boy," I say as if he's my pet, which right now, he is.

I wonder if I'm only having so much fun because I see this as some sort of twisted revenge. I cock my head to the side. It's an exaggerated move that almost seems like it's for him, but since he can't see me, it must be what I expect someone in this dominant position to do.

"Why don't you do a little dance for me?" I ask. He pouts, as if he's not sure how exactly to do this, but I press. "Come on," I say, "You've seen enough movies to know what to do. I want a little lap dance. Let me see this body at work."

His expression shifts to something cool...more controlled. He squats so that his torso is all I can focus on, and he shifts his pelvis about, twisting his upper body in a silly way that makes me laugh. He stops, his cheeks flashing red, and I can't help but appreciate my involvement in his embarrassment. As the color drains from his face, he slows his movements, rocking his pelvis back and forth, those lines in his six-pack distracting me as they put on a slow, intimate show, just for me.

He rotates his hips, his obliques displaying their own serious definition. He starts to put his hand on my leg, but pulls back. "You can touch me," I say, enjoying the sensation within me so much. He presses both hands on my legs and continues his dance. He rubs his hands up and down my legs and as he finds my hands he lifts them and sets them on his ever-shifting abdomen.

Now I'm blushing, and I'm glad his eyes are covered. He moves my hands around his torso so I can feel the thick muscles as they expand. I want these all over me. I want to feel them contracting and shifting like this against my body.

"Turn around," I say. He obeys but continues his dance, swaying his hips. My skin feels as hot as a sunburn. I feel around to his back and lower my hands at his sides, pulling his pajama bottoms down just below his ass, which he sways in my face.

It's the perfect c-shape. I imagine it contracting as he forces himself inside me. I rub my hands across his ass, massaging it with my thumbs so I can feel the soft flesh that I can never get enough of. He pushes it back at me, as if permitting me to enjoy it however I wish. I kiss the base of his spine and slowly kiss up his back, feeling my fingers across his sides, enjoying his lats. Soon, I'm standing and kissing the back of his neck.

I walk around him and he ceases his dance. He just stands before me, his penis rock-hard. I'm pleased to see how much this is turning him on.

I want to tease him. I want him to think I'm about to allow him to do whatever he wants to me. I move close so the tip of his penis touches my jeans. It twitches about, as if it wants to get inside me.

I shove him back onto the bed. He's taken aback, but he quickly settles, lying still so that his legs dangle over the side of the mattress. I crawl on the bed, my legs on either side of his thighs as I press my face against his abs, kissing his muscles. I feel up and down his sides, enjoying his torso and then kiss up to his chest before reaching his face. I kiss him and he kisses back, clearly wanting a deep, serious kiss, but I pull away. "Not until I say so."

I retrieve the condoms and lube and step off the bed. I get on my knees on the carpet so I'm eye level with his erect cock, which is at a forty-five-degree angle. "I think he should be a little harder, don't you?" I ask, and it stiffens and points more toward the ceiling. I lean forward and lick my tongue from the base of his shaft to the tip, and it pivots nearly to a ninety-degree angle. "Much better," I say. I remove the condom from the wrapper and slide it onto his cock. I rub some lube on it, stand, and remove my clothes.

When I'm finished, I crawl back over him and lean down until my lips are beside his ear. I whisper, "Now...fuck the shit out of me."

Before I can even get the 'me' out, I feel his grip on my arm, and in a quick, powerful maneuver, he rolls so that I'm lying beneath him, dumbfounded by his display of power and authority. His dick must have some sixth sense about how to find its way inside me, because it appears effortless for him as he slips inside and pushes his pelvis forward. I throw my head back and groan as he slides in farther. He wraps his hands under my legs and pulls me toward him, entering even deeper. *Fuck the shit out of me, Jarek.*

I want him to make me his, to enjoy me as much as he's capable of enjoying a woman. I don't want him to forget this experience, and when he can't have it ever again, I want it to haunt him through every sexual experience he ever has with another woman, just as he has done with me.

He pushes in deep and moves back and forth. Then he leans down and snatches my wrists, pulling them forcefully over my head, as if demonstrating his renewed dominance.

I love it. I need it.

He holds my wrists tight as he presses in and out of me. I gaze up and down his body, watching his muscles expand and contract, as if he's doing crunches for me. The pressure inside me sends waves of relief rushing through my body. The profound, visceral relief I feel leaves me sure I've needed this for so long, as if I've never been fucked and I've always needed to be.

I wrap my legs around his as he presses his lips firmly against mine, his kiss so intense it's as if he's punishing me for depriving him of my body for so long. My breasts shake and tremble with each thrust he offers. The pain and pleasure that ripple through his movements excite me. I love being under him, having him control me like this. I know it can't last, but I wish we could fuck like this for the rest of our lives. How will I cope when this is gone? How will I find someone who can make me feel like this?

I catch a whiff of his scent, surely a product of this intense workout he's performing on me. I delight in the smell. I can't believe the fragrance is so lovely. How's that even possible? Why is it that every part of me is so attracted to him?

Sweat collects on my forehead. Jarek dips down and kisses my breasts in a frenzy. He's not Jarek anymore. He's a wild animal, a beast taking me, wanting me to have his offspring. As I greet every entry with a push toward him, he must know how much I want his seed inside me.

He teases my nipples with his tongue. His hips' movements surprise me. His heat washes over me and makes me feel whole. My thoughts travel through time, back to our first experience, back to the time when I felt as if he and I were one, and it's as if I'm not just in this moment with him now, but as if I've been transported back to the very first time and am being simultaneously pleasured here and there. My body trembles as sensations from concurrent experiences pulse through me. As he reaches that powerful, forceful grunt and quivers to let me know he's succeeded, I'm concerned since I'm a few beats behind.

Yet he doesn't stop his movements; he continues pressing into me. He leans down. The blindfold scratches against my cheek as he whispers into my ear, "Do you enjoy being mine?" As his breath hits my ear, combined with the feeling of him within me and the collision of past and present experiences, I can't help but feel my body swell with a sensation that swirls through my veins, as if I'm being wrapped in an electric blanket. My muscles jerk in fits. I roll my eyes back as if I'm enjoying a delicious dessert.

The ecstasy consumes me, and the explosion I feel is profound, perhaps more enjoyable merely because I'm primed for my lover's assault. *Oh, yes, Jarek, I do enjoy it. I enjoy it so much.*

I squeeze my legs around him. It's an instinctive response, as if I want to pull him deeper into me. It just feels so good having him inside me, and I find I can't keep from wanting more.

He rests his head beside my neck, his torso pressed against my belly, his chest against my breasts. As he shifts his head slightly, I can feel his breath against the side of my face.

With his hands still binding my wrists, I gasp, descending from my high. My thoughts settle on how much I want to be trapped under him like this always...how I want him to control me like this whenever he wants. However, now that I'm back in my right frame of mind, I know this is a fleeting moment and that soon I'll long for it like an addict for a drug. Only this isn't a drug I can get from any dealer—only Jarek, the one who will be leaving me soon.

He leans down and kisses me again. It's cruel, because the act makes me feel as if there will be more to us than these experiences, and I know the kiss is surely just an instinctual response, but it feels like it's intended to make me imagine us as more than these moments together.

A tear in my eye blurs my vision. I'm not sure if it's from the delicious experience or my fear of losing all this so quickly again. All I know is I'm relieved he can't see me. My pain is invisible to him.

Chapter Eight

The following day, I meet with Janet.

"Sorry about this weekend," she says as she slides onto the stool across the table from me. She sets her latte down and glances out the wall-length window beside us. I sip on the tea I ordered before she arrived. As she plants her purse on the table, I gaze at her with an expression that surely conveys the worry I've felt since the night before last.

"Janet, what's wrong?" I ask.

"Everything's fine," she says, but I can tell by the look on her face that it really isn't.

"Seriously."

"I just wanted to have a good time." *A lie. But what am I supposed to do?*

"Have you seen your therapist recently?" Janet sees her therapist two Thursdays every month. It's not something I'd normally bring up, but considering how sloppy she was at the bar, I can't help but be concerned.

"I saw her last week," she replies.

I can't help but wonder if that's a lie, too. *When did my sister become so secretive?* I recall her being quiet as a child, but not deceptive. It didn't seem to set in until after college. I wonder if somehow my prodding in college gave her a reason to resist honesty. "And?"

"Same as usual. I don't see what your problem is."

"You were wasted, Janet. Like sorority party wasted." She appears apprehensive. I know I risk my freedom to hang out with her, but I feel like it would be irresponsible of me to ignore her behavior.

"I'm fine," she says. "I can deal with my own issues. Now, please. Let's not make this into a big deal when it's not. Tell me about Jarek. How did it go? Any rekindled flames?"

She's trying to change the subject, but I have to acknowledge she isn't budging. Not today, and I'm sure I'm just a few probing questions away from being iced out of her life yet again. Perhaps a wiser strategy would be to continue talking to her, sharing with her, and wait until the right moment when she can't refuse my request to understand her life.

"Nothing's there," I reply.

"Oh, please. You like him. You've always liked him. Don't lie to yourself."

"We're just friends. Like we've always been."

"Mmmkay. Has he mentioned why he left like that?"

For someone who doesn't want to talk to me about any of her issues, she's sure quick to interrogate me about my most vulnerable areas. "Not really. He just told me he moved out west."

"It was probably the stress of what happened to Daddy. He'd done so much for him. I guess he just couldn't be around there because it reminded him of those memories. If I could have gotten out of there for a while, I would have."

"But you would have said something to us about it."

"He told Mom."

"You think he shouldn't have said goodbye to us?" *How can Janet be so flip about this when I dwell on it?*

"I guess if he needed to say bye to anyone, it would have been you," she says. "Me and Kelsey weren't all that close to him. You know that. Kelsey was always off doing stuff at school, and I was always hanging with my friends. You were the ones who just had each other. Am I wrong? That's what it always seemed like on the outside."

"You're not wrong," I say bitterly.

"So why wouldn't he have said goodbye to you?"

Considering the night I shared with Jarek, this question makes me nauseous. Allowing him back into my life has been a terrible mistake. I knew that when I started down this path, but how could I have let it get this far? How could I have been so stupid?

"Who knows?" I say. "It's been so long. He may have said bye and I just didn't remember. There was so much going on back then." She eyes me skeptically. I wonder if I was looking at her like that when she was avoiding talking about therapy.

I sit at my desk, sifting through a series of scanned documents on my laptop, ensuring they're properly filed for our audit. The click of heels outside my office assures me that Stephanie is nearby, and as she enters, she closes the door behind her. She glances around as if she's worried someone might know what she's up to. Why is she acting like a secret agent?

"What's wrong?" I ask.

"There's a bit of a problem. That's a lie. There's a huge problem! I'm just trying to tell you before Mr. Farcon—"

"Where is she?" booms behind her.

Mr. Farcon, all three feet of him, rounds the corner, a grimace on his face, his usually pale flesh red as a tomato.

Oh, no. Whatever it is, it's really bad. Stephanie stands beside the door as he rushes in and stands right before my desk. I start to get up when he screams, "Sit down!"

I've seen him do this with Stephanie before. This is how he responded when he discovered we needed to perform the audit for the last event. I look to Stephanie as if I need her to psychically project to me what he's about to fuss at me about before he can.

"The Frenly Brothers are backing out," he says.

"What?" I ask.

"Evidently one of them had a skiing accident. Broke his arm."

"Oh, God."

"Yeah, you're gonna need a God to get us out of this one."

"Can't you just show them that they were supposed to..." Stephanie says behind him, trying to step in and defend me, which is nice, but useless.

"At the end of the day, is that going to bring money in?" he asks. "If we can't sell tickets and get people at this event, we're screwed. And if we're screwed, you're out of a fucking job! You got that?"

My face must be as red as his, but for a totally different reason. "What am I supposed to do?" I ask. It was a miracle that I booked them, and it's not my fault one of them had an accident.

"Fix it," he says slowly, as if trying to calm himself. "Fix it real fast."

He must know how impossible that is. However, rather than arguing with him, I decide appeasement is the best option: "Okay."

"Good. And if you can't find me an act in two days, don't bother coming back in—even to pack your things, or I'll have you kicked out on your ass faster than you can say 'severance.' Understood?"

I nod. He growls, like he's about to bark at me, but instead, he stomps out, leaving Stephanie and I staring blankly at each other.

"I have to do this in a week?" I ask in a whisper, fearing he may still be close and be even more infuriated by my skepticism about my new task.

"Lana, you can do it," Stephanie says, clearly trying to pump me up. "You got the Frenly Brothers. You can use that same entrepreneurial spirit and wrangle up some other act. Can't you?" Her tone is desperate, like she doesn't really believe I can pull this off.

"I can't—"

"Sure you can. Please. Just see if you can find someone. I have a file of plenty of local performers that you might be able to find someone from."

I know the performers she's referring to, and I might as well not have an act. They're a bunch of wedding singers and no-names who won't in and of themselves draw an audience to the fundraiser. I don't have anything against their work, but considering we're in the business of selling tickets based on the acts we bring to the table, this isn't going to cut it.

"I'll see what I can do," I say.

"Great, Lana. That's perfect."

As she leaves me to my mess of work and the new mess of the fundraiser that was supposed to go on without a hitch, I want to bash my face against the keyboard of my laptop.

I start out the building, flipping through a green binder of performers that Stephanie gave me earlier. *What am I supposed to do? How am I supposed to make this happen?*

My phone vibrates, and as I pull it out, I see it's Jarek. Suddenly, he's not the most troublesome thing in my life right now.

"Hello?"

"You okay?" he asks. "You sound pissed."

"The Frenly Brothers just canceled for the fundraiser, so now I'm totally fucked because I have no time and if people don't show up to this thing, I'm going to be fired for sure."

Silence.

"Anyway," I say, "I'd better go. I have a career that I have to watch go down the tubes."

"Wait, wait, Lana," he says. "What if I could help you get someone?"

"Who?"

"Will you meet me in an hour?"

"Jarek, don't worry. I can figure this out."

"I know you can, but if this is something I can help you with, I want to help you. An hour?"

"Okay."

I shouldn't have agreed. I should be doing everything in my power to fix this catastrophe, but I can't help but feel that wasting an afternoon with Jarek is just as useless as wasting it stressing over the end of my career.

Thirty minutes later, he texts me to wear something nice. Since I really have nothing to lose right now, I obey, and when he texts me to let me know he's arrived, I head downstairs. He's waiting in a navy-blue Mercedes. As I slip into the front seat, I glare at him. His face spasms, as if he's trying to figure out what my look is about.

"A fucking Mercedes? Really?"

"It's just a rental."

"Exactly. Would a Toyota have killed you?"

He smirks. God, I could just slap him right now. "It really didn't even come up," he says.

"I bet it didn't." I set my purse on the floor and pull my seat-belt on. "Now Jarek, it really isn't something you need to worry about." As appreciative as I am that he's offered to help, it's not his mess to fix.

"Not an issue," he says. "Just relax."

I try, but considering how stressed I am about this and the audit, I'm not sure I'm going to make it through today as a relaxed person.

He drives to the interstate and takes it south for fifteen minutes before he drives alongside a fenced off tarmac. The sight of a runway and small white planes makes me uneasy.

"What are we doing?" I ask suspiciously. I already know, but I can't wrap my thoughts around it. *Are we seriously about to fly somewhere?* I could kill Jarek. He should have warned me. *I can't just leave. I have to be back at work tomorrow!*

"You want to fix this problem?" he asks, obviously knowing he needs to curtail my frustration.

"Yes, but—"

"Then you need to trust me on this and get on this plane." I'm even more concerned. I'm about to waste an evening, and for what?

He heads through a security gate and parks in a small parking lot. When we get out, he leads me across the tarmac.

Not fifteen minutes later, we're in the air, flying a private jet he's hired just for this trip. I'm wracked with guilt. He shouldn't have spent all this money on me. Considering the nature of our relationship, he shouldn't be spending *any* money on me.

Jarek snatches a magazine off a table before our chairs. I give him a frustrated look to convey just how uncomfortable I am with this whole situation.

"What?"

"Not everyone can hop on a private jet."

A self-indulgent smirk creeps across his face, and I shake my head. "Where are we heading?" I ask.

"Don't you want it to be a surprise?" he asks.

"I'm not sure I do."

"Oh, you do."

"When will we be back? I have work tomorrow."

"We're having a short outing. No big deal. Relax. Do you want a new performer or what?"

"You are just so frustrating sometimes, Jarek Dean." His smirk broadens. I want to punch it right off his cocky face.

When we land, we have a car waiting for us. I think I liked it better when Jarek's riches were just something I heard about—an intangible mass of money. Seeing the evidence makes me self-conscious. What must he think of my life...of my crappy apartment? The old Jarek wouldn't have thought anything of them. He would have thought I'd actually made something of myself. The new Jarek must think of me as the closest thing to a homeless person he knows.

In the distance, a city rises before the light blue of the afternoon sky. I recognize the spires of the Sears Tower from having visited Chicago a few times to see a friend.

The driver drops us off outside a large building. Condos, I think. Jarek leads me inside and checks in with the concierge, who fetches the elevator for us.

Jarek seems so comfortable living like this, having everything at his disposal. Not only has he amassed all this money, but he's acclimated to the lifestyle that comes along with it. We don't even exist in the same world. *How can this be the boy I grew up with?*

The elevator chimes as it stops on the thirty-fourth floor. "Thirty-four," a female voice announces through the speaker. Jarek leads me through the hall to one of the rooms and knocks.

I have no idea what to expect, but by now I've given up trying to figure it out. I might as well let Jarek have his way with me.

The door swings open, revealing an older man in a sleeveless white shirt tainted with yellow stains. A pair of black skinny jeans sculpts around scrawny chicken legs. The man is barefoot, assuring me I'm not overdressed. As he sees Jarek, a broad smile sweeps across his face. He has rosy cheeks and long strands of white hair that fall just below his ears. *How does Jarek think this guy can help me get a new performer?*

"Garreth!" Jarek exclaims.

"You crazy son of a bitch," the man says. "What brings you out here? Where are my manners?" He shifts his attention to me. "I'm Garreth Pulzer."

Garreth Pulzer? The *renowned pianist with double platinum albums and three Grammy Awards?* That *Garreth Pulzer?* I've seen his picture a few times, but seeing him outside his suit and tie and well-groomed state completely threw me.

Did Jarek bring me here to convince Garreth to perform at the fundraiser? That's impossible. Garreth has lived in seclusion, refusing to perform for five years. Though I'm honored to be in the presence of a legend, if Jarek really brought me here to attempt to convince Garreth to help me out, not only will I not have an act by the end of today, I'll have humiliated myself in front of one of the greatest living musical artists in the world.

Those facts aside, I can see why Jarek thought enlisting Garreth's help would have bailed me out of my jam. Garreth is like the Streisand of pianists. People will fly from all over the country if they think they have a chance to see him perform live again.

But fat chance of that happening.

"Come on in, come on in," Garreth says, waving us inside. He leads us into his condo, his bare feet padding against the coal-black, wood-paneled floor. The wall-length window overlooks the Chicago skyline as the sun sets in the distance. It's as if we arrived at just the perfect time to watch this magical moment.

Garreth approaches a cabinet and pulls down a door, revealing a mini-bar. He retrieves a bottle of red wine and a glass. "This comes from a beautiful winery in Italy. They don't have their license to sell it in the states, so it costs a fortune to have it shipped here. Please, have a seat."

I settle on a gray couch before a wall with a piece of artwork, a three-paneled black and white photograph of a hippopotamus, which looks far classier than it sounds.

After he pours a glass of wine, he hands it to me. I take sip, my face cringing from the sour taste.

"You have a beautiful place," Jarek says, sitting in a brown barcalounger before the windows.

"Thank you so much," Garreth says as he prepares a glass of wine for Jarek. When he's finished, he hands it off to Jarek and returns to the bar.

"Now, what brings you all the way out here?" Garreth asks, pouring his own drink. "You said you needed to ask me for a favor?"

"Yeah," Jarek says. "I kinda was wondering if you wouldn't mind performing again."

I blush. How could Jarek be so tactless in his approach? Obviously, Garreth isn't just going to agree to perform as a favor to him. I want to die from embarrassment.

Garreth gives him the look I'd expect of a man who has a reputation for refusing to perform. "Are you out of your fucking mind?" he asks, his tone cold, severe.

"Probably, because I'd need for you to do it for free, too."

My jaw drops. I drink as much of the red wine as I can manage, hoping it'll ease the tension that's steadily intensifying within me. Despite Jarek humiliating both of us with such a ridiculous request, I acknowledge that this sort of gumption is surely a part of Jarek's immense success.

The stern, insulted look on Garreth's face leads me to believe we're a few moments away from being escorted from his condo. He stares out his window and downs the glass he's made for himself before pouring himself another and drinking half of it. He sets the glass down on a side table beside him with such force I'm sure the glass is going to shatter.

"You came all this way to piss me off?" he asks, his face reddening. He glances at me, a wicked gleam in his eyes. "This guy's got real balls, doesn't he?"

I couldn't agree more.

Jarek motions to me, "It's for my..."

"Yes, what is this divine creature to you?" Garreth asks, again with that same wicked glint.

I'm eager to hear how he introduces me. His trick? His slut? His—

"Very good friend," he says. I subdue a scoff. We aren't good friends, if only considering the amount of time that has passed without hearing so much as a word from him.

"Did he tell you how we met?" Garreth asks me.

"He didn't even tell me this was where we were heading. I'm really sorry. I didn't mean to impose."

"I assure you, madam, you are not the one offending me right now. It's this asshole who needs to be a little more careful with his words." It's amusing that this prestigious musician can be so crude.

"I would think, considering our past, you would be a little more willing to help me out."

"Really?" Garreth asks. "You're going to use that against me now?"

"You're welcome," Jarek says.

"What's going on?" I ask.

"Oh, he didn't tell you?" Garreth asks. "Ha. Well, at least I know he has some discretion."

"Of course," Jarek says facetiously.

"We met six years ago. We were attending a party of Lady Granderly in London."

"It was her and her husband's anniversary," Jarek interjects.

"I remember the goddamn story. I can tell the details." Jarek smirks. It's clear they have a very affectionate friendship, neither seeming to mind the other's teasing or insults.

"I was wasted out of my mind," Garreth says. "Stumbling, falling over drunk. I don't usually get this sloppy, but Mr. Granderly and I have a history that I won't bore you with. Needless to say, our affair didn't come to a great end, but as society has always considered us to be good friends, I arrived and when he didn't so much as speak to me, I just kept downing the wine. Jarek took it upon himself to keep an eye on me, which was nice, but it didn't help."

"He's got a bit of Janet in him," Jarek explains.

"Since Frederick wouldn't speak to me, I chatted up his son, who I could tell from some glares and exchanges had similar tastes as his father, so we ended up heading to the restroom."

"Which was a terrible idea, and I told him that."

"Whatever. I was so loaded, I didn't care. Jarek played lookout and when Frederick was on his way to the loo, Jarek told him it wasn't working and walked him to another restroom across the house. So...he got me out of a pretty serious jam. I can't imagine the fight that would have gone down if we'd been discovered. At the very least, Frederick Jr. would have been disowned. At most, Frederick would have probably slit my throat."

"That's a lot more scandalous than I was expecting," I confess.

"Right?"

"So he kind of owes me," Jarek says with a sly smile.

Garreth stares him down. "Jarek, if you knew what performing did to me, you wouldn't be asking me to do this."

"What does it do to you?" I ask.

"The performances get to me. I head to an event and it nags at my nerves. There's so much pressure with a performance. My hands practically freeze up on the keys unless I have something to take the edge off. And I'm just a fit of nerves. It's a horrible feeling. When I used to perform, I had to drink—a lot. I began my career in the cellars of symposiums. Eventually, I realized I couldn't live like that."

"So why didn't you just give up the drinking?"

"It's what kept me going! It's what made me strong enough to go out there."

I think of Janet. "So you just gave it up?"

"Threw my career in the trash. I mean, look at me, I'm not suffering. I don't have to go out there and perform. I still play here, plenty. Enough for me at least, and here, I don't have to worry about the nerves getting to me. That said, I'm afraid I just can't play. It's too much for me. I don't have the strength. Not at this age."

It's as I expected. He won't perform my fundraiser. Jarek looks disappointed, like he's failed me. Although, considering the lengths he went to get here, he should be more than disappointed. He pops up from the barcalounger. "You mind if I talk to you alone?" Jarek asks.

Garreth eyes him curiously. "What you got up your sleeve?"

"Come on," Jarek insists.

"Alright, but it won't do a damn bit of good."

"Humor me."

Garreth excuses himself, and they step out onto the balcony. I glance around uneasily as they chat, looking out at the view. I can't tell what they're discussing, but I'm sure whatever Jarek has to say to Garreth, it's not going to change his mind. If nerves are his problem, and he hasn't performed live in so long, I doubt anything we say will encourage him.

After nearly five minutes, they step back inside. "You've got a performer," Jarek says quickly.

"What?" I ask, startled by how quickly he's changed his mind.

"One time," Garreth says. "One time this guy gets me out of a hole, and now he expects me to go against everything in me—everything that I've been fighting all these years."

"You love doing this. Come on. I'm not asking you to go on fucking tour. I'm asking you to play one show, trip totally paid."

"We can't afford that," I say, horrified at the suggestion.

"I told you," Jarek replies, "I was planning to make a donation anyway. This will be my part."

This is *way* too much, especially for Jarek, who has no reason to be going so far out of his way for me.

"When is this fundraiser?" Garreth asks, his face locked in a resigned expression.

"Not this weekend, but the next," I say.

Garreth looks to Jarek again. "Seriously? I'm supposed to have something to play by then? You never cease to amaze me."

"As if you haven't been playing plenty already," Jarek says. "Just promise us you'll be there, all right?"

"You can count on me."

Did Jarek just save my job? And why is he offering to pay for Garreth's expenses? This is way too much. Although if I have Garreth Pulzer at the fundraiser, that will draw plenty of people and likely a slew of donations that will ensure its success—and my ability to keep hosting them.

Jarek extends his hand to shake on it, and Garreth takes it, a look of determination in his eyes.

Garreth turns to me. "Lana, looks like we have a show to put on," he says as we shake.

I'm thrilled and terrified. *Will I really have the opportunity to tell Mr. Farcon I landed Garreth Pulzer? Will he actually show?* Considering how stubborn he was when we first arrived, I wouldn't be surprised if he decided to back out like the Frenley Brothers, but if he does show up, I'll have a solid foundation for my future career at Farcon & Williams.

Chapter Nine

With Garreth Pulzer slated to participate in the fundraiser, it appears I have little to worry about. I owe Jarek for his generosity in assisting me, and I'm starting to reconsider these notions I've had about him, all these beliefs about the kind of person he is—was. What kind of man would do this for someone? A rich man, obviously. But why for me? On one hand, we have a long history together and perhaps he isn't just doing it for me, but for my father. Still, what about when he left me? I can't distance myself from that memory, regardless of what he does. However, I can accept being the recipient of his generosity, and as much as I don't want to, I appreciate it.

Two days pass, and it's the night of Mom's birthday party. These past two weeks have been little more than a series of events that have drained me emotionally and physically, and while it's been a lot of work, I'm capable of handling it. I just wish there had been some promise of breaks in between—not a continuous workload to get through from one large event to the next. But that's life.

"Jarek will be here again tonight," Mom says to Kelsey. *Why is he coming tonight? And why is she telling Kelsey?*

I'd considered inviting him, especially after what he did for me, but it was difficult to justify inviting him because he'd be coming as my date, and to my mother's birthday, which didn't seem right.

Mom lounges in a stool beside the table while I organize trays and plates for food. Janet scrubs down wine glasses on the other side of the table while Kelsey unloads the liquor she's brought with her—two crates full, an impressive load that Janet keeps eyeing a little too eagerly, as if she's one step away from escaping so that she can single-handedly delight in the selection. My concern about her drinking only amplifies the more I'm around her, and I've already decided I need to keep an eye on her tonight so she doesn't turn Mom's party into another drunken episode. However, in this moment, Janet's drinking doesn't concern me as much as what Mom just said to Kelsey.

A sly expression sneaks across Kelsey's face. The gleam in her eyes is the sort I imagine she gets when she plots to find herself a new husband. I noted her clothes when she first arrived. A high-collared, bright-red dress molds against her curves, and though it doesn't show cleavage, the way they shape around her ample breasts leaves little to the imagination. A black belt ties around her waist, matching her boots, which make her appear what seems to me a foot taller than usual. Her blonde locks are bound in an elegant up-do that hangs to one side of her face. As great as Kelsey looks normally, it is evident she's spent some extra time on her look, and now I know why. She's eager to impress Jarek.

She and Mom have undoubtedly determined that Jarek is the best option right now, because he's a damn good option. I imagine they've even discussed this already, and I can't help but wonder if they left me out because of my past with him. Although I doubt Mom and Kelsey understand what happened. They're too self-absorbed to think that much about me.

I wish I could say something to Jarek to discourage him from pursuing my sister, but I know that will only make me look jealous and interested. But what am I concerned about? I doubt she'll capture his interest, yet maybe she's what he wants in a woman. Kelsey's the kind of girl a guy like Jarek marries. I suppose I'm destined to be the girl he just hooks up with.

I want to believe he couldn't marry a girl like her, but do I know the real Jarek? Once upon a time, I deluded myself into believing he was someone other than the guy who abandoned me. I can't permit myself to make that mistake again. If he decides he wants to date my sister, I will have to find a way to deal with that. But what would I do if things grew more serious? Would I need to attend their wedding? Would I have to survive family get-togethers with them holding hands and exchanging loving gazes? I wouldn't. I *couldn't!* I'd have to stop attending family events altogether. Become more like Janet.

"How is that working out?" Mom asks Kelsey. *Working out? How far have they gone?* He sure as hell hasn't said anything to me about their rendezvous. *Has he been juggling us ever since he got back in town?*

"Yes, how is that working out, Kelsey?" I press.

"He's coming along. He seems fairly preoccupied with work..." *It's not just work he's preoccupied with.* "...but we've gotten together a few times, so I think it's just a matter of him coming around."

"When have you gotten together?" I ask.

"Just those two times. For dinner and then drinks at the bar that night."

I had him one of those times, so screw you. It's not a competition, but I can't help but feel it is. That's how everything seems to be with Kelsey, so all I can think is, "I'm winning, winning, winning!"

"But he's coming tonight as my date, so..."

"Your date?" I ask. I need to shut my mouth. I can't play cool if I'm freaking out every time she reveals a new piece of information.

"I invited him." *Maybe he doesn't care who he plows.* For a classy guy, this seems like the least classy behavior ever.

The news hurts, but I'm not sure if I have a right to be hurt. I haven't said anything to suggest I like him beyond our flings, but what was I supposed to think when he helped me wrangle up a hermit artist for my fundraiser? Didn't that mean he wanted more? Or did I read too much into it?

If he really likes me, and that seems to be what his behavior has suggested, then why would he go behind my back and make dates with my sister? I'm overreacting. Attending a party he knows I'll be at is hardly 'behind my back.' I have to keep in mind that Kelsey can make things sound a little more dramatic than they really are, especially to satisfy my mother's shallow imagination.

"How's Kirk?" Kelsey asks Janet.

"He's good," she replies as she finishes wiping the inside of a glass and moves on to the next. "He's pretty swamped in Dallas right now, but he'll be home tomorrow. Yay!"

I've never heard Janet sound so enthusiastic about his return. Although, get a few drinks in her and she sounds enthusiastic about anything. But I've only seen her take a few sips from the glass of wine beside her.

"That's good," Kelsey says. "It's amazing how much time he spends away from home. Chad was like that, and that's how I found out about Tara."

Janet's expression shifts to worry. Of course she would worry. Who wouldn't at least entertain that idea if their husband was gone as much as Janet's is? I'm certain Kelsey brought it up to hurt Janet—a dig, perhaps just to make herself feel better about her own failed marriage. Whatever the reason, Kelsey has already found her way onto my shit-list tonight.

As guests begin arriving, Kelsey delivers a glowing hostess performance, demonstrating all the skills she's acquired from Mom over the years. Janet and I make last minute preparations, during which I catch Janet downing two glasses of chardonnay. As much as I would hope a sight like that would turn me off of drinking, it makes me want to sneak my own. I don't want to be emotionally present for this. I don't want to see Kelsey putting moves on Jarek, parading around in front of me like she's won a contest.

As I mix and mingle with the guests, I see Jarek step through the hallway, carrying a bottle of red wine. He approaches Kelsey directly, not even looking at me. Interesting that he would avoid me considering our last encounter, but I shake it off and continue mingling.

Kelsey drags Jarek aside, I guess to accost him with a flirtatious moment. But maybe that's what he wants.

I wish I could slip away and see how she's tilting her head as she bats those long lashes at him. I'm sure she's posing so he can see her figure in its most accessible of positions. I can't judge, because I know I've done the same thing with him. *But I had a right to! He's mine!*

After a few minutes, they rejoin Carol and Melanie and laugh and chat amongst one another. Kelsey laughs heartily and sets her hand on his shoulder. I don't know what's been said, but I know what she's up to. *Get your hands off him!*

My jealousy consumes me. I want to believe it's something else, perhaps my natural rage to protect him from my sister's clutches, but I know better. As much as I want to deny and fight it, I still crave him.

"Hey, Lana," I hear behind me. I spin around, and Charlie Gruber approaches me.

Charlie is Mom's friend Andrea Glider's son. With his hair slicked to the side and his glasses resting on the edge of his nose, he looks like as much of a goober as he is.

"What are you doing here?" I ask, my curtness stemming from my lack of enthusiasm about being assaulted by his advances, which are constant whenever I'm unfortunate enough to cross his path at a party. "I thought you were in Phoenix."

"I am, but I came back to visit the family. You know how it goes." He starts on about his work as a lawyer for his father's firm. He rants on about how much he detests it, but how necessary he is for everyone else to function. I could only imagine the way he would talk about a girl if he was in a relationship, a prospect that doesn't seem very likely.

I do my best to act involved, if only so that I can keep my mind off my sister's work on Jarek, but I can't help but note how, after over ten minutes, Charlie still hasn't asked me to say anything about my life or what I've been up to since we last spoke what must have been two years ago.

Kelsey and Jarek make their way to Mom's cluster of friends, primarily Charlie's mother and Vera Chiles. Andrea and Vera have been Mom's friends since Daddy first purchased this house. Andrea's husband is in corporate real estate and Vera does something with hedge funds.

As Charlie's monologue ascends to an all-time high level of boredom, I find myself struggling to keep from yawning, so I tell him I need another drink. It's the least I need to put up with him. I may need several. I'm just a few more Charlie-brags away from becoming Janet.

I head to the bar, placing myself beside Mom, Andrea, Vera, and their friend Charlene, who always finds an excuse to give me grief about my lack of relationships.

Charlene, my mother's age, with platinum blonde hair in an up-do, wears some poor forest creature around her neck and a set of pearls with an off-white pantsuit. She greets me with a mischievous look, as if she is just waiting to get around to me, to assault me about my life. Fortunately, my rush to the bar and Mom's current conversation with her keeps her from yanking me into one.

"Janet has been doing just fine," Mom says. "She and Kirk are talking about getting married, but they're waiting for him to get a promotion to management."

"He's such a nice young man," Charlene says. She hardly talks to Kirk about his relationship with Janet. None of us really know that much. She just enjoys that he makes so much money and is prize-worthy for our family's collection of prestigious men. I guess that role has to go to someone since Kelsey can't brag about her wealthy husband anymore. Mom has to look forward to some well-off in-law, and I clearly won't be bringing one to the table.

"Is Lana seeing someone?" Charlene asks.

"She has some mystery boyfriend in the city," Mom lies.

"There's no one," I say, speaking loudly so that even Jarek and Kelsey turn my direction. I didn't imagine I'd capture their attention, but I didn't want Mom to get away with insisting I had some secret boyfriend I was hiding from everyone. If Charlene managed to discover the truth from Kelsey or Janet or Charlie, I'm sure she would make a dig, as if I had been the one to perpetuate the lie, and I'm not in the mood for that. "I'm happily on my own," I insist.

"You're not seeing anyone?" Charlene presses, as if she knows better.

"No. I'm actually perfectly content with being a single woman with a decent career and very close friends."

"But don't you want someone?" Vera asks. "Don't you want someone you can come home to?"

"Who says I don't come home to anyone?" I ask. Some wicked part of me is trying to cause a stir. "I come home to whoever I want to come home to, but I don't need it to be the same person—and I don't need a relationship to make me happy. Let's be honest, how many people do we know who are in relationships that they'd be happier without?"

My gaze shifts to Charlene. I can tell by her wide eyes and open mouth she takes it as a jab at her own marital issues—her husband's eager law partner who eventually transformed into his partner in the bedroom. I didn't intend it to be directly related to her own failed marriage, but I don't mind her making the correlation.

The red hue that overtakes Mom's face reveals how scandalized she is. *Is she offended that I said I'd sleep with whatever man I want to or that she thinks I called out Charlene's miserable marriage? Probably both.* I grab my glass off the bar. "I think I'll run to the ladies' room."

As I turn, I catch Kelsey's bowed head, putting on an oh-so-embarrassed performance for Jarek and the group she's collected with. Jarek winks at me. It's a familiar moment, reminding me of when we were young and always on the same team. Angry as I am with him, that same eagerness and excitement returns, like when we had all those jokes and played together.

When I return from the restroom, an all-too-eager Charlie approaches me. Judging by the sparkle in his eyes, he's picked up some hope from overhearing my comment to Charlene. Desperate as I may get, I would never get that desperate.

"What are you up to after this?" he asks.

"She's hanging out with me." Janet leans against the doorframe to the kitchen, a grin on her face, a glass of wine close to the cleavage her black dress reveals, as if she's afraid to let her glass stray too far from her lips. "Isn't that right, big sis?" she asks as she brushes a lock of her dark hair that dangles across her face behind her ear.

"That's right."

"Well," he says, "maybe some other time we should meet up in Atlanta and grab a drink or something." *You can't take the hint?*

Is it just because he's Charlie that I find myself so disgusted by his words? If Jarek approached me the same way, I doubt I would feel so disgusted by this approach.

After I turn down Charlie's offer, Janet and I escape and work our way to another corner of the room. When Janet sneaks away to the bathroom, I saunter about the room on my own, sipping on a glass of chardonnay that, at least for now, is my only friend. To avoid talking to anyone, I chat up one of the caterers at the party, who is pleasant and discusses his desire to create his own catering business with me. He sounds like a great contact for Farcon & Williams, so I ask for his card.

Before I know it, nearly half an hour has passed, and as I scan the crowd, I become increasingly concerned about Janet's absence. I excuse myself from my conversation with the caterer and begin my quest for Janet, trying to appear as if I'm just checking to make sure everything is in place so no one will suspect my real interest.

Between dodging chatter and cleaning up messes here and there, I finally make it upstairs. The faint sound of the ruckus downstairs echoes in the back of my mind, as if it's a memory I've conjured up. I check the bedrooms for my sneaky sister.

Did she leave? I open the door to her old bedroom and hear a sound that startles me. I turn on the light.

Janet sits on the carpet before the guest bed, a bottle of wine in hand, a guilty look sparkling in her eyes. "Really, Janet?" I ask.

She holds the bottle out. "Here," she says, "It'll make you feel better." I take the bottle and sit beside her. It's like when we used to sit in her room when we were little, with the addition of the bottle of wine.

I already feel loopy from the chardonnay I've downed, but being swamped with the prying curiosities of mother's company and forced to endure Kelsey's attempts to snatch Jarek, I'm willing to take the easy escape. I take a swig. Perhaps I can join Janet in whatever magical place she wanders to when she attempts to dilute the sting of this harsh world.

"They having fun down there?" Janet asks as she wraps her arms around her legs.

"I guess."

"And Kelsey?"

"As fun as ever." It's hard to reflect on a time when Kelsey wasn't having a good time. She's always smiling or laughing. Even senior year, when Brittany Krider spread rumors about her blowing Derren Sparks in the restroom, Kelsey smiled, exposing her bright white teeth as she said so eloquently, "I guess we'll need a replacement for the top of the pyramid until you can fight off that muffin top." These sorts of girl-on-girl moments were the only times she revealed her intellect. With men, she never tried to be clever or biting, and I could tell it was because she thought it wouldn't be advantageous to behave that way.

"Kelsey has a way of pissing me off," Janet says, echoing my own thoughts.

"I know what you mean." I dwell on Kelsey's callous nature. "I remember when we were kids. She never liked doing things with us and Dad. She didn't ever get those afternoon outings for ice cream, and I know she didn't understand why Daddy got so upset when she finally found a way to sneak out of them by hanging out with whatever boy she was seeing."

"Do you think she even misses him?"

"Of course she does," I insist, though I don't know. Sometimes I catch myself wondering.

The gleam in Janet's eyes reveals she's more blasted than I initially thought, but her words come out lucidly: "I don't know that she cares about anyone other than herself. Don't know if she ever has."

"I'm sure that, like Mom, she's pissed that he didn't leave a little more behind. I don't think his generosity or authenticity meant much to them." That I'm even discussing this assures me I'm drunker than I realize, and

Janet's so far gone, she'll probably agree about pretty much anything. *Shouldn't I be chastising her?* I should be the responsible one encouraging her to clean up her act, especially at a family gathering. But I don't want to be responsible. Not tonight. *Where has that ever gotten me?*

"He was wonderful to us," Janet continues. "That's the thing about life...cruel, twisted life. You have something beautiful like him in this world, something that makes you feel so special and loved, and then God comes and pulls him right from you."

God? This is the first time I've heard Janet mention anything about God.

"Do you remember when I started going to church?" she asks. "I'm sure you don't. It was for a little while during college. There was this guy, Simon Baker, who attended the First Presbyterian Church. I thought if I went to the service with him, I'd have a better shot at getting him to go on a date with me. It felt nice, this idea that something else could fill that void, that empty place Daddy left in me—us. But no matter how much I prayed, no matter how much I begged for something to fill it, this nagging emptiness lingered within me. That's when I realized I was just trying to shove anything and everything into that void...I've been trying to do that for a long time.

"When Daddy passed, Mom just...well, she wasn't the best nurturer, and I guess she never had been, but she couldn't reach us. Couldn't talk to us about anything. Couldn't make us feel special or loved. She made us feel like we always had to do things to prove ourselves to her. Kelsey was good at that. She did all the things Mommy liked to do. I think just playing sports made Mom think I was from a different planet. And when Daddy passed, if I talked about it with her, she shut down. Like I betrayed her for loving Daddy. It's as if she withheld her love since she didn't understand me. That's silly, isn't it? Thinking your Mom is withholding love from you?"

"I don't know that it is silly," I say, a confession I feel guilty for expressing. I believe she blames us for what Daddy did with his money. Like we could have done something to stop him—to make him more responsible. Because she sure as hell couldn't.

"You remember when he would come into the bedroom and tell ghost stories?" Janet asks. I can't tell if this thought came from something I said or if it's just Dammit Janet's drunken mind wandering. However it arose, I go along with it.

"We were way too young for those," I say.

"I was scared for like two weeks of that damn hand he told us about."

"That was pretty much child abuse."

"He got such a kick out of scaring the living daylights out of us, but he was so good. When he hugged you, he made you feel like he was caring about you. You felt adored all over. When Mom hugs you, it's like a fucking chore. Like it's killing her to put her arms around you. How hard can it be to hug your own kid?"

Her mention of children saddens me. Though I don't desire to have any soon, it's something I would like to get around to one day. However, between work and my lack of a potential partner (and equal lack of desire for finding one), I'm not sure I'll ever have a chance. "I don't think I'll ever know," I say. Despite my awareness that I'm only being so open because of the wine, I take another swig from the bottle.

"Really?" Janet asks. "Lana, you'd be great with kids."

"I don't think I'll ever have the opportunity to find out."

"There's someone out there for you. One day, you'll meet this amazing guy, and he'll make you feel so incredible, and you'll know he's the one. You'll just know it."

"Like you did with Kirk?"

Her gaze sinks to the floor. "Ah, yes," she says, as if the very mention of his name disturbs her, as if she doesn't want to be reminded that he's returning tomorrow. "I do think he's the one," she says. "My one. The one I deserve to be with."

"Why do you say it like that?"

"That hole I feel inside me, the one I tried to shove God into—it's like we both have those kinds of holes, and we fit into each other's just right. That's not the right way of putting it, because we don't make it go away. I think looking at each other's holes makes it easier to deal with our own. Makes the world feel a lot less lonely. That's a terrible thing to say about your husband, isn't it? Kind of a schadenfreude. Looking at his misery and feeling better because I think it's as bad as mine, but it helps on hard nights. It helps seeing how sad and imperfect he is."

"Janet, don't tell me that. Tell me you're really happy."

Her face trembles as she forces a smile. "I'm really happy, Lana. Aren't you?"

My face spasms even more than hers as tears spill from my eyes. I didn't feel as if I was close to crying until those words reached into my soul and yanked out all the pain and sorrow I've been hiding from for so long.

It's just from the wine. I should have stopped. But everything hurts so much, and I just want the pain to go away...if only for a moment.

If I feel this way now, I wonder how sad Janet must feel all the time. "I wish I could help you, Janet. I wish there was something I could do. You know that, don't you? But I'm so scared that if I do anything, you'll push me away—leave like you did before."

"Because that's what I'll do. I don't know what comes over me, but I don't like everyone else telling me what I should do. Mom did enough of that when we were little. Didn't she get onto us enough for everyone for the rest of our lives?" I laugh and nod. "Lana, don't take it personally. I've made my choices, and I have to do everything I can to cope with them."

Is she really that unhappy with Kirk? She's never seemed unhappy. Or is there more to it? Did something happen to her? Is there something she's harboring that she's never shared with me?

"You know I love you, Janet. Don't you?"

"I don't know that love can fix what's broken inside me."

Tears continue streaming down my face. "I don't know if it can fix *anything*. The only thing I think love can do is twist your soul, make you feel rage when you realize those who you love can never feel the same way about you. That the whole world is set up to disappoint you. Not just disappoint you, but torture you with those things that you want so badly...those things that you want so much that it hurts. The world can be so cruel."

"You're talking about Jarek, aren't you?"

The tears just keep coming. Janet wraps her arms around me.

"I'm so sorry, Lana. I didn't really understand the other night. Oh, God. Those things I said...I feel like such a bitch."

"You didn't know. I didn't tell anyone."

"I feel like I need to punch him or something." I laugh. "I'm sure that'll put a dent in that flawless body of his."

"At least we have alcohol. Look at us, talking about it, speaking it, and it's easier. I wouldn't talk like this if I didn't have something in me, you know? But sometimes it just flows right out when I drink because it doesn't sting the way it does without it." However, that's not entirely true, because even with this in me, I know the things I'm not willing to discuss, those things that are deeply troubling me, the ones I don't dare speak if only because I don't want to be so aware of them myself. I'd love to hide them, lock them away, but there are some truths within me that are just too painful to deal with, especially everything I feel about Jarek right now.

Janet pulls away and then kisses my cheek. "Love you, Lana," she says.

"I love you, too."

"We have each other. But then again, I guess what Daddy taught me is that you never know how quickly something you love will leave."

"He didn't leave," I insist. "Leaving is a choice. He didn't have one."

"I'm sorry. I didn't mean to make you upset. Don't be upset with me, Lana. Please."

"I'm not upset with you. I'm just upset with myself right now."

"Don't be upset with yourself. Be upset with me. That's better than being upset with yourself. If you're upset with yourself, this is what happens to you. This is what you have to do to make the day easier. Don't do that, Lana."

"Okay, Janet," I say to appease her drunken concern. I take another drink. What's the point of trying to be sober now anyway? Maybe Janet has it figured out. Maybe this world is just too difficult for sobriety.

Considering how inebriated we are, it's time for us to leave, so I gently nudge Janet. "I think we should—"

"I don't want to go back down there. I don't like those people. Don't make me see them."

"We don't need to see anyone. We need to sneak out of here so no one realizes how wasted we are. Come on," I say. "I'll help you downstairs, and I'll call a car."

"Can't I come back to your place? Let me just come back with you, and we can sleep in the bed together like we used to—like when we were kids. I miss you so much. It's been so long, and we never spend enough time together."

"You can come over."

"And let's watch TV and laugh about the good times, and let's talk more, because we never talk."

As soon as she's sober, she won't feel this way, but it's nice that she's thinking like that, even if just for these moments. "All right, Janet."

She smiles broadly. "Then let's get out of here!" she exclaims.

We start down the stairs. I retrieve our jackets from the coat closet when I hear a loud, shrill, "You guys!" I turn to Kelsey, who approaches so quickly my drunken mind has me thinking I need to raise my fists in case she tries to hit me.

"Where have you gals been?" *Gals?* With Melanie at her side, I can tell her chummy behavior is little more than a performance.

Janet eyes her with contempt, though I'm not sure why. Is it because she's just as disgusted by this performance as I am? "We're leaving!" she exclaims authoritatively.

"No, no," Kelsey says, "I insist you stay. Just another ten."

"We really need to head out," I say. We're too tipsy to talk to anyone.

Kelsey turns back to Melanie. "Would you mind grabbing me a glass of chardonnay?" Her tone says, "Excuse me while I deal with my irresponsible sisters." Melanie consents and heads off.

Kelsey approaches Janet, I suppose because she knows better than to approach me. "Pull yourself together!" Kelsey says, fire in her tone.

I can't help but get defensive. "Don't you yell at her."

"Oh, really? Are you going to join her at the Betty Ford clinic?"

"Don't you have a man to be ensnaring?"

"Oh, please, Lana. We all know what this is about, and it has nothing to do with my interest in Jarek. You're just jealous—"

"Jealous? You think I'm jealous?" I am jealous. If someone deserves to end up with him, it's me. It's not that I want to end up with him, but I would deserve it after how I've ached. After how this pain and heartache has consumed me.

"I know you're jealous. You always wanted my things. If you want to fight, then let's say what this is really about."

"I will. Because there are clearly some things you're forgetting. Like why you're interested in Jarek. Just admit that you never, ever wanted him before."

"He's a different man than when we were kids."

"He's a richer man than when we were kids!"

She doesn't appear ruffled by my accusation. "Just because I like a successful, ambitious man doesn't mean—"

"Ambition doesn't have anything to do with it. You and Mom are the same. You want security. That's all life is to you, making sure there's enough for yourself."

"If you'll remember, after Dad's death, we weren't all that sure there would be enough for anyone."

"And what does it matter? We have plenty, and look at us! Are we perfect? Is everything fine? How much did you get in that settlement and are you suddenly without worry? You have so much money, why could you possibly need Jarek to have more?"

"Stop making me sound like a gold-digging slut!"

"I liked you more when you at least acknowledged what you did."

"What are you talking about?"

"When you were in college. How quick you were to say you wanted to marry rich. How you used to dream about marrying a prince or a politician, because you wanted to go to all the nice parties, and—"

"You're using my childhood dreams against me?"

"You still want the prince because you're shallow and vain."

"I'm realistic, Lana. We have to be realistic. I'm not like Dad who went and wasted all our money on ridiculous endeavors."

"Endeavors? You mean charities? He wanted to help people. And we have—"

"The damned trust. That's what we have. Please. A trust we can pull from yearly. Maybe you're just too young to realize what we could have had before."

"That trust sets us up for the rest of our lives. Tell me, between that and your ex-hubby's money, what could you possibly need Jarek for?"

"There are more important things in the world than money!"

"Prestige? Looking good on a wealthy man's shoulder? Do you really want to spend the rest of your life as a prop?"

"Why am I even fighting with you about this? You're so over-dramatic. I actually like Jarek."

"You don't know him," I insist. *But maybe I don't either.*

"I know him just as well as you do."

"You never knew him. You never even liked him."

"Things change, Lana. Haven't you noticed? They aren't the same as when we were teenagers, and they never will be. I'm sorry you can't move on, but the rest of us are trying to."

I'm not finished with her, but I can tell this conversation isn't heading anywhere, so I don't plan on pursuing it further. "Goodbye, Kelsey. We're heading out." Janet finishes putting on her jacket and we head out the door.

I stop in the doorway and turn back to Kelsey. "Tell Mom we said bye."

"And I'm just supposed to clean up after all this?" she asks.

I feel as if I should be reeling with rage after the comment, but there's a quiet to everything, perhaps some sobriety in knowing I'm in the right. "Yes, you can clean up, Kelsey. Perhaps then you'll be a fraction closer to being even with me."

She stiffens her neck, as if trying to stay strong despite my accurate accusation. "Have a good night," she says.

Without acknowledging her further, I step through the doorway behind Janet and start down the driveway. "I hate her," Janet mutters.

Even with the fight, I can't say I *hate* Kelsey. I could never say that. I'm mad at her, and at times, she's too much for me to deal with, but she'll always be my sister. I'll always care about her.

As we approach the street, I fidget with my phone to call a car with an app. An oh-so-familiar car drives up.

It's Jarek. *Of course it is. Why wouldn't it be?*

"Hey, there," he says with that charming smile.

"You," Janet growls.

This is not the time for Janet to blow my cover. She starts for his car. What does she think she'll do? Sucker punch him? I grab her arms and restrain her. He eyes her curiously.

"She's had a little too much," I explain. "Haven't you, Janet?"

"Lana, just let me do this."

"Let her do what?" he asks. "What does she want to do?"

"Nothing," I lie. *Except maybe punch you in the face.*

"Did you need a ride?"

I can't help but enjoy the innuendo. "No thanks," I say. "We'll get a car."

"Come on. I'm heading downtown anyway. Hop in."

We don't have a good reason not to. Although if Janet plans to make a fuss, I'm not sure that's such a great idea.

"Janet, we're riding with Jarek. Is that okay?"

"What?" she asks, eying me as if I've lost my mind. "Don't you let him—"

"Janet!" I shout, giving her a fierce look that silences her. She presses her lips together, as if to suggest her compliance with my wishes. I help her into the backseat and sit shotgun.

This is the second time Janet's been wasted in Jarek's backseat. He must think she's a drunk. Well, perhaps that's appropriate.

"Too much wine?" he asks, a hint of humor in his tone.

"My head's gonna be hurting tomorrow," Janet says with a giggle.

Why did I agree to this ride? Janet is so wasted she'll probably reveal what I told her about Jarek. Although I'm hoping my mentally projecting, "Don't say anything! Don't say anything!" will work.

As we reach downtown, I'm fading. I'm not sure I can stay up much longer. The streetlamps, stoplights, and road signs fuse together in my blurred vision. I haven't been this drunk since college.

Jarek parks outside my building. Janet's passed out, so I help Jarek carry her to my place. We escort her into the guest room and lay her across the bed. I stumble into the kitchen, leading Jarek to the door. I lean on the kitchen island, but I guess I miss, because the momentum carries me to the floor, but I stop before I reach it. I feel arms wrapped around me. I turn around, disoriented, confused.

Jarek's right behind me, holding me tight. He scoops me off the floor so that he's holding me in his arms, gazing into my eyes.

I don't want him to see me like this. He doesn't need to know what a mess I can be. However, there's something nice about being in his arms right now. I feel safe. I feel as if he's caring for me.

A wave of rage rushes through me, and I hit my fist against his shoulder. Not hard, but I'm so mad at him for leaving me all those years ago, and I have to do something.

"Whoa. What was that all about?"

I can't tell you, but you should know. I want to yell at him, to scream at him for what he did. *How can he not know what that did to a young girl? How could he have not known me well enough to know how much that would hurt? And how can he stand here now still not comprehending how wounded he's left me?*

I burst into tears. *Get it together, Lana.* But I'm not in control of my emotions anymore, and the tears keep coming. *Stop it! Stop it!* I can't, and that just makes me cry even more. *Why did you leave me, Jarek? Why?*

The pain of his rejection overwhelms me, and being in his arms confounds my logic and senses. *How did we get to this? Wasn't I in control? Or was that just something I tried to convince myself of?*

The more I try to keep it together, the more my face contorts and twitches in spasms as I continue to cry. He carries me into my bedroom, pulls back the sheets, and lays me across the mattress.

"I'm sorry," I say, despite not actually having anything I should be sorry about. He's the one who should be sorry.

"What's wrong, Lana?" he asks, sitting on the edge of the mattress. *You're the last person in the world I can share that with.*

I consider giving up this ruse, telling him off as I should have told him off when I first saw him, as I thought about doing time and time again before he came back into my life. *If I do, does that mean it's over? Does that mean I won't see him another time before he leaves once again?*

"I'm fine," I insist, wiping the back of my hands furiously across my face.

He sets his hand on my arm, suggesting his support in my moment of grief. But there's nothing he can do to soothe this pain. Daddy left me with a gaping hole, like the one Janet described, and Jarek made it even wider.

"Do you need anything?" he asks. "Water? A trash can to throw up in?" He says that playfully, like he's trying to cheer me up, and it makes me smile through the tears.

"I'm fine," I insist. Although, considering how the room is spinning, I can't help but wonder if I shouldn't have been so quick to refuse the trash can.

He gazes into my eyes. "Are you sure everything's okay?"

I shake my head. "No." He looks sad for me, but I can't help but wonder if he's reveling in my misery, pleased to know he was wise enough to keep away from me all these years.

He leans down and wraps his arms around me, embracing me in a supportive hug. It sends my mind through a confusing maze of thoughts. If he's here for me, then where was he back then? Where has he been all this time? Like everything we've shared this past week, this is just another lie—just like before. Why does he do this to me? Why does he give me this false hope when he knows he doesn't want me? Is he one of those guys who's so cruel to the people that like him? One who toys with the minds of women whom he knows he has an influence over? But his hold feels so honest, so sincere...but isn't that how it felt before? *Jarek, why do you always do this to me?*

He releases me and stands. "I guess I'd better head out," he says. He starts for the door. I fixate on his ass, sculpted perfectly in his black suit pants.

"Wait!"

He stops and turns back to me, his eyes filled with concern.

"You don't have to go," I say.

I don't know why I'm saying that. I'm sure as hell not in the mood to do anything with him. He returns to me, kicks his shoes off, steps around the bed, and slides onto the mattress. He crawls to me, urges me onto my side, and wraps his arm around me. He's so warm, and as I feel his breath on the back of my neck, I remember how he held me the night after Daddy passed.

My scrambled thoughts focus on that last day. I sat on the rock, watching my tears, which didn't feel like they'd ever end, leave scattered blotches across his jeans. His strong arms held me close as we shivered together. I felt so safe. And his hold gave me hope that maybe one day I'd make it through the nightmare.

Considering our past, it's sick how good lying together in this bed feels. It disturbs me how much I want to stay in this moment, even when I know how this ends. He was just as attentive back then, and it didn't keep him from leaving.

I tremble as my body convulses through another fit of tears. Even though this feels so good, it burns at a wound within me, one that's been there for so long, but feels so fresh.

I let him hold me close, because I need this, and I drift off.

Chapter Ten

The next morning, I'm drowning in paperwork, nearly too consumed to dwell on everything that happened last night. Nearly, but not entirely, because I can't help but reflect on that kindness, that generous nature of Jarek's spirit. Would he lie with any girl overnight without expecting intimacy? Or just me? And why do I care so much?

I attempt to distract myself with my work, particularly the necessary tasks to make sure the fundraiser this coming Saturday goes according to plan. If only I didn't have this painful headache nagging at me, then it might be easier to focus, but it's so painful that it's a struggle. I wonder if Janet always feels like this after a stupor or if it's easier for her since she's so used to getting trashed.

When I return home that afternoon, I continue my work, scattering files across the table as I sort them into appropriate stacks. After dedicating a few hours to that, I move on to cleaning, which I'm thinking is a nice break from work.

I guess this is what my life will be about: cleaning my damn house and being a spinster forever. Maybe I need to get a cat...or a dog. A pet would be good. Oh, God, what am I thinking? I don't want to deal with little hairs everywhere. No, no. I like having my space to myself. And I'd feel terrible about not having time to walk a dog.

My phone rings. I walk across the kitchen and look at the screen. Jarek. Another booty call, I'm guessing.

I answer. "Hey."

"How's it going?"

"I'm having an amazing night cleaning out my kitchen."

"What do you say we go out tonight?"

"Go out? I figured you'd be with my sister."

"We have about as much in common as a lion and a gazelle."

"So you just like playing the gazelle at parties?"

"Ha ha ha. Seriously, though. I want to do something tonight."

I don't know if this is a good idea, but I can't help but think it'd be a nice break from having to clean my place. "What do you have in mind?" I ask.

"You know, the symphony...maybe an art gallery."

"Oooh...exciting!" I jest.

He laughs. "I was thinking we could hit up a burger joint by the mall."

I burst into laughter. I don't know why it's so hilarious. What's not hilarious about a millionaire eating at a shitty burger joint? "That sounds good to me."

What am I going to do with you, Jarek? It's a question I seriously consider, because am I really going to let myself fall back in love with him? I guess I've given up, but I feel like I might need to fight...if only for my own sanity.

While I'm getting ready, putting on fresh clothes, my phone rings again. As I straighten my blouse, I glance at my phone and see that it's Janet. She might want to hang out, but as I recall, her husband's back in town, so I don't figure she needs me for anything.

"Hey, sis, what's up?"

I hear a soft whisper. "Lana, please get over here."

My face drains as I realize she's in serious trouble. "Are you okay? Janet?" I check the screen, which assures me the call has ended. I try to call her as I grab my keys and race down the stairs to my car.

On the way over, I quickly dial Jarek's number. "Hey—I have to cancel. Janet just called. I'm heading over to her place to make sure she's okay."

"Do you need—"

"I'll call you when I find out what's going on."

"Okay, okay. Thanks for letting me know."

At a time like this, it would be nice to be with Jarek—or anyone—to share my worry. But right now, I'm on my own. I continue trying to call her on my way over. Still no response.

Is she hurt?

When I reach her building, I park and head up the stairwell, to her place. I hear shouting. I turn the knob. Locked.

I knock as loudly as I can. The shouting continues. It's clearly Kirk.

Are they having a fight? If that's what all this is about, then I'm going to put a stop to it right away. I continue knocking until I'm pounding and my fists hurt.

The door opens. Kirk stands in the entry. His face is red as if he's just returned from the gym, but I know better.

"Hey, Lana. How's it going?" he asks, taking a breath as if to soothe whatever rage I heard him releasing just moments ago. His words are friendly, sincere-sounding, but I know what I just heard, and I am not happy.

"Where's my sister?"

"She's just...she's..."

I push past him, through their living area. Through the entry to their kitchen, I see her on the other side of their dining table. She sits on the tile floor, her back against the entry to another hallway. Tears stream down her face as she holds her legs close.

"What the hell do you think you're doing barging in here like this?" Kirk asks. His tone isn't like anything I've heard from him before. He's aggressive, severe.

Janet's hair is disheveled, some of it pulled loose from the ponytail she has it in. Her mascara runs as she rubs her arm, as if it's where he was holding her before I barged in. As I spy a red mark on the arm she rubs, I know what he really is, and I'm not interested in discussions.

"Come on, Janet." I say, kneeling and wrapping my arms around her.

"What do you think you're doing?" Kirk asks.

I stand tall, realizing that Kirk could effortlessly punch me to the floor. But like with a dog, I can't show fear. "I'm taking Janet home with me. She's not staying here."

"Really? And you're just gonna come in here and take her? You don't know us. You don't know our lives. You don't get to judge what goes on in the fucking privacy of our home!"

He approaches me, his chest pushed forward and his hands balled into fists. I never realized how closely his face resembles that of a bulldog until this moment, as he stands there, round faced and droopy-cheeked. He's scowling, his eyes cast in the shadows of the kitchen light.

"Lana," Kirk says, "you don't have any business here, so why don't you just step out and let me tend to my business."

"My sister is my business, and she's coming with me. Come on, Janet."

Kirk snatches me by the hair and yanks me back to my feet. He shoves me across the room. I trip over a chair at the end of the dining table and stumble past the stove. I throw my arms out to break my fall against the fridge, but the handle gets me right in the ribs.

As I recover, I turn sharply, and Kirk is heading for me. "You don't let me take her, and I swear to God I'll call the police!" I exclaim, hoping my threat will at least make him pause before deciding to tear off my head, which seems more than likely at this point.

However, he doesn't appear discouraged. He keeps heading for me, a wicked gleam in his eyes, as if he plans to do far worse to me than just break my arm. I leap to the side and grab a frying pan from the stove and swing at him.

He catches my wrist. "Naughty, bitch," he says. It's eerie how calmly he speaks, and the look in his eyes assures me I should have been more prepared before I came over.

He twists my wrist and forces me back against the fridge. I struggle to break free when a loud crunching sound fills the room, and he releases me.

I turn and see Jarek throwing him against the kitchen counter on the other side of the stove. He lays blows into Kirk's torso.

"Fuck!" Kirk cries as he unleashes a series of expletives while Jarek continues his assault. Kirk swings about, but Jarek's blows are more precise and hit with a powerful impact. His face is red as his blows crack against Kirk's body.

Kirk collapses against the counter, and as I see that he's obviously delirious, incapable of fighting back, I work to soothe Jarek. "He's finished, Jarek. He's finished."

Jarek snaps out of whatever rage compelled him and hurries to me. "Are you okay?" he asks, scanning me over. He checks my wrist. "What did he do? Where did he touch you?"

"I'm fine, I'm fine." My insistence about my well-being doesn't relax his aggression. He turns back to Kirk, grabs him by his shirt collar, and throws him across the room so that he smashes into the pantry on the other side of the kitchen and collapses to the floor. I want to scream, "Enough fighting!" but Kirk deserves every bit of Jarek's aggression.

I hurry to Janet and help her to her feet. She's lost in a fit of tears, clearly overwhelmed by everything that's going on.

Jarek hurries to our side and leads us out of the apartment. As we reach the car and I regain my composure, waking from those primal impulses that Kirk's behavior stirred, I'm filled with appreciation for Jarek's presence. "How did you know where we were?" I ask.

"I called Kelsey and asked—since someone," he says severely, "wouldn't tell me what was going on."

"I'm sorry." I realize what a horribly moronic idea it was barging in like that without letting anyone know where I was, but I've dealt with Kirk on plenty of occasions, and I never believed he would become violent. *At least everyone's fine now.*

We head to the hospital, where Janet is tended to by physicians and police offers. Jarek and I offer our statements about the events that transpired, and after several hours, we're permitted to leave. We head back to my place. I tuck Janet into the guest bed and return to the living area, where Jarek awaits me, sitting on the couch.

"Thank you so much," I say. "If you hadn't come..."

He rises from the sofa. "It's nothing," he insists, as if he doesn't want my appreciation. It reminds me that there was a time not so long ago when I didn't believe I'd ever be appreciative of anything from him.

Glad as I am that he was there, it disturbs me, because it's so much easier when I don't see the good in him, when I believe he's a horrible, insensitive man. But I can't believe that. I've seen too much evidence to the contrary, and it leaves me feeling like he couldn't be with me back then because I wasn't worthy of his affection. Maybe I really wasn't.

He approaches me quickly. His swift movement alarms me, I suppose stirring some of the same instincts activated when Kirk attacked me. As I gaze into his eyes, I don't see the usual appreciation and gentleness I'm used to. I see something angry, furious.

"When I saw him doing that to you," he says, "I thought I was going to kill him." The tone in his voice convinces me he's serious, and I'm glad for everyone's sake it didn't come to that. He wraps his arms around me and holds me close, filling me with a sense of security that feels so good right now, after such a twisted moment. He shifts his face so his nose presses against my ear. His breath rushes against me as he whispers, "If something had happened to you, I don't know what I would've done."

"You would've been fine," I say curtly, because it's a painful truth— one I don't want to acknowledge, yet one I'll always be all-too-aware of.

"What?" he says, releasing me and pulling away. I wish I had kept my mouth shut, because right now, I really need his arms around me. I need him close. He's the only thing keeping me together.

He gazes at me as if I'm insane for suggesting he'd be fine. All I want to say is, "Look at you— you've managed this long without me. You ran off, lived a perfectly fulfilling life. You didn't need me back then and you sure as hell don't need me now."

I keep quiet. I don't want an argument or to see him feign defense for his feelings. That won't do either of us any good.

"Don't you know how much I care about you?" he asks. "Can't you feel it?"

I want to believe he feels for me the way I feel for him, but my feelings mislead me, as they did all those years ago. I can't tell him that, though. Maybe he believes he feels this way, as he believed he did back then, but I know how easily he can walk away from these feelings, and I'll never distance myself from that knowledge.

As he stands there, expressing these deep feelings, whether I believe them or not, I can't help but despise him. I want to demand an answer to why he left, but to keep myself from giving into this hate, I do the only thing I know will silence these impulses. I kiss him. His arms are soon back around me, making me feel as secure as I felt before. It's wonderful...it's delicious...it's as if I don't have to worry about anything ever again.

His kisses are frenzied, passionate, as if the encounter with Kirk left him realizing how quickly he could lose me. *Wishful thinking.*

He kneels, lifts me off the floor, and carries me into my bedroom. All I know in this moment is that I'm his.

He rests me on the bed, and as I remove my blouse and bra, he takes off my shoes and slides my jeans down my legs. Once again, I'm lying under him, vulnerable, exposed, knowing that I'm being offered one more night.

I wish I was stronger. I wish I could fight him. I wish I could scream, "Why don't you feel for me how I feel for you?" Gazing into his eyes only makes it worse. It's that same look I remember so long ago, that look of love and appreciation...or maybe that's just what I mistake it for. Maybe it's something else. As he rests his arms on either side of me, his face just inches from mine, his breath hitting my face, I can't help but think that surely what he feels is real. *Still, that's what I thought back then!*

He kisses me again, powerfully, allowing my thoughts to release all that pain once again. He strokes a hand up and down my side and as his lips release mine, he whispers against my cheek, "I care about you so much, Lana. Ever since we were kids. All I ever wanted was for you to be happy."

It's a lie. How could he look back at those days and think about anything other than what he did? Anger swells in me, but I know it will pass.

He kisses down my chest, and as his face reaches my navel, he grabs the sides of my panties. He slips them off and leans back, throwing his shirt over his head, revealing those abs. He adds his jeans to the mound of clothes he's created.

As he undoes his pants and hurries out of them, I crawl across the bed, open the drawer, and retrieve the condoms and lube. He wraps his arms around me and pulls me so that my back is pressed against his chest. I feel his lips behind my ear—the warmth of his touch crawling across my flesh, wherever he touches radiating with delightful sensations.

He grabs the condom and lube from me and I hear him preparing himself behind me. I rest my hands on the mattress. Then I feel the pressure. It builds and builds as he slides into me. His arm wraps around me as he continues to thrust. He kisses behind my ear. I lean back and he follows until we're upright, him continuing to penetrate me, filling me with his shaft, which feels so erotic.

This is how I want him to fuck me. I don't want him to see my face, see my weakness. I want to be treated like any girl he'd fuck on the street—like the object he uses me as.

He massages his fingers across my belly and kisses softly across my back. He leans back so that my back is arched and my breasts fall to either side. He cups his hand around my neck. I feel like I'm totally in his control—his to use how he wants. Because that's all I've ever been to him.

If that's the case, why would he say that he cares about me? Why lie to me about how he really feels? Why can't he just fuck the shit out of me and shut up?

He releases my neck and slides out of me. I turn to him and he scoops me up again, laying me on my back. He descends so that we're looking into each other's eyes. I preferred it when he couldn't see me, when he could have just been fucking any girl. *Not me.*

There's that soft look, the one that always makes me feel as if he cares so much. He kisses me, spreads my legs, and inserts himself. The pressure feels delightful, and as he thrusts, he tucks his face against my cheek and whispers, "Lana, I care about you so much."

He thrusts so hard I gasp, but I can't tell if the gasp is from the surprise of his movements or his words. *Why would he say that?*

It kills me, because I've wanted to hear these words so badly for so long, and now that they're offered freely, it seems cruel. Surely he's just caught up in the moment, confused as men sometimes are in the middle of sex. It doesn't mean anything to him right now...not what it means to me.

My body tenses because suddenly I wish he wasn't inside me. I wish I wasn't enjoying this so much because I hate him. I hate what he did to me. I hate what he's doing to me. I hate that I really want him to feel the way he says.

Try as I did to convince myself I could enjoy these experiences knowing they wouldn't last, I've always known it was a lie, because with each encounter, I feel more and more attached to him. And knowing he must go pains me to my core.

Another push sends a pool of delicious sensations rippling through me, shaking me from my anger and reminding me that, though I know it can't last, if this is all I have to look forward to, then I should take advantage of it as I would a finite amount of water in the desert.

Take me, Jarek. Do whatever you want to me. Hurt me as much as you want, because no matter how much it hurts, it'll never be as bad as it was before.

Each kiss, each turn of his head, each stroke of his finger, draws me back into him, and evokes a little girl within me, begging, "Please don't leave me. Please don't ever leave me." I don't feel bad for myself, but for her, because I know how sad she can get.

He pulls out of me and stretches out beside me, lying on his back. He props his dick up and eyes it. "Come on," he says with a playful smirk.

I quickly obey and straddle him, sliding him back inside me, allowing him to fill me. He strokes his hands back and forth across my thighs as I push off my knees to give him leverage. His pelvis bobs up and down, each entry exciting more nerves than the last. He rubs one hand under my breasts, his thumb sliding across my flesh as if he's just appreciating my body. With his other, he slides it and cups it so that he can thumb my clitoris, exciting the nerves so much that it forces my muscles to twitch and pulse in surprising ways.

He releases my clitoris and sits up, wrapping his arm around me and pulling me close as he kisses my lips. He rolls me onto my back, kicking his legs out so that soon he's on top of me and forcing his way in again. He grips my shins as he continues forcing himself in and out.

All I can think now is how much I want him to make me his, to own me once again. As I look up, his eyes are closed. *Is he imagining someone else? Some prettier girl? Someone he's fucked in the past?* But soon he reopens his eyes and scans my body over. The pressure inside me intensifies as he grows harder. He swoops down so that his face is right before mine again. I feel his thumb against my clitoris, stimulating me so that I can feel how close I am. "Lana," he says, reminding me of that time so long ago when he said the same thing.

What could he possibly have to say to me now? Why can't he just fuck the shit out of me and leave it at that?

"You're everything to me."

The words hit my ear, electrifying every part of me and coupling with my current arousal so that my body transforms into a fit of quivers. My head jerks around violently as I come, feeling overwhelmed with sensation, my body shaking as he grabs my wrists and pins me down as I hear him cry out. His expression twists as his pelvis slams into mine and he collapses in a similar fit of convulsions.

As he lays on me, I feel each breath, and his warm, damp flesh against me. I can't help but feel a terrible crash, so much worse than anything I've experienced before.

Those words that did me in, that gave me such satisfaction, fill me with guilt. Why did I have to enjoy them so much? I hate myself for having basked in the lie, the deceit. How stupid am I that even for a second I believed him?

My guilt transforms into rage. *What kind of bastard is he to say something like that to me—to a little girl? But I'm not a girl! I'm a woman. I'm a woman he's done this to already. He must know how I feel. He must know what he's doing to me. What he did to me. Why did he hurt me like that?*

As he offers soft kisses, I can't kiss back. I'm in shock, hardly knowing how to respond to what just happened. Surely I should just forget it, as he no doubt will. But I don't want to forget. And I hate myself for that.

Chapter Eleven

"I owe you a big thank you," Janet says as she scratches her fork through a layer of syrup across the pancake I've made her. It's what I used to make her for breakfast when we were kids. I guess I should say it's what I attempted to make her when we were kids. It took a long time for me to get the consistency just right, but by thirteen, I was a pro.

I'm not so liberal with my own caloric intake. I've prepared yogurt with strawberries and blueberries, which I've also made as a side for Janet.

I set her bowl of yogurt beside her pancakes. "It's not an issue," I say as I head to the fridge to retrieve some orange juice for her. "I assume you know you'll be staying here for a while." She smirks. It's the following day, the day after discovering what an ass Kirk really was and hearing Jarek express his feelings to me.

I pour a glass of orange juice for her, which she quickly thanks me for, but it's evident she's thanking me for a lot more than orange juice.

I set the carton on the table. "Janet, I love you so much. You know that, right?" The sad look in her eyes assures me she knows where this is going. But she should expect it after last night.

"He was upset," Janet confesses. "Although I don't think he had much right to be upset." A guilty look flashes across her face. "I checked his phone. I know, that's awful, but...We've had issues before."

I sit across from her. "Oh my God."

"Not everyone's perfect, Lana. A relationship is about compromise, and working through things. And so we worked through it. I thought. And when I checked his phone, I didn't see anything, right? All good. But Kirk's pretty smart. I figured he'd delete the texts, so I decided to check his pictures. I mean, why would he think I would check there, right? And there was this early-twenty-something girl. I just got so fucking mad."

"Shouldn't you have been the one kicking his ass?" I ask.

"When I confronted him, he just got so mad. Said it's no wonder he did that in Dallas, because I obviously didn't trust him. And then he just got aggressive...and...well, you know."

"I'm assuming this wasn't the first time he's gotten..." I let my words trail off, because she must know what I'm referring to. She shakes her head.

I just can't believe that all this time that I've known them, I never found out. That's surely why Janet kept me at a distance all of these years—so I wouldn't find out, so I wouldn't see her battle scars. However, Janet never seemed like someone who would just sit back and take it.

"How did it get that far?" I ask. Her lips quiver. She glances around as if she doesn't want to confront me directly. I feel like that's how she got into this mess to begin with.

"You remember the beginning?" she asks. "It was so wonderful. I mean, the boyfriend I had before him was Rodney Berger from senior year, and he didn't even remember my birthday. But Kirk remembered everything. Every little thing I said I liked. One time, I told him how much I loved Hall and Oates, and the next time I came over, he played a mix CD so that 'Maneater' played right before he dropped me off. Then he acted so cool about it, and it was the most adorable thing I'd ever seen. And the notes he wrote...telling me how much he loved me, how much he wanted to be with me. I'd never had a guy want me that much. Need me that much. He was perfect.

"I know what you're thinking. There had to be signs. And there were. I had this friend, Steve. He was a gay guy I'd met in Bio 101, but Kirk used to get so jealous. This guy was practically riding in on a unicorn when he entered a room, but Kirk just couldn't take how close we were. He said it made him uncomfortable when I hung out with him. Said it wasn't appropriate to hang out with a guy—any guy—behind his back. I'm not sure if he actually had a problem with it or if it was just his way of getting me to cut off my friends. Everyone had some fault. The girls were jealous of me, and he didn't like the way they undermined me or the guys looked at me the wrong way. He didn't like you or Kelsey telling me what to do. Said I was letting you all get away with murder because you were big sisters. And I bought it.

"Some part of me didn't. Some part of me knew there was something off. And when he got mad, oh he'd get so mad. But Lana, when he did love me...I felt like I was the whole world. You remember the way Daddy made us feel. That's what it felt like with him. He knows how to make you feel like nothing else in the world even exists to him, and the moment he looked away, oh, it just made me want to die.

"The drinking...I guess that made it easier. But after a while it didn't because he'd yell at me about that, too. And the fights. That's how it started last night. I'd been drinking when I decided to check his phone. Seemed like such a good idea, and then confronting him seemed like just as good of an idea. I should have known better. He's so irritable when he comes back from a trip. He just gets so angry, like he's furious when he's reminded that we're married. Like he'd rather be anywhere but with me. Sometimes I would catch him looking at me while I was reading a book or watching TV, and there would just be this hateful look in his eyes. And I thought I deserved it."

"What in the world made you think that was what you deserved?"

"I'm not you, Lana. I never believed that good things would come my way, or that I could face everything in the world fearlessly. The world's a scary place. When Daddy..." She doesn't finish. I understand why. "It was just a lot. Before that, I thought I was like you, that I was fearless and that I could take anything on. And then when that happened, I realized that everything was a lie...the world was a mean, terrible place that could take anything good and wonderful from you in a moment."

"I was never fearless," I say. "And I never thought I could handle anything."

She eyes me skeptically. "Yes, you did. Especially when we were kids. Don't you remember sneaking off into the woods at night?" As a kid, I enjoyed running through the woods at night. One time, I made her go with me so that we could sneak into this little ditch I'd discovered. I brought a flashlight and a book so I could read to her. It was a stupid idea because it scared the shit out of both of us, but I used to get into all sorts of trouble like that.

"I was so scared," she said.

"I was just as scared."

"But you did it, and if you hadn't been pushing me, prodding me, I wouldn't have. I never did it again after that night. But what did you do? You kept doing it, because you didn't want to be afraid. That's not me. That's never been me."

"Well, some things are a lot scarier than the woods at night," I say.

"It's not just the woods," she insists. "It's your life, your job. You see an obstacle and you face it. You aren't afraid of a challenge. I've always taken the easy way out because...it's easier."

Janet's version of my life is a childish dream, because as I look at my relationships and lack thereof, I know there are some things I'm too afraid to approach because I'm not willing to feel that way ever again.

"I just want you to be happy," I say.

"It's a little late for me," she replies, "but you need follow your heart, Lana. You can only fight it so long."

"What?"

"You're still not over him."

"What I said the other night..."

"This isn't about the other night. I see the way you look at him—even now, after all these years."

I blush. It's as apparent as I feared. "I understand why you think that," I reply. "But Janet, if there ever was a chance for us to be together, to be happy, it's passed, and it can't return."

Her expression shifts to one of concern. "I don't know what happened, but don't you think you can move past it? Clearly you're willing to forgive him enough to talk to him again..."

"I don't want to talk about it, but what Jarek did was so cruel that, as much as I care about him, as good as he seems to be now, I can never distance myself from what he did."

Lana presses her fork into her pancake. "Was this in college? Was it why he left?"

"It's about that."

"What happened, Lana?" I shake my head. "You can't bottle all this up forever," she says. "You were always so private, so quiet, and you never let anyone help you with anything. Sometimes you have to open up. You don't have to do everything by yourself."

Yes, I do. I gaze at the clock on the stove. "Oh, look at the time," I say, trying to change the subject. "I guess I should head to the store. I need to pick up a few supplies for the get-together tonight."

Janet rolls her eyes. "Are you seriously going to that? We *just* had her birthday party."

"And now her Women's Club needs to have their post-fundraiser meeting. You knew this was the busiest time of the year. We don't have to do much more. Aren't you coming?"

"Yes, but I thought you might have wised up after that last one. Ugh. If I see any more snooty people after this, I swear I'll scream."

"Thank you for helping me with Janet...and Kirk."

"Anyone else would have done the same thing."

After breakfast with Janet, I meet Jarek for lunch at the pizzeria where we met previously. He enjoys a slice of pepperoni pizza while I snack on my rabbit food. Considering everything that has transpired, it's strange meeting him out like this. It feels as if we should be meeting in a more intimate setting to discuss something so close to my heart, but that's not the sort of relationship we're in. And though he offered to come over to my place, it's my job to set boundaries.

Jarek glances around uneasily. "Did your Dad ever tell you about my life...before I started staying with you guys?"

It's strange to hear him bring it up. Back when he stayed with us, it never came up, and though I was curious, I could tell by the look in his eyes, by some darkness within him, that it wasn't something to press about. "You were abandoned by your mother."

"Kind of the truth, I guess. But there's a little more to it than that. Back then, I just avoided talking about it altogether." He hesitates, as if he's considering not continuing. But then he does. "She had issues. I didn't even know what they were at the time. One day, she'd be the most delightful person in the world. Social, caring, charming. The next she would be a nightmare, filled with rage and fury. I couldn't ever determine which side of her I'd be getting when I came home from school." From my limited knowledge of bipolar disorder, this sounded familiar. "Once when I was fifteen, she was particularly upset when I came home. Crying. As a kid, I wanted to cheer her up—or at least figure out what was wrong, so I approached her, but she lashed out at me. She beat on me with her fists and shouted at me, saying I was the reason her life was so fucked up. She said if she hadn't met my dad then things would never have gone wrong. And then she told me who he was. She'd never mentioned it before. She had been sixteen, and he was a cop. Evidently, he was the boyfriend of a mutual friend, and one day he showed up at her place, she thought just to talk. She didn't think it was a good idea. She tried to keep him from coming in, but he insisted that he was worried about her friend. She let him in and it wasn't long before she figured out what he really wanted, and she fought and screamed out, but it was useless."

I'm disturbed, not because he's sharing this with me, but because I'm amazed I've never heard this before. Because I feel that it's something I should have known.

Jarek stills, as if he's thinking about what he's just shared. He rubs his thumb along the rim of his plate, his gaze on his half-eaten pizza. "The day she told me that, she grabbed a knife from a drawer and came at me with it. She said she should have taken care of this a long time ago—that she'd had the option plenty of times, but she just hadn't had the strength...and now she did. It's a really fucked up thing when that's what you remember most about your mother.

"I managed to get her off me, and that's the day I ran off."

I reach across the table and set my hand on his. "Jarek, I'm so sorry. You never said anything?"

"What would I have said? That my mom couldn't even stand looking at me because every time she did, I just reminded her of what had happened? Don't feel bad for me. I don't need anyone pitying me. I'm just telling you because when I walked into Kirk and Janet's and saw him attacking you like that, it just reminded me of back then...that day. It was like I was there all over again, screaming at Mom to get off me. Begging her to stop calling me a bastard."

A solitary tear shifts in his eye before falling. He quickly wipes it away, as if his act will prevent me from seeing it. "I know what I did was wrong that day."

Hope wells within me. *Is this it? Am I about to get my apology? Is he finally going to admit that what he did to me was wrong?*

"I knew I shouldn't have broken into your family's house. I knew I shouldn't have stolen that shit. I can't even really tell you why I did it. I honestly think I was just so pissed since you guys had everything, and I didn't have anything." I feel foolish for assuming he would have been thinking about our night together. "And then, when the police picked me up, I thought, 'Here we go. Now I've really gone and fucked shit up.' I kind of wanted them to throw me away. I didn't feel like I belonged anywhere else. And then I met your dad, and everything changed. In just a few weeks, I went from thinking I was nobody to having a family—a better family than I ever could have hoped for. A better family than I deserved."

Then why did you leave?

He shakes his head. "Sorry. I guess you don't need to hear my sorry-ass story now. I'm just...I owe your father everything in the world, and I'm glad I was able to be there last night, if only to help save Janet from that asshole she married."

I'm in shock from all he's revealed. "I'm so sorry," I say. "You didn't deserve to be treated like that. No one deserves that. Not from a parent." Suddenly I feel like my mom isn't nearly as bad as I make her out to be.

He tries to smile, but I can tell it's a struggle. He stares at me for a moment, as if considering something, before saying, "What do you say we go out tonight?"

"Go out?"

"Yeah. A date. Ever heard of it?" His words are lighter, more at ease. I wonder if he's trying to lighten the mood. If that's the case, he's only doing it for himself, because the very thought of going on a date with him makes the muscles in my chest constrict. As appreciative as I am for what he did at Janet's and as sorry as I am for what happened to him when he was younger, neither will make me forgive him for what I carry with me. Because that can't just go away. Still, I want to go on this date. I want to be with him, and the more I try to convince myself I'm trying to tease him along for the sake of revenge, the more I'm lying to myself, because I don't want that. I don't even believe it's possible to hurt him the way he's hurt me.

Maybe things can be different. I want to believe I can put all this behind me—maybe the part of him that has changed was the part that left me so long ago. I don't entirely believe that, but I'm holding out a speck of hope, because I like him. He's not just an asshole, as I hoped he'd be. There's so much of him that's the same—the Jarek I fell in love with. *But isn't that what I should be afraid of?*

"What did you have in mind?" I ask.

He smirks. "If I just told you, that wouldn't be much of a surprise. Would it?"

"A surprise?" I say, and now I feel playful and light again. As much as I want to enjoy the moment with reckless abandon, I can't distance myself from the sense of caution that lingers within me.

"Yes, a surprise. You remember those?"

"Vaguely."

"Seriously, though. I want to take you out."

If this has been a game all along, then I've lost.

"I'd really like that."

Jarek told me to look my best, but I'm horrified I won't wear the right outfit. I don't have anything that would be appropriate for something extravagant.

I put on the best dress I have, one I bought for some of our functions and fundraisers at work. I usually wouldn't wear it because it hangs a little lower than I'm comfortable with, but tonight, I want to draw attention to the girls...for Jarek's benefit.

I spend some time before the mirror, perfecting my makeup. Though I usually wear makeup to work, I invest my time in applying foundation and a lipstick that is fairly close to my natural tone. Tonight I want to up the game a little bit, so I apply mascara, rouge, and some other essentials that I usually ignore. I'm not Kelsey, so I refuse to cake it on, but I'm trying to look a little nicer than usual—trying to stand out just a bit more. As I fix my lipstick, I gaze at my hair, locked in white curlers, with amusement. The amount of work involved in looking nice is incredible. I can only imagine how much effort the drop-dead gorgeous Stephanie invests in her appearance every morning before work.

Once I'm finished, I assess myself in the mirror. Jarek texts to let me know he's five minutes away. Eagerness fills my belly. *This is really happening.* This moment I've dreamt about so many times...this moment I thought would never come to pass.

For tonight, I'm vanquishing my fears—those creeping nuisances of thoughts—so that I can just have a good time. I deserve that.

When he arrives, I greet him at the curb in his Mercedes. He steps out and opens the door for me. He's in another gorgeous suit, of course. I expected no less.

"'Evening," he says kindly as he lets me in, his gaze shifting to my chest, and judging by the expression I catch through my peripheral, I made a good decision.

As we head to this secret destination, I'm wildly curious about what awaits us. I imagine we'll be stuck in some stuffy restaurant with the sort of people Jarek is accustomed to. That's the way it would be with him, but if I have to endure that sort of night, I'm fine with it, as long as I'm with him. Childish impulses rise within me, making me want to skip about.

As Jarek approaches a stoplight, he reaches over, opens the glovebox, and retrieves a black scarf. "I'm afraid," he says, "I'm going to have to ask you to put this on."

I eye it curiously, then him.

"I told you, it's a surprise."

It reminds me of the night I made him wear the blindfold. Perhaps this is his revenge. Regardless, I'm delighted by the game of it, and quickly put it on so that I'm trapped in darkness.

"It's just killing you, isn't it?" he says, though judging by his tone, he's more excited about revealing his surprise than I am about receiving it.

As we come to a stop, I hear him get out and open my door. His touch comforts me as he guides me out. "Careful," I say. "I'm a mess in heels."

He's a perfect gentleman as he helps me out. I reach up to remove the scarf, but he snatches my wrist. "No, no," he says. "Wait for it." He guides me along what feels like concrete.

Where are we going?

He gently brings me to a stop and I feel him untying the blindfold. As it slides down my face, I see moonlight glistening in water. I gasp.

It's Lake Dreyfus.

Two high floodlights illuminate a table with two chairs set up before the shore, where I see my rock. At another table a few yards away, closer to a cluster of trees beside the lake, a man in a suit juggles his time between aluminum covered containers and various boxes. I glance at Jarek, baffled.

"What's the point of having all this money if I can't do something extravagant?"

It's more than extravagant. It's sincere, thoughtful...amazing. This was my spot—our spot. This was where we came so many times to talk about life...the place where he soothed me when Jacob Wilder broke my heart, the place where he found me after Daddy passed, because he was the only one who knew me well enough to know this was where I'd come. And now here we are again, and it stirs tears in my eyes.

I fight them back, because I'm not just happy, I'm elated. I don't know that anyone could ever do anything sweeter for me, because no one could know me this well.

We walk across a path of stones that leads to the table. He pulls out a chair for me. "Madam," he says facetiously. I sit, feeling giddy, but at the same time feeling bad for the poor waiter who has to serve us out here in the middle of nowhere, though I assume Jarek has thoroughly compensated him for this gig.

The waiter approaches the table and pours red wine in two glasses before us. Jarek eagerly sips his, and as he looks at me, he has that same conceited look he always has when he's read me so well. "You like it?" he asks.

Judging by the expression on his face, he already knows the answer, and I almost don't want to give him props, but considering how elaborate this is, I have to acknowledge how beautiful it is. "I don't know that you could have done anything more perfect." He grins.

"What's on the menu?" I ask.

"Another surprise," he says.

"I can't wait."

The waiter spends a moment away before providing us with breadsticks. Perfect. I'm starving since I figured we'd be spending far too many calories on this meal, so I made sure to be good today.

The waiter sets a salad before me, and I eye Jarek.

"I figured I had to make sure to get you something you'd like," he says. I notice it has everything I'd put in the Caesar I'd made at the sandwich shop we ate at the day he found me at work.

"Is this dinner just meant to poke fun at me?" I ask.

"Basically. Is that going to be a problem?" He winks.

When we finish our salads, the waiter swaps our bowls for tin-covered trays. When he pulls the lids off, he unveils dinner plates of ravioli and garlic bread. My jaw drops and my gaze goes right to Jarek, who appears to be glancing at me desperately, as if he's hoping I'll enjoy the present, but how couldn't I? It's almost too perfect. Here I was thinking he was going to try to win me over with filet mignon or mahi mahi, but instead he provided another callback to the past.

"For old times' sake," he says.

I'm struggling to keep my cool. I can't believe how thoughtful this is. *Why did he go to such great lengths to remind me of those nights when I'd make him ravioli and garlic bread?* It seems like such a stupid meal now, but looking at this, clearly a far better version than the can of ravioli I used and probably homemade garlic bread, I'm so impressed.

My smile must reveal how pleased I am with all this. "Thank you," I say, not just appreciative of the lengths he went to, but because it's the most thoughtful thing anyone's ever done for me. I dig into the ravioli and it's delicious. The garlic bread is far better than anything we could have warmed from a frozen bag.

When the waiter removes our plates, he announces, "And for dessert, we have..." He sets a glass before me. It's filled with strawberry milkshake and has a straw sticking out from it. "Strawberry milkshake! And for the gentleman...we have cookies and cream!" He sets Jarek's before him.

Our days of getting milkshakes! This might do me in, because those were some of the happiest days of my life. The laughs, the jokes, the fun, the playfulness, in a time where I didn't even feel anything other than friendship with Jarek… But now, to be confronted with those memories when I've been working so hard to hate him, it's difficult.

I leap up, rush past the waiter, and dash into the cluster of trees a few yards away. I don't want Jarek to see my face. Not when I'm about to fall apart.

I look at the ground cautiously, working to keep from ruining the dress, but I know that I can't be near Jarek right now, not while I'm filled with all these conflicting emotions.

It's too much.

Why is he haunting me with these beautiful memories, ones that have been tainted for so long by what he's done?

I bow over. I'm about to burst into tears when I hear behind me.

"Lana." His voice is soft. He's near. I turn around. His eyes glisten with moonlight. "Are you okay?" he asks. "I'm sorry, I just thought—"

I shake my head. "It's perfect. It's beyond perfect. It just...it stirs up a lot." The change in his expression makes me wonder if he knows what I'm really referring to.

"Lana, I care about you so much. You have to know that."

Seeing this display, thinking back on the past few days, I have to admit he's right. I want to tell him that I don't know that, that he's made it impossible for me to even consider it, but I can't...I'm swept up in his spell. He has me now, as he always manages to.

"It just reminds me of all those good times...with you...with Daddy. I'm sorry. Let's just get back to the table."

We head back, and I sip on my milkshake, though not as much as I would have when I was little. Not so much for my diet — this extraordinary display has made me lose my appetite.

When dinner comes to an end, we leave the waiter, who packs everything up. He's surely also responsible for handling clean-up, which is strange for me, since I'm usually the one in charge of cleaning up messes.

We get into Jarek's car and he drives us back to my place.

"Mind if I come up?" he asks as we arrive. "I have another surprise for you."

"I don't know if I can handle any more surprises."

"I think you can handle this one."

The wicked gleam in his eyes makes me suspicious, but what could I possibly have to lose? I lead him up and open the door.

He carries a bag and asks, "Mind if we take a changing break real quick?"

Does the bag contain some sexual experiment? I head into my room and change into more casual clothes while he changes in the bathroom. When I step out of the bedroom, he's wearing his pajama bottoms and a white sleeveless tee.

I burst into laughter. He really is going out of his way to take us back, and right now, it's mesmerizing.

I hear something on the TV. He's obviously queued up something for us to watch together. I step into the living room. An RKO Pictures logo appears on the screen, and I know what it is.

"Bringing up Baby?" I ask, even though I don't need to because the opening credit sequence is unmistakable.

He nods. My mood transforms from pleasantly surprised to horrified.

He doesn't realize that as he's taking me back to these moments, he keeps bringing back what I'm desperately working to forget. I can't help but think of that day, and suddenly I'm that girl again, waking up and searching around for him.

Get out of my head!

"What's wrong?" he asks, approaching me.

I retreat back to the entry to the hall.

The sensations of that night return, the feeling of joy as I thought we would be together for the rest of our lives—that I might never be happier with anyone but my Jarek. These images collide with those of the following day and the subsequent weeks where I cried my eyes out in the privacy of my room, though I told everyone it was over Daddy because I didn't want them to peer into those private moments I'd shared with Jarek.

I'm not angry with him now. Just hurt. So hurt. Like that morning. I want to ask why he left. *Don't I deserve an answer to that?* But I'm filled with so many other questions. *Why is he doing this? Why does he want to be with me now? Why is he back?*

"I just can't do this—" I say.

"Do what?"

"Whatever it is that you think all this is leading to."

"Lana, I care about you...so much."

After tonight, it's hard for me to deny that, but it's equally impossible for me to deny what he did to me. What I'm thinking is *I wish you really did care that much about me, but I know that any day you could up and leave, without a word, and I can't live like that.*

"I can't feel that way about you."

They're the most honest words I could have said, because I can never feel the way I once felt for him after what he did. I'll always have to live with it. I wish I could shake free of that feeling, but I don't think it can happen. Ever.

"You don't want this?" he asks.

"I don't think I can do it." I reword his question, because I want to so badly, but that's not what this is about. "I think you should go."

He stares at me, dumfounded. "I thought—"

"I don't know what you thought, but I'm not ready for a relationship. What we had...I told you it was just for fun."

"When I first got back, I just assumed that since then, things had—"

"—changed?" I chuckle. *You're such an idiot. You don't know what I'm really getting at?* And I hate him for not knowing. "They have changed," I say. "But not the way you think. I'm so sorry. This was a wonderful night, and you did everything you could do to make it perfect. But I don't want that with you, Jarek." I'm lying. I want it, but that's the easiest response to keep him from prying into my true feelings.

I wonder if he deserves to know the truth, but considering all I've done up to this point, I can't tell him that I've been leading him on, for my own selfish sake, especially not after all he's done for me since the day he arrived. How out of his way he's gone to be generous and kind to me.

Jarek's expression turns sad. Some traitor within me wants to console him, but I have to be strong. This is my moment. My revenge. Shouldn't I revel in it? Shouldn't I be happy I finally have the chance to get him back? If so, why do I feel like I'm about to fall apart?

His eyes water. He nods. "Fine," he says curtly. He heads to the VCR and removes the VHS.

I wonder how long this awkwardness will last. *Will he change back into his regular clothes?*

He rushes into the bathroom to retrieve his bag, and without another word, dashes out the door.

Once again, he leaves without a goodbye.

This was it. I know that. I took what could have been a beautiful night and spoiled it...just as he spoiled what could have been a beautiful morning. I should feel vindicated, but I don't.

I head to the window and gaze out, once again watching as he heads across the street. This time, there's no interruption. He slips into his Mercedes, and as the headlights flash on, I know this may very well be the last time I ever see him. I suppose that's not such a big loss, considering I already thought that moment had come so long ago, but this one confuses me just as much. *What did we share? What were we?* I secretly wanted more. I wanted things to work out in a way I shouldn't have wanted them to work out, and things grew into something more so quickly—him coming over, staying over. Giving me this dinner and setting me up with Garreth. Will Garreth even come? I doubt Jarek will ask him to refuse my event, but who knows? I don't know Jarek as much as I'd liked to believe. Isn't that what all this is really about?

Chapter Twelve

It was a difficult night. To see Jarek so hurt by my words, to know he worked so hard to make it special filled me with guilt and sadness.

A few days pass, and though I feel terrible I cut Jarek back out of my life, I know it's for the best. I had to, for my own sanity, for the sake of feeling secure and like I won't wake up one day and find myself alone and scared and miserable all over again.

As mom's get-together for her Women's Club begins, I stand at a table covered in pamphlets, creating a more aesthetically pleasing arrangement than the mess Janet left it in. But it's a lot more help than anything Kelsey has offered since she arrived. She stands a few feet from me, at the bar, as she pours Melanie a glass of wine. Melanie's hair has toned down a few shades since I first met her, so I imagine my initial assumption about hair dye was correct.

"You look stunning tonight," Melanie says, which annoys me since Kelsey doesn't ever need more flattery. But she does look lovely, her hair resting at her shoulders in a flip. She wears a cream dress, a lot less attention-seeking than the red dress she wore to impress Jarek.

"Thank you," Kelsey says. "Dress to impress."

I'm all ears, slowing my work with the pamphlets so I can stand here as long as I need to in order to hear more.

"So he's interested?" Melanie asks.

"Oh, yeah. He's interested all right." I'm sure they're talking about Jarek. *After the other night, is he still pursuing my sister?*

"Have you..." Carol, who stands beside Melanie, asks as she sips on the wine Kelsey's already poured for her. I can tell by the tone in her voice that she wants to ask if Jarek fucked the shit out of Kelsey.

"Oh, please, Carol," Kelsey says as she hands Melanie her glass. "Have you seen him? You think I didn't snatch that the first night?"

"Slut!" Melanie exclaims.

Heat flashes through my face. The pamphlets shiver in my grasp. Here I was, actually believing Jarek was interested, and he's getting it from both Raeven girls.

A gazelle, indeed! I set the pamphlets on the table and start out, maneuvering through the guests as I navigate through the main hall and step out onto the front porch.

I need some air. As I step through the doorway and feel the cool air against my face, I nearly collide with a guest.

It's Jarek.

Of course it would be him! Universe, why do you hate me? He glances at me uncomfortably. I roll my eyes and fly past him.

"Lana? What is…? Lana, will you just talk to me..."

I feel his grip on my arm and I whirl around. "You greedy son of a bitch!"

He stares at me, dumbfounded. Though his focus is on me, I can't help but look around to see if anyone's caught my outburst. A cluster down the hall in the entryway to the living room glances our way.

"What are you talking about?" Jarek asks.

I lower my voice but maintain my level of fury. "Kelsey! If you'd been honest with me about what you'd done with her, I wouldn't have given a shit. But really? You didn't think I'd find out from my own sister?" I doubt she would have told me, but he doesn't have any reason to know that.

"I didn't do anything with Kelsey."

"Whatever." I head back inside, darting up the stairs. I can hide in my old room until the party's over. Then I'll help Mom clean up. It'll be like a sober version of the night Janet and I consoled each other in her old room.

"Lana! Please just listen to me."

He follows me up the stairs. I turn around halfway and scream, "Just leave me alone!"

The cluster that first overheard us turns and stares at us. Fortunately, I don't recognize any of them, so it will at least take some time before news of our display reaches my mother.

I know I'm behaving like I did when I was mad at him when we were teens, but it's all that I can do right now. I feel so hurt. Of course he would find yet another way to hurt me. He's just so damn good at it.

I barge into my old room. I start to close the door, but Jarek forces it open. I put my foot in the path. He sticks his arm in, but I try to close it anyway. If he wants to feel the pain, that's on him.

"Lana, seriously?"

"You are a lying asshole, you know that?"

"What the fuck? Just let me in."

"No!"

The adult in me reminds me that there's a party going on downstairs and that screaming at Jarek probably isn't the smartest idea, so I surrender. "What?" I ask.

He steps into the room, looking at me as if I've lost my mind. He closes the door behind him, I assume to prevent my rather loud confrontation from making it downstairs. "*What*? You make that big fuss and then you ask me *what*?"

Be tough, Lana. Don't let him get to you.

It's way too late for that.

"I don't even get you," he says. "You said you didn't want anything serious."

I want to mean it, but I can't help but want him, like I've always wanted him, and it hurts that I can't just tell him that. "That doesn't mean you have to lie to me. She's my sister, for Christ's sake."

"So what if I fucked her? What does it have to do with us?"

"Don't say that word about my sister," I snap, slapping his shoulder.

"Jesus, you don't have to be so fucking physical about it. What is this: an MFA fight?"

"So you're admitting that you did?"

"No. I just don't understand how, even if we had done something, it would have to do with you."

I glance around uneasily. "I don't know...I just...well, there's no reason to lie about it."

"We...didn't...do...anything."

He appears sincere, but when doesn't he? Isn't that the sign of a great con artist, the ability to manipulate people? However, when I think about my Jarek back then, I'm not thinking of someone manipulative, and I have a hard time believing he's really changed that much. Still, it doesn't seem wise to just trust him.

He approaches slowly, as if he's waiting for me to snap at him like I did before. "Lana, the only reason I came here was to make up with you. I want *you*. I know you don't feel the same, but that's how I feel and I'm not interested in Kelsey. Never have been."

As I reflect on her discussion with her friends, I realize I'm putting faith in the wrong testimony, considering Kelsey will say pretty much anything to sound cool to her friends. *Still, how do I know she's not telling the truth? What if he's lying?*

Before I have time to reflect on the validity of his account, he kisses me. It feels so good, so intoxicating, so delicious. Just like it does every time. I want to slap him. I want to kick him in the balls for the audacity of doing that while I'm still pissed at him for potentially having fucked my sister.

The intense energy that rushes through me is too much for me to deny, and I wrap my arms around him and kiss back. He falls against the door.

What if he really did fuck her? What if this is all a lie and he just wants to fuck me again? As much as it may be the case, I don't care, because I need him one more time so I can remember how good it feels...how good it can feel.

He forces me back onto the guest bed, which has since replaced the one from when I was a girl in this room. My face feels like it's about to explode from the heat.

He gropes at my body, his hands moving under my blouse as he feels my flesh. I lay back on the bed, my legs folding over the sides. He pulls my blouse up and kisses my belly, his nose gliding as he moves up, before it catches on my button.

You don't want him! I scream at myself. But I do...so badly. *Will I ever be able to resist him?*

He lifts my skirt and kisses around my panties, softly, tenderly, his hands cupping around my sides, his fingers massaging my back.

Can't it be like this forever? The swirling sensations that ripple through me...that make me feel like it's the very first time I ever touched myself...the first time I learned just how good it could feel?

He abandons his kisses and removes my shoes. I unfasten my belt and slide my skirt and panties down my legs. Jarek grabs them from me and pulls them the rest of the way down before setting them beside my shoes.

He kicks off his own shoes and removes his slacks and boxers, piling them on top of my clothes. He kneels down and reaches into his pant pocket.

A condom and a pack of lube. I eye him curiously. "Did someone expect to get lucky tonight?"

He smiles cockily. "I was hoping the opportunity would arise."

Take me. Just take me. I don't care anymore. I deserve this.

I must deserve to be hurt by him, because I should care that he may have fucked Kelsey. I should care that he could be lying to me, but I can care about that later, after this is over. He slides the condom on and covers it with lube.

He lifts my legs and squats, positioning me for easy access. He pushes in and then undoes the rest of the buttons on his shirt and pulls it off. As I realize I'm still in my blouse, I quickly do the same.

Once I'm naked, we gaze into each other's eyes. I don a stern glare, because I am still mad, and it turns his expression serious, as if he would rather not feel attracted to me either. However, he's a man, so I doubt that's what he's thinking.

He pushes farther in. It feels so right having a dick inside me that fits as if it was manufactured just for me. He lifts my legs and holds onto my ankles as he pushes in farther. The tension I've felt since I heard Kelsey—the rage that consumed me—dissipates, my tight muscles loosening.

I spread my arms to my sides and grip onto the sheets, preparing for that last inch that is just the right level of intensity. He scoots my body across the sheets and crawls onto the bed, still inside me. He leans down and presses his lips against my breast, as if he's drawn to it.

He kisses up to my neck, each kiss growing softer until he reaches my lips and kisses me passionately. He pulls himself out and then thrusts in quickly. I can't help but cry out as the speed surprises every nerve within me.

Why are we doing this? Why aren't we still fighting? Why don't I even care about the answers to those questions?

I gaze at the window, my old window from when we did this before. This is the room he fucked me in. The one he left me in.

I wrap my hands around his thighs and cup his ass cheeks. They're so firm, and I can feel each forceful push as he invades my body. I wish we didn't have to use protection. I wish he could come inside me over and over again, filling me. I know that thought is wrong, but I wish I could just take him completely, that I could contain him in a way I never have. But I know we'll never get to that place. Because this is what we are. This is all we can ever be.

His hot breath hits my face as he gazes down at me. *What is he looking for? What does he see in me? Does he see someone he really likes, as he claims? Or am I just like every other girl he's ever fucked?*

As he pulls back, I see an angry expression locked on his face. I know he's pissed because I told him I didn't want anything more. Each entry is so intense, as if he's taking out that anger on my body. But I want him to. I want to hurt because of how much I've hurt him, because of how much I've hurt myself.

A sharp sting within me forces me to cry out. He gazes down at me worriedly.

"You can fuck me harder than that, can't you?" I ask, because I don't want him to let up. I want him to fuck me as much as he thinks I deserve to be fucked. I want him to hurt me as much as he needs to, because I deserve to be punished for how I made him believe there was a chance we could be together.

Because we can't be.

I start to cry out again but he cups his hand over my mouth. He glances back at the door. I can tell he's concerned about my noise reaching the guests of Mom's party. *But what do I care if they're annoyed? What do I care about anyone right now?*

His hand over my mouth is so hot. And each thrust is more arousing than the last. I grab his ass and pull it toward me, encouraging his entry. As he grunts, I can tell he's close. And I'm close...so close.

The fury in his eyes isn't like anything I've seen before. *Is he really this pissed at me? Does he really resent me this much for denying him?* Though each penetration is forceful, severe, as if designed to make me feel pain that he believes I deserve for my cruelty, that they would come from his desire to be with me leaves me wanting it to hurt even more.

He leans down, his teeth gritted, his stare cold as he looks into my eyes, his palm firming against my lips. He inserts himself particularly powerfully and I lose control, that delightful rush of energy jolting through me so powerfully that I think I might pass out.

I come. The jerk of his pelvis, the cringe on his face, and his guttural cry assure me that he's reveling in his own bliss.

A silence settles between us. He looks at me, his gaze rife with guilt as he pulls his hand from my mouth. His scans my body as I slide out from under him, feeling ashamed of how much I've enjoyed myself once again. Without words, we pick up our clothes and scramble into them, returning to the party. Jarek beelines for Kelsey while I handle my daughterly responsibilities around the house.

Chapter Thirteen

I'm as rattled as ever.

What am I supposed to do about Jarek? I should have been smarter. I shouldn't have caved to those initial impulses. I should have fought harder, been stronger. I should have said I wasn't going to fall apart in his arms, but when he's around, that's all I want to do. It's the most important thing in the world to me. I just want him, and now I'm paying the price, because as much as I don't want to cave to these urges, I can't help but imagine what it would be like if I could bury that thing in the past and love him for the beautiful man he is today. Can I do that? Is it possible? I want to believe it is, but what if it's not? What if I'm lying to myself?

For the first time, I know he wants to be with me, but what am I supposed to do with that?

As I head into the office, I spot Geoffrey Brenner— Mom's attorney, the man in charge of our estate, with whom she's worked for the past few weeks to wiggle money out of the trust for a face-lift. He stands at the desk, dressed in a dark suit with an emerald-green tie. He speaks with Victoria before he spots me and offers a smile, but judging by how his thick gray eyebrows pull together, I can tell he has something serious on his mind.

"Hello, Geoffrey. What brings you to this side of town? Business?"

He flinches, as if bothered by something in the air. "Yes. With you, actually."

"Is Mom filing a suit against me?" He laughs in a way that suggests my joke isn't entirely unreasonable, and knowing Mother, it isn't.

"It's funny you mention your mother," he says with another twitch. "That's why I'm here. I'm supposed to meet with her this morning about the contents of your father's will."

"The face-lift?"

"It's a little more than that. Apparently, she'd like to purchase some new property, and she'd like to pull from some of the funds of the trust. She wants to make a few rather substantial investments, actually."

Little liar, I think as I reflect on Mom's little nip/tuck that she claimed was all she desired.

"Of course," I say. "You know Mom and her way with money."

"Yes, I do, which is why I want to tell you, if there's any way you can impress upon her that she shouldn't pursue this, I highly recommend it."

"Why?" I ask. I wonder if he is as apprehensive as I am about Mom making these sorts of business decisions against Daddy's wishes.

"I think you know how your mother's spending habits are, and I'm worried that if she gets any more money, it'll run out faster than is necessary."

"What do you mean?"

"She's a large part of the reason why there wasn't much available when your father passed. You know that, right?"

"Know what?" I'm totally thrown. No one's ever discussed anything like this with me before. In fact, I've only seen Geoffrey on a few occasions at Mom's parties, and never to discuss business.

"While she was with him, she spent a substantial, extravagant amount of money on fairly superficial things—parties, clothes, etc. She bought as if he was going to be making millions forever." *She probably thought he would be.*

"But Daddy was also spending quite a lot on his charities," I insist, trying to take some of the blame off Mom. I know how Geoffrey is liable to blame Mom for everything, considering his opinion of her, but as her daughter, I feel it's my duty to stand up for her here.

He eyes me curiously before the same nervous tic resurfaces. "A couple hundred thousand. Nothing compared to the amount of money your Mom was pulling."

"A couple hundred thousand, you say?" I ask.

All this time, Mom has been leading us to believe that he was the one who squandered the money, but it'd really been her all along.

Bitch!

When I finish at work, I decide to pay Mom a visit.

I've been fuming since my exchange with Geoffrey where he offered further details of Mom's extravagant nature, which made it very clear how much she'd deceived us about her spending habits. How could she lead us to believe that our father was responsible for our financial ruin? Looking back, it's easy to see how she was the one using the money, considering her extravagant tastes and her desire to go on endless shopping sprees.

I'm not sure how I'll forgive her for this treachery. *Does she even deserve forgiveness when she tried to turn her daughters on their own father? How dare she poison us with such foul thoughts about a man who she knew we adored?*

She knew she was in the wrong. She must have known. *That selfish witch!*

As I pull into the driveway behind Mom's car, I eye the house as if *it* lied to me.

I hope for Mom's sake she's in a mood to fight, because I sure am! And I plan on drilling this into her so severely she won't know what hit her. She'll feel bad about what she did, whether she likes it or not.

I knock, far more calmly than I imagined I would knock. I feel as if I'm in the eye of the storm. My rage has generated a surge of energy within me—it makes me feel powerful, invincible. Where was this the night Kirk attacked Janet?

She opens the door, a surprised look in her eyes. In white pants, a leopard-print blouse, and red shoes that match her belt, it's clear she was planning to head out. "Oh, Lana. I didn't expect you to come here today. You should have called."

Her words evoke further aggression. "I can't just come see my mother?"

"Don't be like that. You can come see your mother whenever you want. I was just surprised, that's all."

I follow her inside and she leads me into the kitchen. "What have you been up to today?" I ask.

"I'm about to have dinner with Shelley Rigby and Deanna Kower. I've been meaning to chat with them about the next Women's Club meeting for some time now, you know."

I spot a glass of what's clearly white wine on the counter. I guess she felt she needed to get a little alcohol in her before the meeting. At least I know where Janet gets it from.

"Do you want me to put on some water for tea?" she asks.

"That'd be lovely." I'd never agree to have tea with Mom, but considering the circumstances, I don't mind dragging this out a bit.

"How's that fundraiser for work going?" she asks as she fetches the kettle and takes it to the sink.

"It's coming along. A few odds and ends I'm trying to sort through, but other than that, fairly well."

She sets the kettle on the stove and turns the burner knob. "That's good. I've been trying to get ready for this next Women's Club meeting. Megan thinks we should work with the community theatre on their production of Fiddler on the Roof, but I don't know how comfortable I feel being associated with the theatre. That's not really any of our concern. Beneath us, don't you think? It's my fault for insisting we contribute all that money to the symphony. Now we're supposed to be there for all the arts. It's all just so time-consuming—you don't even know. Of course, back in the day, your father would have thrown money at the theatre or any other cause he deemed worthy of taking all his hard earned money."

And here it is—not within five minutes of speaking with her, she's talking about the very thing that's pissing me off. "What did you say?"

"Lana, I won't hear your defending him right now. I just spoke with Geoffrey today, and he is stubborn as ever that we shouldn't go to court over the trust."

"To court?"

"I just believe we should contest the will so that we have total access to what's rightfully ours. If he had known he was going to leave us in that state, I'm sure he would have granted us access to that money, aren't you?"

"I think Daddy was wise not to let you have access to it all at once."

"Me?" she asks, totally thrown by my obvious accusation.

"You're the one who blew through his money," I say, my words severe and bold. I won't let her sneak her way out of this. Not after how horrible she's been about Daddy. "You're the one who held your extravagant parties and bought all those designer clothes. You're the one who bought a second condo and a third. Did you think the money would last forever?"

"How dare you suggest—"

"I'm not suggesting, Mom. I'm flat out telling you that you wasted our money. Because that's what you did. I wasn't relying on Daddy's money. I'm still not relying on it, because you've hoarded what you've managed to get and used it on every frivolous thing you could ever think of, so don't tell me that he did this to us, Mom, because you did this to yourself."

"What's gotten into you?"

"I spoke with Geoffrey. He told me the truth about everything you've been lying about all this time, so next time you try to turn me against Daddy just because you feel so guilty about how horrible you've been with our finances, tell it to someone who'll believe you, because it won't be me. Not anymore."

She shakes with rage. I know the look because she used to look like that whenever we tracked mud into the house...or just before she and Daddy got into an argument.

"You think it was easy on me when he went and left us like that?"

"Left us? You don't know what it means to be left. Left is when someone has a choice. He didn't, Mom. He died of a brain aneurism, and you know there was nothing he could have done."

"I was devastated. I had three girls I still had to raise."

"Raise? Is that what you call what you did? You didn't raise us any more than you did before he died. You never cared about us. You cared about your greedy, narcissistic pursuits, and *how dare you* try and convince us that our father was this wasteful asshole who didn't give us two thoughts, when in reality he was the most caring and nurturing man that we could have hoped for."

"You give me fits, Lana. Are you trying to give me an anxiety attack?"

"God forbid I do anything that could lead to one of your anxiety attacks. Here. I'll make this real easy on you. I'm going. And if you need anything else from me, for any party or get-together, you know where to find Kelsey. I'm sure that even when she finds out what you've done, she won't give a flying fuck."

"Lana!"

"Grow up, Mom."

I don't spend another moment in her house. I'm done with her. I'm furious. I can't deal with her lies anymore. Maybe I was a little too hard on her, but it's how I feel right now, and in some ways, I'm unleashing all my rage about the whole Jarek situation on her. I don't feel guilty about it, though. I hurry into my car and leave.

I don't make it very far before I pull over, my face twisting in spasms and my eyes filling with tears. I grip the steering wheel and brace myself as I cry.

It can never be easy, can it? Something always has to go wrong. I just can't take it anymore.

KNOCK. KNOCK. KNOCK.
Great. I totally need a visitor right now.

I lounge on the couch. The sound of a particularly violent horror film fills the room. I don't know why, but right now, I'm drawn to the violence, the bloodshed. This girl, desperately running from the slasher, reminds me of myself. Like I'm running from all these demons within me.

To think this is how I'm spending my Friday afternoon.

My anger and frustration at Mom and Jarek has settled. Though I'm still pissed with Mom, I'm just confused with how Jarek and I left things. *What did our experience at Mom's mean? Did it mean anything?*

I've tried to reject these thoughts, but they come unbidden, invading my mind, like a slasher chasing me through the night, stalking me. And even when I think I've lost him, I'm constantly searching around, waiting for him to leap out from some unknown hiding spot.

The knock at the door forces me out of my brooding. I rise and answer the door.

Jarek stands on the doormat just outside, wearing jeans, a tee, and a pout.

"What are you doing here?" I ask. The expression on my face must reveal my disapproval of his presence. However, I'm pleased that he's here, because it will perhaps give us a chance to establish where we really stand now.

I don't want him out of my life. I'm not that good at resisting him. Yet I know better than to allow him as close as I have.

"I'm sorry," he says.

"What?" *Jarek Dean, you've totally thrown me yet again.*

"You were very clear from the get-go what this was, and I went and changed the rules. So I'm sorry for that." It's not the apology I was hoping for, but it'll do for this moment. Any apology from Jarek Dean is cathartic. "But just because we can't..." He stops himself, his gaze finishing his sentence. It's as if he wants to say something naughty, but I know what he's really reaching for is "be in a relationship."

"Can we at least be friends?" he asks.

I don't know that I can, but after all that's happened, after how far I let it get, I can't help but think that I want him to be a part of my life in whatever way he's willing to be a part of it.

"I'd be fine with that." It's not true. I know it, because the girl in me is screaming at me, begging me not to accept it, reminding me of what he did. However, after all he's done, after all I've seen, I want to believe I can move beyond that.

His smile fills me with relief. "If you're willing, I'd like to take you somewhere. I have something planned for this evening. Something I think you'll enjoy."

I eye him suspiciously. After the other night, I'm not sure I can take any of his surprises.

He raises his hands, suggesting he's unarmed. I laugh, and I wish I hadn't, because he shouldn't be able to make me smile.

"What are you talking about?" I ask.

"If you come with me, I'll show you."

I could make up an excuse. There are so many reasons I could be unavailable tonight. A date with Janet. A date with Mom. A date with a man. However, if I dismiss him, I won't get to know what surprise he has in store for me. It reminds me of when we were kids and he'd keep a secret just to make me beg for him to tell me.

What am I going to do with you, Jarek? He smiles, because he knows he's won.

I prepare to head out, dressing in casual clothes to match his less-than-glamorous outfit. He leads me to his car and drives us downtown.

He hasn't spoken to me since we left my apartment. I can't even begin to speculate what surprise awaits me, but as the car slows down, I glance around, trying to figure out where he's led me.

He passes a few tables set up on the side of the road with a large banner that reads, "Atlanta Hearts & Hugs." AHH is the organization we used to volunteer for when we were younger. Has he brought me here to remind me of those times?

As he slips into the parking lot across the street, the one where he used parked his truck, I check the time: 7:00PM. The stand opens at 7:30PM. He's brought me here to volunteer.

I reflect on the conversation we had where I told him that I was bothered by my job because it wasn't the same as helping people face-to-face. I glare at him. This is along the same lines as what he did the other night, when he duped me into going on that date with him. Where he reminded me of all those wonderful times we had together. *How could he do that to me? How does he do this to me?*

We approach the stand together. A few teenagers prepare the dishes across two fold-out tables. Some remove trays and paper plates. An older man wears a red apron, the sunlight reflecting off his balding scalp as he flips a burger. Behind him, beneath one of the tables, a woman riffles through a box of plastic silverware.

I don't recognize anyone here. Surely everything has changed since we were younger.

I feel guilty for not volunteering more. Certainly, there are plenty of opportunities like this available, but life always seems too busy to take a moment to reach out and help. The gentleman behind the barbecue glances our way and approaches. "How are you two today?" he asks, leaving me wondering if Jarek bothered to sign us up or if we're just crashing the stand.

Jarek reaches his hand out and shakes the man's hand. "Good to see you again, Dirk. This is Lana."

"Do you know each other?" I ask Jarek.

"He was here a couple of days ago," Dirk replies. "Guy's got a knack for the grill."

A few days ago? Jarek just came down here and helped out? Now I'm really thrown. Surely a guy with a camera is about to hop out from some hiding place to let me know this has all been part of a cruel and humiliating reality gag.

"Lana, do you think you could help me?" the woman riffling through the box of plastic utensils asks as she rises from her work. "I need to get some boxes from the van, and it's just going to take me forever if I try to do it on my own."

"Certainly," I say with a smile, happy there's a way I can contribute. I eagerly follow her to her car while Jarek takes his place at the grill.

After I help with boxes, I return and help scoop out various food items from aluminum tins onto the trays of some of our visitors, who have started lining up at the stand. "How are you today?" I ask a man who has two kids on either side of him.

With a five o'clock shadow and a disheartened smile, I can tell he's not eager to accept the charity, but I figure he's doing it for his children more than himself. And while it pains me to see that expression on his face, I'm pleased I'm offering him something of value. This reminds me of why I enjoyed volunteering so much—why I enjoyed helping people, why Daddy enjoyed helping people.

Jarek steps up beside me. "What'll you have, young lady?" he asks the young girl beside the father.

The girl grins broadly, clearly pleased that Jarek is paying attention to her. "A cheeseburger, please," she says as she nestles her head against her father's khakis.

"You got it. And for you, man?" he asks the boy, who equally beams.

It really is just like back then.

The boy asks for a hamburger. Jarek's glance shifts to the father, who seems even more bothered now that he has two of us assisting him. "You've got two beautiful kids there," Jarek says.

His words soften the man's expression. "Thanks."

Jarek takes the man's request and then heads back to the grill to get the burgers as I finish piling food onto their trays.

This makes me feel that what I do for a living is trite. While I appreciate the opportunities it's provided, it's not the same as this—being here, really assisting people who are struggling to survive.

We continue for three hours before the line has cleared. Then we pack up.

Once we're finished assisting, Jarek drives me to his hotel so I can clean up some of the grime I've collected on my arms and face, which feels like it's been collecting grease from all the steam I've been around for the past two hours.

As I enter his suite, I'm as impressed as I figured I'd be. The wide room is packed with décor I don't usually see in hotel rooms. Peculiar, modern artwork that surely only a designer with more eclectic tastes than myself could appreciate fills the room. French doors on the far wall open out to a balcony that looks down at the city lights.

Jarek shows me to the bathroom, where I rinse my arms and face before returning to the living room where Jarek lies stretched out on an oatmeal-white couch. He appears so at ease, so relaxed. He's clearly as exhausted as I am from the workload, but the look on his face reveals that he's just as satisfied as I am by what we've accomplished. "You want a drink?" he asks.

I consider, but I know he wants more than a drink. I want more than a drink as well, but I don't think that would be wise. I know where this will end up, and I have a feeling that if I get too close to his freshly acquired barbecue fragrance, I might lose control of myself.

"No, thank you," I say. "I'll call a car and head home, I think."

He pouts, then rises and approaches me. "You don't have to." Those beautiful blue eyes pierce through me, and I feel that same sensation welling up within me, the one that was so powerful the night we fucked at Mom's party.

No. Don't. Not again.

Every time I give in, every time I don't fight, I'm left feeling weak. Like I've lost a part of myself to him, and I don't want to give him any more of me.

I can't do it again.

"I'm sorry," I say, "but I have to get home."

He moves in likes he's about to kiss me, but he's waiting for me to offer some sort of approval.

I won't. Not tonight.

I slip past him and walk to the door before turning back around.

He gazes at me, as if in awe that I've managed to escape his charm. I'm not proud that I have, but I feel that I'm finally wise enough to do the right thing.

"Thank you," I say.

"For what?"

"For today. For being my friend."

Though he appears disappointed, I feel more at ease than I ever thought I could feel around him. Because while I can never have him the way I want him, at the very least I can keep myself from destroying my own life with these masochist impulses that keep bringing me back into his arms.

I want to ask him, to end the questions, the confusion, about why he left that day, but I stop myself. We'll never be together, so what's the point? Why dig that back up right now?

"I'll see you Saturday for the fundraiser?" he asks. I nod and head out.

As I make my way to the elevator, I realize this is the first time I've walked out on Jarek. It feels cathartic, though it doesn't take away the sting of the memories, the one that I know can never heal, no matter how much good Jarek may do. No matter what he could possibly do to make up for leaving.

Chapter Fourteen

I've scrambled around for hours, tending to VIP seating, catering, and equipment rentals. Derren and Stephanie have stepped up their game, helping me juggle the many tasks that must be handled immediately, assuring me that it's only mundane, day-to-day jobs they choose to neglect.

Jarek texted me ten minutes earlier to alert me of his arrival, but I haven't had a chance to meet up with him yet, as I've had so much to take care of. Though I made my intentions with him clear, considering how much he helped me, it would have been insulting not to invite him as my date. He's here as my friend, and though I'll never shake these feelings that linger for him, at the very least I can get through one night.

I haven't spoken to Mom since our argument at the beginning of the week, and I don't plan on reaching out to her, though she's left several voicemails—none of which I've listened to. She doesn't deserve my response. I did, however, tell Janet she could invite Mom to the fundraiser. If she chooses to come, I'm willing to consider a truce.

As I meet up with Stephanie, she assures me everything is in order. She stands with Garreth, whom she fetched from the limousine Jarek hired to bring him to the event. He sips from a glass of wine as he rubs his hand up and down the side of his tux, as if he's trying to scratch something in his palm. I'm sure it's a nervous tic. That and his wandering gaze are the only physical mannerisms that express his stage fright.

"You'll do fine," I assure him.

Garreth shakes his head. "Easy for you to say when you're not the one who has to do it. I don't know why I let Jarek talk me into this. I think I might just slip out the back."

"Oh, no you don't. You're going to go out there and give an excellent performance, okay?"

"If you say so."

Everyone in attendance is expecting this incredible performance from the legend, and I wonder if he's up for it. It's been a long time since he's had to worry about being in public. And if his nerves really do affect him, I worry he might lose it completely and become incapable of delivering. My hands shake at the mere thought of introducing him, a responsibility I'm used to Stephanie handling as the primary event coordinator for the company. Considering how nervous I am for the five seconds I'll be on the stage, I can only imagine how much pressure Garreth feels to give a magnificent performance.

Stephanie slides her arm through mine and pulls me aside. She looks as fabulous as ever—in a cream blouse, black skirt and a pair of heels that make me look like a child next to her. As she leans into me, one of her extensions grazes my cheek. "You did an amazing job," she says, the light in her eyes assuring me she's pleased with my work. "You know how many people are going to be here? We have some serious money coming. I don't think you'll have anything to worry about from here on out. You'll definitely be moving up the ranks."

"Thank you," I say. She gives me the run-down on some of the ins and outs she's tended to and then insists I should enjoy myself while I have the chance—relax before I need to present Garreth. I take her advice and head to the main auditorium. Guests scatter around various tables, arranged for the dinner that precedes the performance.

A massive crystal chandelier hangs from the ceiling, shimmering with the glow from the light of the faux-candle bulbs that wrap around circular tracks in three tiers ascending from smallest to largest. On the far end of the room, a jazz band plays beside an untouched piano, where Garreth will perform in less than thirty minutes. A few lively guests, dressed up for the occasion, dance before the stage—only a few confident enough to show off their old school swing moves. Several tables are arranged around the dance floor, each table carefully positioned to provide everyone with the best possible view of the show.

Near the tables, against the wall, I spy Jarek beside the appetizer table. I navigate through clusters of guests meeting and greeting with one another, some whom I politely greet, as I recognize them from Mom's various parties and fundraisers. As I make it to the table, I take a breath, allowing myself just a moment to relax and appreciate the nearly successful event.

Jarek looks gorgeous in his suit. He's gelled his blonde locks to the side. I miss the stylized messy look he normally creates—perhaps because it's closer to the Jarek I remember when I was younger. Though I'm not in love with this more refined look, any hairstyle suits a face like Jarek's.

The blue in his suit glistens in the overhead light. He looks like he could appear on the cover of Esquire or GQ, and considering how successful he's become, and how attractive he is, I wouldn't be surprised if that happened in the near future. When I was younger, I never imagined him fighting his way into all this money, but I have to say he seems as if he was born to be wealthy and successful. I can understand what Kelsey sees in him because he doesn't look like the rough, untamed boy that stole my heart.

He retrieves a cheese-ball on a toothpick from a plate on the table and pops it in his mouth, his cheeks sticking out, indicating there's more than one cheese-ball in there. He slides the pick back out from between his lips.

I chuckle as he makes a face that shows just how much he enjoys the taste. I should be so lucky if he made that face when he was tasting me.

"I guess you didn't eat today?" I ask with a smile as I approach him.

He shakes his head and takes a moment as he downs what must have been a hefty amount of food. "Saving it for tonight, so say goodbye to the dessert table. Isn't that how you do it?" I giggle.

"Lana!" I turn. Janet throws her arms around me.

"I'm so glad you came," I say. Considering everything she's been through, I didn't pressure her into coming. I just told her if she felt like it, she should. I figured it would be better than moping around my place, feeling sorry for herself.

"Me, too."

"Mom?" I ask.

She shakes her head. "But I talked with a therapist today."

"And?"

"I'm going to start going to AA meetings."

"That's really big of you," Jarek says.

"I figure it's about time I started making some changes."

"I'm proud of you, Janet," I say. She looks as if she's happy to hear that, but she doesn't know how relieved I am to hear she's doing something to help herself—to pull herself from the misery I know she's been feeling for so long.

"Lana, you mind if I talk to you in private for a second?"

"Oh, please," Jarek says. "I'll go find something to keep me busy."

I smile. "Thank you."

"Although I fully expect a dance when you're done."

At first, I think he must be talking to Janet because of the dance they shared in the bar that night, but as I gaze at him, he's looking at me. *Me, dance?* Perhaps he wants an opportunity to laugh at me. "Of course," I reply.

As he walks way, Janet's expression shifts to worry. "Why did you bring *him*?"

I understand her concern, considering the last time I spoke to her about him it was to let her know how much he's haunted me. "He's the only reason this event is going to be a success."

"Sneaking off into the woods again?" *Perhaps.*

She gazes at me like she empathizes with my dilemma, but I don't think I get to act like I've come to some great crossroads considering everything she must be dealing with right now.

"Is Kelsey coming?" she asks.

I shake my head. "Something mysteriously came up after our...disagreement the other night."

"She'll settle down."

"You're the only one who's not mad at me right now. I managed to piss all the other Raeven girls off."

"There's still time," she says with a wink. "Just playing. Everyone will come around. Just give it time. We've made it this long, haven't we?"

"Have we?" I ask, as I reflect on how much time we've spent together these past few weeks but how little we've really talked. Not me and Janet. We've talked plenty, but what about Kelsey and Mom? Do I really even know them? I thought I knew Mother, but considering what she's been telling us all these years, I'm starting to question that.

"Everything's going to turn out all right," Janet assures me.

"Who are you? Dad?"

"Just your bestest sister in the world," she says with a gleam in her eyes. "Now, go on. Appreciate that you brought all this together! Just let go and enjoy tonight." That would surely be the best thing for me, but until it's declared a success, I'm not sure I can. "Have fun dancing," Janet says, her tone disapproving, but the gleam in her eyes encouraging. She heads to our table, and I greet Jarek beside the open space where the guests are dancing eagerly to the music.

"Shall we cut a rug or whatever the kids say?" I ask.

He chuckles. "They don't say that, I promise." He takes my hand and guides me onto the dance floor.

Jarek Dean dancing. *This will be interesting.* However, as we begin, I see it's not interesting. It's fantastic. He takes my hands and leads me, and I'm in awe of his skill, his moves, and how he guides me so effortlessly. I suppose because it's easy for me to let my guard down with him. I want him to guide me, to tell me where to go, and as always, I feel so safe in his arms. I reflect on his comment about Kelsey being a lion and him being a gazelle. I feel as if I'm the gazelle and he's the lion, and he's just luring me in so he can break me once again.

Being here with him, like this, I'm reminded of how difficult it is to refuse him. I may have had a solitary victory the other night, but judging by the feelings that arise within me, it was a fluke. Before it has a chance to build, I vanquish the thought to allow myself to return to the pleasure of this moment once again, allowing myself to enjoy the movements. However, in a moment, I gaze into those beautiful blue eyes, and I want to be lost in them forever. I lose track of where we are and everything that's happened the past few weeks. I even forget what's transpired between us as I allow myself to pretend that the only thing that's important is the moments we've shared together today.

It's a scene from a dream, one I might have had when I was younger but since then I haven't allowed myself to enjoy, because of how heinous it would be to even consider such a dream with him.

Could we make this work?

I wish I hadn't thought that. Aren't I beyond these sorts of thoughts? I know better. My confidence that I'd maintain my stance on Jarek was nothing more than a delusion. I could refuse him for a night, and while it was empowering, it couldn't shake this deeper feeling within me, one that I can never shake.

He's not the man I imagined he'd become, but he's still Jarek, and even though my feelings about the past linger and burn, maybe one day I can find a way to release them. Is it possible? Could I learn to put them aside so I can enjoy being with this beautiful man? He clearly loves me— otherwise he wouldn't have insisted on taking our relationship to another level. He wants to be with me, and I still want to be with him. Maybe I can do this. Maybe I can finally let go of the past, release all those fears, and just be with him, as we are now.

"Lana," a voice comes from beside us, shattering Jarek's hypnotic power over me. Derren stands beside me, and I've seen that look in his eyes before. It's panic, but over what?

"What's wrong?" I ask.

"I'm having a hard time finding Garreth."

"What? I saw him not ten minutes ago."

"I know. But he's not in the green room, and I've turned the place upside-down searching for him." I sincerely doubt Derren has worked this hard. The only thing he ever expends that much energy on is the games on his phone. However, since he's been so good today, I'm willing to give him the benefit of the doubt.

I turn back to Jarek. "Back to putting out fires, I guess," I say.

"I'll help you look for him." It's nice having someone on my side, someone to help me when things go awry. Just like when we were in high school, and we were each other's best friend.

Jarek agrees to search upstairs while I check outside, asking around in the most discreet way possible. I approach one cluster and ask, "By any chance, have any of you seen Garreth Pulzer run by?"

An older man replies, "Not yet. But boy am I excited about getting to tonight."

"Right?" I reply. "I'm just as excited as you are. Won't it be nice when that happens?" I hurry off to continue my desperate search.

I could lose my job over this. Sure, Stephanie could vouch for him being here earlier, but I know that if he isn't here for the performance, I'm the one who'll be blamed for this. I won't just get yelled at by Mr. Farcon. I'll be fired, and who will employ me if I can't even get a reference from this job? That's silly, though. Mr. Farcon would absolutely give me a reference. It would just be written on my epitaph.

I scold myself for not having kept better track of Garreth. I knew he didn't want to do this. He even suggested that he might slip out, and considering his history with being mysteriously absent from the stage when it came time to perform, I should have taken better care to keep an eye on him.

As I start around the corner, I spot Mr. Farcon heading around the building. I turn to dash off, but I hear behind me, "Lana!" I whirl back around.

Act cool. Remember that you just have to keep yourself together for a little while. "Mr. Farcon!" I exclaim.

"Where did Garreth go? Stephanie said he was here, but I haven't seen him."

"He had to get a breath of fresh air. He's just doing a little ritual he does before shows."

He eyes me suspiciously. Though he seems tame, I'm waiting for him to catch on and fuss at me like he did in the office the day he discovered the Frenly Brothers wouldn't perform for the event.

"If this all goes well, I have to say, you're definitely looking at a bright future at our company, you hear?"

"Oh, thank you so much, Mr. Farcon. You can't know what that means to me right now."

He starts to head off, but turns back to me. "I'm so excited about seeing Garreth Pulzer!" he says. He's clearly a fan, which makes the prospect of not finding him even more horrifying.

"Me, too!" *So excited about seeing him and possibly killing him once I find him!*

A little ritual he does before shows? My excuse reminds me of when I first met him. He said he used to sneak off to drink in private in the cellars of venues.

Does this place have a cellar? When I was first scouting the venue, I recall the guide showing me a set of stairs that led to a storage area. It's a long shot, but it's the best thing I have right now. I creep back inside and try to act calm and together as I head to the doorway. I make my way down the stairs and enter the small storage area. It's my only hope.

Sure enough, he's sitting on the floor, leaning against a stack of boxes. He drinks from a tin flask, one I'm sure he brought.

"Garreth! You're on in ten minutes!" I exclaim. "Are you insane?" He smirks, his eyes alight with enthusiasm. It's a look I'm used to Janet making.

"Just wetting the palate a little bit, you know?" He stumbles to his feet, and I hurry to assist him. "Do my fans need me?" The aroma of Jack fills my nostrils, assuring me that I could be in a lot of trouble.

"Yes. They need you right now. Can you do this after you've been drinking?"

"Are you kidding? I was loaded for all my best shows."

"You're a pianist, not a rock star."

"I'm a rock star to my fans!"

"I bet you are."

He grips the rail for support as I lead him up the stairs and out the door. Perhaps not finding him would have been better than forcing him to perform in this state, but I'm desperate. At this point, I'll do anything to get him on that stage.

As I come through the main entrance, I see Jarek walking across the auditorium. When he sees us, he approaches and we meet halfway. "Everything okay?" he asks.

"Just fine. I'm going to get him to the stage. I'll be back in a minute."

"I'll be waiting at the table," Jarek says. I gaze into those beautiful, sincere eyes.

I believe him. Me, the girl who was so upset after he left, who didn't think she could ever trust him again really believes that he'll be here for me.

I can do this. I can be with him...if that's what he really wants.

I take Garreth to the stage and wait on the sidelines to make sure he doesn't try to sneak off.

As nine o'clock rolls around, the jazz band ceases and I approach the podium. I'm nervous as hell, but I just have to get through this and then I'll be done for the night, and it will have been a success. I spot Jarek at the table beside Janet, giving me a thumbs up. It gives me the boost I need to go through with this.

"Hello, everyone. I'd like to thank you all for joining us tonight for this fundraiser and performance from Mr. Garreth Pulzer." I ramble on about his accolades and awards, nervously picking at the edge of the podium as I contemplate being scolded by Mr. Farcon for bringing a far-too-inebriated Garreth Pulzer onto the stage. Vanquishing that from my thoughts, I say, "Without further ado, Garreth Pulzer."

Garreth walks on stage, smiling brightly, his eyes filled with that same gleam as in the cellar, but his movements are far more seemingly-sober than when I was leading him up the stairs. If he can pull off this act, perhaps we can both get out of this unscathed.

He sits on the piano bench and pauses for a moment before beginning, smiling once again at the audience.

This could be utterly tragic. Will I find another job if this blows up in my face?

I scratch at my arm. *Please let this go well.*

He plays with the keys for a moment, then stops, looking at them as if he doesn't even know what they are.

This is the end of the fundraiser and my career.

He says into a mic before him, "They seem to have moved all the keys."

Every muscle in me tenses. *What?*

He turns to the audience, a wicked, playful gleam in his eyes, and the room erupts into a fit of laughter. As it settles, his hands move across the keys, fingers tickling the ivory as a beautiful melody fills the room. I glance around to behold mystified gazes and broad smiles.

Whew!

I head out to the table, but when I arrive, I see Jarek is gone. "Where's Jarek?" I ask Janet as I sit beside her.

She glances either way. "Oh, I hadn't even realized he left."

Where could he be? My eyes water, not just because he's gone, but because it's stirred up everything all over again—all those things that less than ten minutes ago I thought I could so easily overcome, all those painful memories. Now they're back, and with a vengeance.

Surely he didn't just ditch me. That's ridiculous. Impossible.

But is it? It happened before.

Not again.

As absurd as it seems, I can't fight the avalanche of thoughts that return just as powerfully as ever. I'm losing my strength, my ability to keep my cool. My breath quickens. I feel as if the entire world is shrinking around me.

I hurry to the main entrance, trying to appear calm and collected, but desperately hoping that when I open this door, I'll see Jarek, who will have some reasonable excuse for his disappearance.

I open the door, but the room is empty. I back up to a nearby column, taking deep breaths, trying to calm my nerves.

"Lana, Lana, that was amazing!" Stephanie says as she steps out from the auditorium. She must have seen me leaving and followed.

Oh, God why did it have to be right now? Not now!

"You really impressed everyone."

"Thank you," I say, but I'm still searching the room. Surely he's here. He has to be somewhere.

He must be in the restroom. That's all it is. Over Stephanie's shoulder, I see Derren step out of the restroom nook, wiping his hands against his pants.

"You need to speak at more of our fundraisers," Stephanie continues.

"Oh, really? I'm just glad it was coherent. Just one minute. Derren," I say, stopping him before he enters the auditorium. "You didn't happen to see Jarek in the restroom, did you?"

He shakes his head. "Nope."

Maybe he's in a stall...or maybe he's really gone again. As Stephanie and Derren return to the auditorium, I look for the nearest exit.

Two dual doors open out to the side of the lobby. I scramble for it and walk casually down the steps, onto a patio. Between Garreth's and Jarek's wandering, I need fresh air.

Maybe he's out here—but a few moments of searching are enough for me to see that that isn't an option. I sneak through a cluster of ferns, into a garden lit by a light hanging from the building, illuminating a fountain with water flowing in arcs into the pool around it.

He's really gone.

I collapse onto a marble bench before the fountain.

This is what I get for letting him back into my life. This is what I get for believing he could be different. *Why was I so stupid?*

My thoughts spiral back to that day, as I'm looking for his truck. As I'm waiting in my room, believing at any minute, he'll return to me. For two days, I thought he would return. Surely Mom couldn't have been right. He couldn't have left me. She had misunderstood the reason he needed to leave. Something must have happened to him. I thought, "He loves me. He must feel for me the way I feel for him."

But I was wrong. So wrong, and I'm clearly wrong again. I wrap my hands around my freezing arms and bow over, crying into my lap. I hope no one comes out here and discovers me in this weakened state. I hope the freezing chill in the air protects me in this moment that I need to unleash all the hurt that's lingered over all these years.

I feel warmth on my shoulder. "Lana?"

I jerk away and leap up from the bench. He looks at me with wide eyes.

A part of me is relieved, but another part is trapped in this awful mood his absence has stirred within me.

"What's wrong?" he asks. "I saw you walking out here and—"

"Where were you?" I ask, my tone hostile.

"I had to take a call from work. What's wrong? Tell me."

I wipe the tears from my eyes. What am I supposed to say? That I'm out here because I thought he left me just like back then? I thought I could do it. I thought I could shake all that and leave it behind me, but clearly I can't. "I can't do this," I say. I start past him. He snatches my arm and whirls me around, pulling me close to him.

"Lana, talk to me."

As good as I've been about keeping all this hate within me, I can't hold back anymore. "I can't do this with you." The look in his eyes assures me he knows what I'm referring to.

"Why?"

"Because I can't live my life, every time you run to the bathroom or take a call, thinking that you've left me again."

His expression shifts from confusion to guilt.

"Did you really think I'd left all that behind me?" I ask. He shakes his head. "Ever since you came back, it's all I've been able to think about. It's consumed me. When I first saw you again, I kept telling myself I just wanted revenge—to make you pay for what you did. I let you in because I wanted to hurt you as much as you hurt me back then, but I don't think that's possible, because obviously leaving me wasn't all that difficult. I can't spend my life always afraid that one day I'm going to wake up and you'll be gone. I don't deserve to live in fear that I'm going to be alone."

"I would never leave you."

"But you did!" I scream, now overtaken with rage rather than fear. "You left me when I needed you most. My father died, and I thought I had one thing in the world that could make it all better, and then he left me. *You* left me! How am I ever supposed to live knowing that? Tell me, Jarek, because when tonight began, I convinced myself I could do it—that I could find a way to make it work because I wanted to be with you so much. Now I know that's just a lie. That fear will never go away, because I'm still that little girl wondering why you up and left me all those years ago. Well?"

"Well what?"

"Why did you leave? Can't you just tell me that much? Tell me there was a good reason. Tell me there was something beyond my understanding that will make it all right."

His gaze shifts to the ground. There isn't a good answer, because there can't be. My face trembles and a rush of tears pours from my eyes. He starts toward me, as if to console me.

"No!" I scream. "I don't need you to be here for me. Not now. There was a time where that was the only thing in the world I wanted, but it's passed, and I can't ever let you hurt me again."

"Please, Lana. Can we just put all that in the past?"

At a moment like this, all I want to do is say yes. Can't I? Can't I just release all this hate? He's still such a beautiful person. He's still that boy I fell in love with. And that's the problem. Because as much as I care about him, as much as I desperately want him to be happy, I know that what he's asking can never be.

He gazes at me with those loving eyes, and though they're disarming, I can't help but feel the rage well up within me. "I wish I could say yes. That day, when we went to the lake, you made me laugh. I hadn't laughed in such a long time before that moment...and I didn't know that I'd ever be able to. And we teased and played and I actually believed I could see a future. One where I could be happy. I didn't even think I could be happy without Daddy. But you made me believe I could. One day. I trusted you so much...I guess that's the problem with being a kid. You trust everyone and you believe the people close to you will never hurt you. You took me in your arms and gave me something so beautiful...so magical...and so enchanting. I never knew a person could feel that way. You gave me a high that I didn't ever want to come down from, and then I didn't just come down from it, I came crashing down.

"When I woke up that morning and realized you were gone, I thought, surely he's just downstairs. My perfect Jarek, just waiting for me. I was sitting there imagining a future with you. Imagining the things we could do together. The life we could have. Oh, God, I don't even know how I can stand here telling you all this. I guess it's just because my feelings now...When I came down, and Mom told me that you'd gone and that you weren't coming back. My *mom*! Not even you. Do you know what that did to me? Do you have any idea how that destroyed me? You didn't say anything. Nothing! Is that what I deserved?"

"No."

"Why? Please...just tell me why I meant so little to you that you didn't do me the honor of saying goodbye—of giving me a reason why you were leaving."

"I—"

"How could you leave me then? You knew how much I needed you."

He hesitates, his gaze shifting before him. "Because I knew you couldn't be happy with me."

As if I'm not furious enough. "That's not a good enough answer! That's not a reason not to tell me why you were leaving. That's not a good enough reason to abandon me and my family—to abandon those who Daddy cared about. He cared about you like you were one of his own, and you ditched us. How can I ever forgive you for that? Do you think my father could forgive you for that?"

His expression sobers, as if he's considered my words and come to some realization, but it isn't sadness. It's certainty. "I know you can't understand this," he says, "and you won't ever, but if you'll trust me in saying that I left because I was doing what was best for everyone, then—"

"Trust you? I trusted you with everything. I gave myself to you in a way I can't ever give myself to another person. But you ruined it. You soiled my heart by tearing from me the last good thing I believed there was in the world, and you showed me that it never really was good. It was just like everything else...a wicked, tortuous disappointment. No, Jarek, I can't trust you. I can never trust you again—just like I can never bring myself to trust any man."

"Lana, please, don't—"

"You need to go."

My words are cold, severe. I'm glad, because I've given him too much of my time, and I let him hurt me again. As much as I tried to guard my heart, as much as I tried to maintain control, I know I never really had it, and that when he leaves this time, it won't be any easier than the last.

He nods, his lips trembling as if he's fighting back tears, and though I can appreciate his weakness, I can't help but feel that he deserves to feel the pain that I endured so many years ago. As sad as he might be that I've slighted his heart, I don't believe he can ever feel the depths of despair I felt after he left me.

I worry I may never recover from this moment, that it will be too much, but I never truly recovered from the first time, so perhaps it doesn't really matter.

Chapter Fifteen

The following day, I call Mom. Since I've ejected Jarek from my life, I need the support of someone close to me. She and Kelsey are heading to dinner later, and she invites me to join them. It's the perfect opportunity to repair the damage that's been done between my heated argument with Kelsey and the one with Mom. They are my family, after all. I can't just exile them like I did with Jarek. It'll take time for these wounds to heal, but I trust they will. And perhaps this new transparency will even make us stronger in the long run.

The front door's unlocked, so I let myself in. I hear Mom and Kelsey chatting away in the kitchen.

"I just can't believe it!" Mom exclaims as I head down the hall. I stop. It sounds like they're in the middle of a serious discussion—one I may not want to intrude on.

"Who were you talking to?" Kelsey asks. I start to turn around when I hear—

"That was your father's attorney on the phone!"

I whirl back around. This is a subject I don't mind being nosy about, as Mom has clearly worked to keep me out of the loop about her exchanges with Geoffrey.

"That money I've been fighting for him to give me—I can't have it."

"But you're contesting it, aren't you? I thought you filed a suit to strip Geoffrey of the executor title." *So that's the real story.* More deceptions from my mother.

"That's just it," Mom says. "I can't contest it."

"What?"

"It's not your father's money. It's Jarek's."

"Jarek Dean?" my sister asks, astonished.

"He's the one responsible for the trust. It turns out he made an agreement with Geoffrey a few years ago, when he allegedly discovered this mystery trust, that he would put money into the trust on our behalf, but none of it was your father's money."

"Why would he do that?"

"I guess he feels responsible since Mike helped him so much, as he should. The amount of money he spent taking care of that delinquent..."

"Mother!"

"I'm grateful for what he's done, but you remember what he was like back then. He was a stray. He didn't have a future. At least, none that was obvious. Oh, he wanted to go off and fix up cars...a mechanic, I thought. Not an engineer. It's a miracle he's gotten as far as he has. If I'd known where he would be today, I wouldn't have kicked him out."

"You kicked him out?"

"Of course I did. He was starting to get a little too close to Lana, and one morning, I just did what I needed to do."

Everything's come up so quickly I almost can't keep up with it. All I know is that I can't stand back any longer, because now that Mom's opened Pandora's box, it's time to bring on the monsters.

I step into the kitchen. "Mom," I say to get her attention.

She turns sharply, clearly shocked. She shouldn't just be surprised. She should be terrified, because right now, all I see around her is red, and everything in me tells me to attack. I fight the primal impulse as I approach slowly, like a predator about to pounce.

"Lana, I didn't know—" Mom begins.

"What did you say to him?"

She glances around, as if inspecting the kitchen for knives or sharp objects that I might try to use against her.

"Lana," Kelsey says, stepping between the counter and Mom, defending her.

"This is between me and Mom!" I shout. My veins are surely popping forward in my neck and my face must be bright red because Kelsey steps back, allowing me to continue toward Mom, who backs up against the counter along the far wall. "What did you say to him?"

Her expression turns serious. "I told him what any loving mother would have. When I came home, I saw your jacket and your jeans on the floor outside your room and I knew—I just knew what was going on in my house. I can't say I was surprised. I'd always felt something between the two of you. I just believed, I guess foolishly, that we'd gotten beyond that. And the next morning, when he came downstairs, I made sure to be the first person he saw, so I could advise him, to protect you."

"What did you say to him?" I repeat, unusually calmly, like the day I came to the house to discuss her lies about Daddy. I'm in the eye of the storm.

"I warned him about how crippled he would leave you if he ever considered taking things beyond your fling. How he could so easily ruin your life by forcing you to live the nothing of a life that a man like him could provide. He didn't have a future back then. You're thinking about him now. This success. This ambition. We never saw that. He was perfectly content to live a mechanic's life."

She starts to approach me, as if she somehow thinks that will make her point better than her words. "That wasn't the life I wanted for you. You were meant for bigger things...you deserved a man with real dreams—"

"You mean real *money*? Like you want for Kelsey?"

She balls her hands into fists. "Lana, don't act like that's such a terrible thing. You don't know what it's like to be poor. Not really poor. You don't know how hard the world can be. You've seen us scraping around for what's left of the estate, but if you only knew what it's like to really go hungry—to really be deprived—then you'd thank me for what I did."

"And what about love?"

Her gaze shifts again. It's the thing I know she doesn't want to talk about, but it's the piece I'm obsessed with. "How could you deprive me— your daughter—of that?"

"Love is a fleeting, silly thing. You would have loved him for a summer or two, and then who knew who you'd be on to next."

"If you'd thought it was so fleeting, you wouldn't have felt the need to step in. Admit it! The only reason you got involved is because you were scared to death that we would end up together."

"All right, I'll admit it then. I could tell. I told you I sensed it from early on, but you deserved better. Look at you, Lana—you have never really understood how beautiful you are. Not to Kelsey's degree, but—"

"What kind of mother compares her daughters' beauty? Do you think I ever wanted to be like Kelsey? Do you think we've ever had anything in common? I don't even know her." I look at Kelsey, because I'm not just trying to attack Mom now. "You think I wanted to be a selfish, money-hungry bitch who never thought of anyone but herself?"

"Lana!" Kelsey exclaims.

"You spent the entire time Jarek was here trying to woo him. For what? For love?"

"You don't understand!" Mom insists. "You've just never thought clearly about these things. Some of us have to live in the real world."

"I live in the real world, Mom. I was there when Daddy died, and I was there when the man I loved left me. And now I'm here realizing that all along my mother has been at the heart of one of the most painful experiences of my life! How could you do that to me?" I'm not angry. I'm hurt. "Didn't you see what that did to me? Didn't you see how crippled I was after that? Do you think it's helped me form healthy relationships? And what about Jarek? How was it fair to him to say that? And so he went off, and he did all that. For what? For our family—because you made him feel like he was nothing?"

"If you were thinking about this clearly, you would realize you should be thanking me. If I hadn't had that conversation with him, he'd never be the success he is now. You'd never have the money from—"

"I didn't want him to be anything other than what he was!" I scream out, my voice echoing through the cabinets. "I just wanted *him*! But look at how much time we've lost because of you. If there was one thing Daddy ever cherished, it was the time we had together, and of course God would leave it for a great man like him to reach an untimely end, but how did you think this would end for me? Would you have preferred I lived a long, miserable existence instead of one where I had something that I cherished? Would you have preferred I know a comfortable life instead of a passionate one?"

"You and your way with words, Lana. You always had a way of making me sound like a villain. I did it because I love you."

"You have a twisted notion of love. Is that what Kelsey would have had for Jarek? Love?" I laugh a nervous laugh, the sort of laugh I assume only people who've lost their minds make. How can I not laugh at the absurdity of all this, though? "If you had only known that all along the man you were trying to force your daughter on was the very person feeding our twisted, greedy family, you wouldn't have had to go to such great lengths to whore her out."

I feel a sharp sting on my cheek. My head jerks to the side. As I regain my composure, I see Mom's hand in the air beside my face. My cheek smarts. She certainly didn't hold back.

"Don't you dare suggest that!" she exclaims. "You don't understand what a mother would do—"

"I do understand what a mother would do—how she would go out of her way to take from her daughter the only person who ever meant anything to her! To deprive her of the man she desperately loved because she had the gall to insist he wasn't good enough. Look at him now, Mom. Is he finally good enough? Of course he is. It's the two of you who are malicious, greed-driven monsters."

I turn to head out, but I stop in the doorway and turn back around.

"At night, sometimes I would get on my knees and pray to God to bring Daddy back to me. I would ask because I wanted him to be here to see all the great things in my life. I wanted him to see my accomplishments. I wanted him to see my success. I wanted him to be there with me to enjoy all these wonderful things, and now, I wish he could be here to see what a cruel, sadistic person you really are."

"How dare you!"

"How—dare—*you*! You didn't have the right..." A fit of tears overtakes me, and I fall against the doorframe. I look at Kelsey, who has a scornful expression on her face. "Kelsey, just tell me you really liked him. Tell me you loved something about him that was more than his money. Tell me you would have been happy if he just gave it all up and wanted to spend his life with you as a mechanic."

The cringe she makes at the word 'mechanic' tells me all I need to know. I bow my head. I give up. For the first time with this family, I just give up. "We didn't deserve Jarek's help, because we're terrible people. I hope one day you both realize that."

I dash through the hallway, and as I make my way through the living room, I hear Mom calling after me, "You don't have any right to talk to me like that after all I've done for you! I was just doing what I thought was best! It's so easy for you to cast that boy in a positive light now that it's years later and you don't have to think about shelter or putting food on the table, but it wasn't that easy back then! I was alone and scared and—"

She shouts from the porch as she follows me out. I get in my car and close the door, which muffles her words. As I start the engine, the radio volume amplifies, effectively drowning her out entirely.

She is my mother, and I know I won't be able to entirely cut her off from my life, but I can shut her out today. I deserve that much considering all the damage she's done.

I drive straight to Jarek's hotel and pound on his suite door. It takes a moment before it opens, and he stands there. His eyes are puffy, as if he's been crying. He looks at me, hopeless, defeated.

I won't waste his time. Mom has already wasted too much of our time. "I just spoke with Mom."

He opens his door more, and I step inside. "And?" he asks.

I look behind him through a doorway where I see clothes piled up on the bed beside a suitcase. He's clearly getting ready to leave. *Is he actually going to leave me again?* Although, considering how I refused him, considering everything I now know, I guess he didn't feel he had any other choice.

"She told me about that day," I say. "I should say I accidentally heard about that day. So I want to know the truth."

He doesn't appear ruffled by my words, though I detect a hint of guilt in his eyes as he looks at the floor, as if he would have preferred I never discover the truth.

"Your mom did the right thing," he says through his teeth, as if consumed with anger. "You remember me back then. I was nothing. Your mom just reminded me of how selfish I would be to destroy your life by being with you."

"Why didn't you just tell me?"

"Because I knew all it would take was one look, one sad glance from you, and I wouldn't be able to do it. I would've done anything for you."

"Clearly not anything."

He appears hurt by my suggestion. "Do you think I did all this for me? Do you think I did any of it for me? I spent the last decade doing everything in my power to become the best person I could be, someone worthy of someone like you. You have to see that."

"It clearly wasn't all for me when you just happened to be here on business."

His look tells all.

"Oh, God. You weren't here on business?"

"I spent a lot of time, after all this, convincing myself that it still wasn't a good idea. That I still wasn't enough. But no matter what I did, no matter how hard I tried, I couldn't shake you from my thoughts. You were my business. I thought if I came here, maybe I could get you back."

My thoughts scramble. *How could I have been so wrong? How could any of this be true?* And yet, it's the only thing that makes any sense.

"Don't you get it, Lana? The only thing that has kept me going—the only thing that has gotten me to this place is waking up to the thought that one day I might be with you again."

"But you never even called..."

"And every day I didn't, it killed me a little more. But I never stopped loving you. I never stopped doing everything in my power to become the sort of man you deserved."

"The sort of man I deserved? Is this what you thought I needed? A man with money? Really? Do you think that I'm so shallow that—"

"No, you never thought like that, but it doesn't keep it from being true. We were kids, and we couldn't have made the kind of life you needed—the kind of life you knew."

"You and my mother, trapped in the 1800s. I didn't need some man to take care of me. Look at me! I'm doing just fine. I didn't give a shit about whether you had fifty dollars or a million. I wanted you!"

"I couldn't have lived with myself if I couldn't give you the most basic of things in the world. If we'd had to live in some trailer park...or some shitty split-level..."

"But you didn't have the right to make that decision on your own! You didn't have the right to leave me out of it!"

"I did what I thought was best at the time."

Tears rush down my face. I glance around, as if looking for an escape. I don't know why, but I just need to get out of here. I need to process all this. I've never been so confused in my life.

"Were you just going to let me go yesterday? Was that it? You were never going to tell me what really happened?"

"If you didn't love me, then I didn't see a reason to keep torturing myself." His words stir a fire within me, and I know I'm about to unleash all this pent up hostility on him once again.

"You abandoned me! I needed you, Jarek. I needed you more than I needed anyone in my entire life. My father died and the only other person in this world who I felt knew me ditched me. I lost the two men I loved the most over the course of two weeks. What was I supposed to say when you came waltzing back in? That I was appreciative? That I wanted you in spite of all that? Were you really just going to let me walk out without ever knowing the truth?"

His expression is rife with guilt. "I know it seems like what I did was unforgivable, but I promise you, Lana, it was all for you. If you knew how

much it was all for you, you'd never question how much I care about you."
He takes my hand. I want to pull away, not because I don't want to be near
him, but because it's all too much to handle right now.

"I'm begging you, Lana. Give me a chance. Give *us* a chance. I know
I've been shitty, and I know I don't deserve your forgiveness, but if you'll
let me, I will be your slave for the rest of my life, and I'll do everything in
my power to make you the happiest woman alive."

I sniffle. The tears are pouring so fast, and they don't show signs of
letting up, but what am I supposed to do to stop them when he's assaulting
me with all the attention and adoration I've always wanted from him?

I gaze into those sincere eyes, desperate as I remember them being
after Daddy died, and I wonder if I look just as he does.

I don't know what comes over me—some latent rage, something I've
held within me for so long, but it comes out with a few pounded fists
against his chest and me screaming out, "You left me! You left me! You
left me!" inarticulately through a fit of tears.

I collapse into his arms and he holds me close, though I'm still trying
to flail about in rage. "I'm so sorry," he says, kissing my cheek repeatedly,
soothing this powerful aggression I feel. His touch and his kisses fill me
with relief. I turn so his lips touch mine with his next kiss, and I grab the
back of his head and pull him close.

I won't sort through all of this now. All I want is him—all of him. I
don't care how much he hurt me, because now that I know he truly loves
me—has loved me all this time—it's too much for me to resist him.

I need him so much. Now more than ever.

*How could he have carried this secret for so long? How could my
mother have driven him away from me so quickly?*

The past only reminds me how quickly the things I love most can be
torn from me. I kiss him passionately, and he reciprocates, holding my
back as he leads me so that I'm lying on the couch.

He kisses down my neck, quickly sliding my shirt over my head and kissing down my body, feeling his way, as if he's just as scared as I am that this may be our last moment together—even though after all the confessions, I can't imagine, even with all this lingering hate I feel toward him, how I can ever be without him.

His lips send jolts of excitement rushing through me with each touch against my flesh. I roll my head across the fabric, reeling in the ecstasy that surges through me, which wars violently with all the other emotions I'm feeling right now. He unfastens my jeans and pulls them down with my panties. Removing my shoes, he kisses my clitoris. Softly, gently, his lips as skilled as his thumb in stirring excitement within me.

I relax into his appreciation of my body, because this excitement, this arousal is the only thing keeping me sane right now. He rubs his hands up and down my thighs as his tongue rims around my entry.

He ceases and rises. He scoops me off the couch and carries me into the bedroom. Laying me on the bed, he retrieves condoms and lube and sets them on the mattress beside me as he undoes his jeans and slides them and his boxers down to his knees. He doesn't remove them any farther before assaulting me with frenzied kisses.

"I love you so much, Lana," he whispers between kisses.

"I love you, too." He puts a condom on and lubricates before easing inside me. I'm still in my shirt and his jeans are still at his knees.

I need him filling me, and as he slides in and out, I writhe in delight on the mattress, pleasuring in every nerve he hits, every bit of arousal that swells within me, climbing and escalating with total abandon. I groan with delight as his thrusts become more powerful, the pressure intensifying.

I can't believe this is happening. Not more than twenty-four hours ago, I despised him for what he did, but now that the truth has been revealed, I realize I've never loved him more—not even when we were just kids. I don't just love him, I trust him with all of me. All this time, he's worked so hard so he could be with me. What kind of man does that? A crazy man, surely, but now I know he really has felt all those powerful emotions that have surged through me all these years, and that brings me such relief. I wasn't just a crazy, lust-hungry teen. I'd felt something special with him, something beyond those feelings I'd had with other men, something meant to last. Though I resent the world and my mother and even him for interrupting our time together, now I can't help but feel like all that heartache, all that pain has evaporated.

As his breath rushes against my ear and he kisses my cheek tenderly, filling me so powerfully, sating this burning need within me, I feel that this sloppy, desperate moment is the most flawless of all those we've ever shared. Here we are, making love because it's all we've wanted all this time, without fear or anxiety about the other's feelings because we've both been so clear about how much we've wanted each other. We're vulnerable, open, as we should have been all along, and yet without all that time, I would never have understood the depth of Jarek's love—that he really would do anything in the world for me.

He leans back, his pelvis continuing to beat against mine, and I see that soft look in his eyes as he scans my body, seemingly at ease for the first time. As I survey his body, his ripped abs and his bulging pecs, I can't help but feel that I not only deserve them, but that they won't flee, that I'm not just a toy for this beautiful specimen. I'm so much more, and always have been.

He slows his rhythm. A smile forms on his face, and I smile back, but it seems my emotions are still getting the best of me because I burst into tears again, though this time I know it's not because I'm sad. It's because I'm so incredibly happy.

As my tears fall, he kisses my face and relieves me of them. He gently continues pushing and pulling, each time the sensation forcing a radiant energy to swell within my pelvis. Swirls of delight radiate through my head and prick at my cheeks. Goosebumps rush up and down my body as a wave of heat captures my face.

I unravel, calling out as I reach the most satisfying of climaxes, one that I release entirely because I know I'm with a man I trust. The pressure in me builds, and he cries out before planting another kiss on my lips.

We kiss each other softly, not nearly as desperately as when we began, as if we've consummated this new stage of our relationship, and as he props himself on his arms, I feel as if I want him to stay in me forever.

I slide my hand down his back, cupping it around his butt. As I look into his gentle eyes, I know that's my butt. And I'm content with thoughts of seeing it every morning for the rest of my life.

Epilogue

"I think you'll really like this one," Farrah says.

Jarek and I follow her into a bare condo with white walls and stray specks of sawdust scattered across the concrete floor. It's the fifth place we've looked at this week.

"Nice," Jarek says with several nods, the way he has about three of the other places we've looked at.

We walk through the living area, adjacent to the kitchen, which is separated by a wall with a rectangular opening stretched across it. A window on the wall opposite the front door opens out to a view of the city, which looks like it will be nearly as brilliant a view as the one Jarek had in his hotel room.

Farrah whirls around to face us. I'm startled, as I was when we first met up with her, by her cleavage, which is remarkably visible in the tight, chocolate-brown blouse she wears. The sides of the blonde wig she dons fall just over her shoulders while the bangs cover her eyebrows, making it difficult to read her expressions at times.

"It's plenty big enough," I say, assessing the space, which is twice as big as the living area in my apartment. This is the first place we've seen that is empty, part of a new structure on Peachtree and 17th Street. Something about the emptiness makes it feel like a good place for a fresh beginning.

"I knew you'd like it," Farrah says with a smile. "It's three bedrooms, two baths. Just right if you're wanting to start a little family."

I gaze at Jarek. He smiles, confirming his excitement about building a family with me. We haven't had many discussions about it. Only enough to know it's something we both want, though we're not in any rush. We'd rather let it happen naturally.

A loud tune fills the room, startling Farrah. She glances around, perplexed by the noise. Then she fishes into her purse and retrieves a cell in a neon pink case. "Feel free to take a look around. I have to take this. It's my kid."

Judging by her age, I can't imagine why she would need to take a call from her certainly twenty-something child, but considering how frequently she receives calls from her children, I figure they're awfully dependent on her. Her black skirt waves as she spins around and heads out onto the balcony.

I lead Jarek on our own tour, turning into an entry on the other end of the condo. I follow it down a hallway, passing a few smaller rooms, before we reach what must be the master bedroom. Plenty of space to work with. A hallway passes through what, judging by the shelves on either side, is some sort of closet. Past the closet is an entrance to what I'm guessing is the master bathroom, scarcely lit by the daylight from the window in the bedroom. We walk through the closet, and I feel along the wall inside the bathroom for a light switch. As I sense a circular, plastic knob, I twist it. White light pours across sparkling white marble tiles.

"This is very nice," I say, stepping inside. It's spacious and has a large bathtub on the other side. I can only imagine the sorts of fun we'll have with that.

"Yes, it is," Jarek says, a wicked look in his eyes, as if he's fantasizing about the sort of trouble we'll get into here. He hurries across the tile floor and kisses me. I can tell by his kiss that he wants far more, but this isn't the time or place. *Now, Jarek? Really?*

Nearly a year has passed since we admitted our feelings for one another, since I abandoned all those fears I had about him, all my insecurities from that day when he left me. Since then, Jarek started teleworking for his company from my place. About a month ago we decided we wanted a place that wasn't his or mine, but ours. That's when we reached out to Farrah, a friend Janet met through her group therapy sessions. Though we're eager to upgrade, I want to pay half the mortgage for whatever we purchase. Even though Jarek has millions, I'm not interested in mining his wealth. I'd rather this be a 50/50 relationship, unlike those Kelsey so eagerly throws herself into. We've quarreled over the details involved in making that happen, but despite those small battles, I'm relieved to have Jarek back in my life. For the first time since he left, I finally feel complete. It's as if something that had once been constricting my throat has released me and now I am free to breathe.

Jarek unfastens the top button of my blouse. I push him back. "What are you doing?" I whisper.

That sly smirk rushes across his face. I can see a mischievous plan formulating in his head. It's the most calculating of looks, and it stirs desire within me. He creeps back to the door, closes it, and turns the lock.

"You naughty boy," I say. He unfastens his pants and pulls them down his legs with his boxers, revealing his hard erection. "Oh my God," I say as heat rushes to my face.

He shouldn't be able to make me blush like this! I'm impressed with how hard he is already. But I'm just as aroused. I can already feel myself getting wet.

I glance around as if Farrah is about to magically pop out of some nook and scold us for our childish behavior. However, recalling how long she usually is on the phone with her kids, I'm not too concerned. I slide my shoes off, quickly remove my jeans, and throw off my shirt. Before I even have a chance to take off my bra, Jarek squats, cups his hands under my butt and hoists me into the air. I start to squeal but stifle it. I have to keep from advertising.

I wrap my arms around him as he whirls me around and pushes me up against the door. He shifts my weight in one hand, pulling his opposite arm back and gripping my knee in it. He moves the other the same way so that my legs are held up by his arms.

He studies his dick as he pushes the head so that it presses against my vagina. He takes his time, moving his hips back and forth until the head pushes in. As always, it has a way of finding its way inside me. He slides right in. Apparently I'm wetter than I realized.

The radiating energy that swirls from nerves deep within rushes across my body. I roll my head back, enjoying the pressure, how it builds and then relaxes. I enjoy being trapped between him and the door, completely in his control, trusting Jarek's skill and awareness to keep me safe. I love having him inside me. I remember a time when I didn't feel so at ease, when I was wracked with guilt over these sorts of experiences. Now I just feel this wild passion burning within me as he takes me like an animal, ravaging me, making me his. It's splendid.

His pelvis jerks back and forth, driving into me, his primal gaze meeting mine, as if he just wants me for this one act, as if I'm just an object to him. Though this is admittedly not the most comfortable of positions, the spontaneity of the moment coupled with being under his total control, trusting his hold, makes it feel so erotic. He kisses me in a frenzy as if at some point I might just take this from him. His saliva tastes as good as always, and his scent sends a rush of energy racing to the back of my skull, as if my nose has just climaxed.

He kisses down my jaw and attends to his favorite place in the cleavage between my breasts. As he continues fucking me, his intensity grows until the door rattles against the frame.

I hope Farrah doesn't hear us. Even if she can, I don't care. I want this. I *need* this.

"Fuck me, Jarek. Fuck me hard," I beg. As he looks up at me, his face is bright red, surely from holding me up. His teeth are ground. He grunts, and a bit of spit rushes past his lips and hits me in the face. I love it because it just makes me feel like I'm even more his than before.

The sensations within me are like waves of excitement vacillating in various parts of my body, making me shake my head about as my muscles jerk and twist, some in discomfort from the position, others so stimulated by the sensations of Jarek's cock inside me.

"You're so fucking beautiful," he says. "I love you so much."

"I love you, too."

We've said it at least a thousand times since we confessed our feelings, but it feels like we can never say it enough. It's as if we're making up for all those years that we never had a chance to say it to each other.

I turn and catch our reflection in the mirror, Jarek's ass muscles contracting powerfully as he takes me. He leans in and whispers into my ear, "Wouldn't want Farrah to catch us in the act, now would we?"

His breath against my earlobe is too much for me, and I feel the delightful rush of energy, the warmth across my flesh, and the shaking of my body as I erupt into a sea of pleasurable sensations. A tidal wave of emotions feels as if it has pounded against my soul, just as Jarek has pounded against my body. "No, no," I whisper as I shiver in his grip.

He grunts into my ear as the sound of the rattling door against the frame quickens until I feel a powerful force, followed by gentler thrusts as he empties himself into me. Knowing he's inside me, filling me with his seed, fills me with a sense of ease. It's all I've wanted ever since we started fucking again. Something I was so pleased to receive after we tested together and agreed to become exclusive. Now I can have it whenever I want, but each time feels as special as the last. Yet with all the experiences we've had since we've gotten back together, it never feels like enough. It feels like we should be fucking until the end of time. Perhaps it has something to do with how long it's taken for us to come together.

"How goes the condo hunting?" Janet asks, a broad smile across her face.

Jarek and I make ourselves comfortable in the chairs across from her at the small, round table she's sitting at in the cafe where we agreed to meet.

"I think we found the one," I sing out.

"Oh, really? Pics?" she asks. I eagerly retrieve my phone, pull up the pictures, and pass it to her.

Janet stayed with Jarek and me throughout the divorce. Just recently, after she found work at an elementary school in Norcross, she began renting an apartment a few blocks from my place. I'm proud of her, because she's finally taking care of herself. She started attending group therapy sessions and seeing her therapist regularly. Though I was concerned in the beginning that she would find some equally repugnant man shortly after breaking it off with Kirk, she hasn't dated since, as she says she'd prefer to find herself before finding a man. Meanwhile, Kelsey is with a new CEO, one who meets all the criteria that Mom and Kelsey surely have on their long list of requirements for suitors.

I haven't spoken with Mom since I confronted her about Jarek, and I'm not sure when I will. I'll call her again...at some point. I know that much. However, I'm not sure I can ever forgive her for what she did. One day, I'll reach back out to her. Because she'll always be my mother. I can't just exile her from my life—not permanently. I do love her. But I question her ability to love me. It's sad that someone has to think that about her own mother.

"That looks perfect!" Janet exclaims as she finishes surveying the pictures of the place.

"We're putting an offer in today," Jarek says, beaming. He looks like he used to when he was excited about getting milkshakes with me. It's so satisfying seeing that look in his eyes. It reminds me of how happy I am now. Nearly as happy as I would be if Daddy were here to see how happy I am.

My phone buzzes in Janet's hand. "Oh," she says. "Farcon & Williams is calling."

"Of course they are," I say. Since the success of the fundraiser, we've acquired several major clients, most of whom I'm responsible for. Though I enjoy the work, I've made an effort to volunteer at Hearts & Hugs with Jarek at least once a week, because as satisfying as it is to help people through these fundraisers, I don't think anything can top the feeling of being there on the street, making connections with people, as Jarek reminded me when he took me out there on that magical day.

Janet tries to hand me my phone back, but I wave it away. "No, no. It's my weekend. I am so not dealing with any of that right now."

"Good for you." She sets my phone on the table. "I'm going to get another drink," she says before heading off.

"Well, they just don't want to leave you alone," Jarek says.

"Thanks to you, I don't think they ever will."

"Thanks to *me*?"

"You think I'd be anywhere right now if it hadn't been for you swooping in with your Garreth Pulzer rescue?"

"Well..."

It really is thanks to his efforts that I am where I am today at Farcon & Williams, and I'm incredibly appreciative of that. Even if I'd had the Frenley Brothers, my event wouldn't have been even half as successful as it was with Garreth Pulzer.

A thought suddenly crosses my mind, one I haven't thought about since the day we met Garreth at his condo. "I know this is going to sound strange, me asking now, but with Garreth, when you guys went out on the balcony, what did you say to him to convince him to do the fundraiser?"

Jarek beams. "I just told him you were the girl I wanted to marry, and I already fucked it up once, so if he could help me out of this jam, I'd be really appreciative."

The look in his eyes reminds me that all this time—all the years of insecurity and feelings of abandonment—were a sham, because he never stopped loving me. And though at times I regret that we didn't come together sooner, as I reflect on how everything transpired, I'm not sure we could have come together more perfectly if it hadn't played out exactly as it had.

www.ingramcontent.com/pod-product-compliance
Lightning Source LLC
Chambersburg PA
CBHW070558130626
46556CB00001B/208